Tabith

Never Knocks

by SJ Townend

Break in. Break down. Break free.

Dedicated to my mother - the reader of books. Rest in peace. Also, thank you to my sister, Victoria Clark, for reminding me to write THE END at the end.

CHAPTER ONE -- THE ALTERNATIVE LIFESTYLE

To do list:

1. *Finish year 7 marking*
2. *Print out worksheets for Thursday*
3. *Collect Oscar's Christmas gift (Argos)*
4. *Book Doctor's appointment (me)*
5. *Clean inside oven*
6. *Big food shop (Sainsbury's)*
7. *Break into number 37*

Patchouli. It absolutely reeked of the stuff. And there were unidentifiable layers present even less pleasing to the nose. Tabitha pulled her t-shirt up over her face. Then from her bum bag, she withdrew a brand new head torch and fastened it over her scraped back hair. She'd been looking forward to her evening off to attend the Women's Institute social since her last experience. In all honesty though, Tabitha hadn't a clue what the ladies were doing down at the church hall today and she had absolutely no intention of finding out. She'd simply used it as an excuse to get out of the house for a few hours; an alibi of sorts. Her recent *ad hoc* tour of Mrs. Burrows' home had left her deeply saddened and a dolorous, grey cloud of pity had followed her around. Protracted grief bayed quietly at her during the more stagnant moments of her week like a trepidatious puppy with its tail tucked under. The very least she could do was help the elderly lady with her party-loving neighbor quandary.

Most of the equipment she might've needed to put an end, at least temporarily, to the fractious outbursts of noise that'd been troubling Mrs. Burrows had been easy to get hold of. Tabitha had carefully planned this evening's outing in between changing nappies and marking homework. Pulling up her black hood, like an incognito Robin of Sherwood, she set about her first self-designated task... this evening, she would be helping the needy and coincidentally, this also provided her with a great deal of enjoyment. She always chose to turn a blind eye to the minor issue of legalities.

Zipped in the bag which was fastened tightly to her waist were several miniature screwdrivers, some pliers, cable cutters and a tube of super glue. She'd also managed to fit into the outer pocket a pair of gloves, her mobile phone (in silent mode) and a protein bar. Having spent a disproportionate amount of time considering which snack to pack, she'd opted eventually for one which would shed minimal crumbs and thus leave no evidence of her fine-dining experience.

It'd been surprisingly easy to find online tips for breaking into residential properties and taking the advice she'd been freely given, she approached the back door 'unarmed', using her nearby Corsa as a stash spot for the larger tools. Travelling light had allowed her to assess the situation better and it turned out that she needed very little, as the careless fools had left the back door unlocked. Turning the handle and pushing the door open, she stepped inside with guarded feelings of excitement.

Adrenaline was flowing. She'd already broken into a gentle sweat as her heart pounded faster, like a washing machine on an overzealous spin cycle. She took a slow, deep breath once inside the property and quietly pulled the back door closed behind her. Thumping vibrations as the blood flushed around her eardrums were apparent only to her, the atmosphere was otherwise silent. No-one was home and at last she was inside of the dusty, musky student hole so she securely fastened the back door from within, leaving the key resting in the lock. She felt safe; protected by the walls of a stranger. The filtration system of her top was poor however and the smell of student life permeated everything.

Now in, she needed to assess the situation.

Snack time.

She peeled back the wrapper of her 100% organic fruit and nut cacao bar which she'd chosen due to its perfect combination of natural sugars, fibre and low glycaemic index. It was the perfect aid to help her complete her mission. Additionally, it was packed with protein which was essential to repair the muscles she'd exhausted marching up and down the back lane for quarter of an hour.

The first bite was delicious, if a little powdery. The second, not so much, as the reality that it was not chocolate and tasted nothing like it kicked in. On the third bite, she wretched a little and spat it out into a tissue, which she tightly folded and placed back into her bag. She should've packed a Snickers.

Irrespective of her poor snack choice, her commitment to the task in hand was firm. She'd expended so much emotional energy already; the planning, circling the block in her car and hanging around in the lane trying to be inconspicuous whilst waiting patiently for the last of the students to leave. She was tired, but the excitement and the justness of what was about to take place seemed to power her forwards. A Snickers might've helped though.

Tabitha had been tracking the movements of the students for a few weeks already. She'd created an Excel spreadsheet onto which she'd scrupulously logged times and dates of each of the inhabitants entering or leaving the property. A separate column contained the rough timings of any lights being switched on and off too. She could see all this clearly from the comfort of her own bedroom and as a general rule of thumb, if any of the students were home, there was loud music blaring from the terraced building, shaking the surroundings like a tsunami. Now, at 8.13pm on this chilly evening, the house was silent. All except for the snuffling sounds of a thirty five year old lady, dressed head-to-toe in black, spitting out a health bar.

Tiptoeing through the unlit kitchen, Tabitha fought the urge to clear some filthy plates dashed over the hob and the mound of washing up stacked in the bowl like a game of ceramic Jenga. She resorted to pinching her nose over the top of her faux gas mask as the smell from the drains or possibly some kind of rodent infestation was overbearing. The kitchen was painted sloppily with a mixture of oxblood red on one wall and occasional patches of deep maroon on another. Its mosaic appearance may have been an attempt to make the place seem bohemian or perhaps it was just a bodged DIY job. The kitchen cupboards were doorless and filled to the brim with glass bottles and Ikea kilner jars holding everything from homemade herbal tea bags to star anise, chutneys to chia seeds. Fancy food. She was pretty sure that she'd have to be near starving to want to eat anything prepared here though, with the dirty hotchpotch of random cutlery and chipped, mismatched plates.

Where the rest of the house lacked coordination, organisation or pride, Tabitha, even with her untrained eye could see that somebody had spent a great deal of time and effort installing speakers carefully into every corner of the room. Carefully fastened and concealed, cables trailed around the top of all four walls, a theme which continued throughout the house.

She followed the cabling, like a wildlife expert tracking an animal's foot prints through the mud. Although Tabitha felt more like Officer Ripley than Steve Irwin, stepping off the Nostromo and onto a derelict spacecraft following a series of indecipherable radio transmissions, unaware what hideous alien creature may be around the next turn. Every muscle in her system flooded with feverish expectation. She used the narrow beam of light from her head torch to locate the living room without crashing into the wall. This short journey took her to the front door where she quickly bolted herself in inside in case any of the reprobates were to return home early and then entered the lounge. She could scarper out of the opposing exit.

The students' main living space seemed to be the source of the mephitic essential oil stench and from the hallway, she spotted two oil burners and a joss stick tray on a small table below the windowsill in the corner of a room- a spot most would choose to home a television.

She stood on something lumpy and looked down to find a metallic puddle of discharged cream dispensers. She recognised these from a drugs education lesson that she'd prepared last year. They contained nitrous oxide, or laughing gas which was apparently the drug of the day with teenagers due to its 'quick acting buzz' alongside its non-illegal status and pocket-money value. She had experienced quite a lot of it herself whilst giving birth to her son – possibly the only enjoyable part of labour other than when the baby was out, screaming loudly at the end. It had made her feel totally enveloped by the sounds of each exhalation. She was fond of the patterns that she'd seen whilst on it. They reminded her of elaborate ceramic work from Moroccan buildings like the ones she'd photographed whilst back-packing around Marrakesh many moons ago. Other than the stunning geometrical shapes only visible to her, and the midwife wrestling the nitrous mask out of Tabitha's mouth after she'd delivered, she couldn't remember much else about the birth other than severe pain. The mind has a clever way of blocking out unwanted memories. As she looked down at the pile of empty silver canisters, she placed her hand on her belly and thought about Oscar and smiled. No one had given birth here. If they had, she hoped they were up to date with their jabs.

These kids were so messy. She resisted the temptation to sweep the pile flat against the corridor wall with her foot, instead stepping over it and entering the front room. How could people live like this? The tea-light candles underneath the oil burners were burnt out, thank goodness, but the smell of the oils was deep-seated. She'd read an article a while back linking oil burning and joss sticks with an increased chance of developing lung cancer.

Tabitha no longer needed to follow the cables as there in front of her, standing boldly like an upright, silver-back gorilla, was the largest stereo set she'd ever seen. Bingo. The Mothership. One of her few memories of her father pinged into her mind. They'd been visiting Tandy's. She must have been eleven or twelve and she'd been bored stiff. He'd acted like a child at Christmas, queuing up behind the other middle-aged men to press the black button to open the tiny drawer on a shop display model of the first portable CD player. He had died shortly after.

The set-up in the front room before her looked so much more complicated than what she had pictured in her mind and after her nostalgic wobble, she panicked briefly, doubting herself and her abilities. The large speakers either side of the stereo stack looked like huge, black storage boxes, balanced precariously on top of each other in descending size. They were symmetrical and arranged either side of the box of buttons in the middle. This control centre consisted of six thin, flat sections, aligned on top of each other like a vertical loaf of sliced robotic bread. As she tried to locate the switches to turn it on, she hesitated. She must locate the volume control first. The last thing she needed was to bring any unnecessary attention to the property.

Tabitha patrolled the room with her eyes and noticed that there were more large speakers. These ones were shaped like double-ended loud hailers used by hostage negotiators for shouting at buildings in films from the 80's. They were facing inside and outside of the house. Why would they deliberately project their atrocious music to the outside world? If they want to damage their own cochlea then so be it, but no one else on this residential road wanted to hear 'Life 4 Land' or 'Ragga Jungle Mash Up' - whatever that was - especially not at 3 o'clock in the morning. She placed back down the vinyl sleeves she had found atop of one of the record decks and then shined her head torch again, up towards the window-mounted speakers to see if they were permanently connected to the system.

Tabitha's father had himself been a vinyl collector but was more of a classic rock kind of chap. He always said that good music didn't need to be played loudly as good music spoke for itself. Her father had also said that he thought young hoodlums blasting out loud music from their trashy 'twin-turbo-exhaust vehicles' was the teenage equivalent of a sexually frustrated bird's mating call. Retrospectively, Tabitha actually agreed with her father's point which always made her picture plucky blue-footed boobies strutting their stuff every time she saw a young lad in a souped-up Nova zoom past, tunes a-blaring.

Swimming in nostalgia, Tabitha coughed as some dust tickled the back of her throat. There were several large circular knobs, flat switches, sockets and holes on the control panels of the stacked units and on closer inspection Tabitha spotted two knobs marked '*Vol*' and turned them both right down to be safe. In between the sofa and the deck-stand was a single wall socket from which splayed an array of various four bars, spaghetti junction fashion. She followed the cable from the amplifier to one of the four bars. After unplugging everything else, she plugged the amplifier directly into the wall and heard only the sibilant sound of electricity running through the wires for a split second, followed by the switching on of motors, movement of magnets, mice on a treadmill or whatever else was hidden inside of this noise production box. Next, the lights; a spectrum of neon luminosity flickering on then off then on again, spreading across the display, winking at her like reflective eyes peering back through a possessed forest at midnight. Whipping out her screwdriver set, she perched on the elephant-themed sofa and started to unscrew the back of the three pin plug.

The brown fuse popped out of its AC nest and she crimped it with the cutting section of her pliers. It shattered; the wire inside severed, but the housing remained intact enough for it to be pushed back into place. The now defunct plug was easy to put back together and, joy of joys, as she flicked the socket switch to red, nothing happened.

The neon lights that had previously fired up across the face of the sound system no longer glowed. The first part of her mission had proven successful. However, confident that a broken fuse would not be enough to keep these students quiet for long, she started on the second part of the Saturday evening sabotage.

Tabitha carefully pulled out the top section of the stack. She slid the heavy unit onto her lap and admired the combination of sockets, holes, input and output options and red and black ports. She had no idea what the majority of these parts were for but she did know that cheap super glue was awesome. Revelling in the meteoric pounding of her heart, she gently unscrewed the tube of adhesive and tipped it into each of the holes. Problem solved. She threw her head back and chuckled uncontrollably like a Scooby Doo villain but on catching sight of herself in a mirror, she closed her lips immediately and exercised total restraint. Maybe she was starting to get carried away; crossing the boundary between local sound-police heroine and psychotic axe-wielding lunatic? Nah, she was just having the most fun she'd had in months and it was all for a good cause.

Tabitha slid the unit back into place and reconnected the cables as best she could, despite most of the holes now being full of semi-solidified glue. Hopefully it would take them a while to figure out what was wrong.

Her next step was to slowly hack at some of the cables that were running along the floor leading up to the window speakers to try and recreate a 'mouse- nibble' effect. Bent down on hands and knees, she pushed her slightly blunt Swiss Army knife back and forth on the plastic sheath until she was through to the fine coppery strands below. This was followed by sporadic snipping with the scissor-option which Tabitha continued for several minutes until her index finger started to blister slightly from the friction.

Feeling satisfied with her work, Tabitha drew out her smart phone. As the slate grey fascia vanished and the digital display appeared over a gorgeous photo of little Oscar sat on the beach, she blinked and rubbed her tired eyes, regaining focus. 8.42pm. Still plenty of time left until she had to be home, so she decided to head upstairs to explore.

This house felt promising; perhaps because it was so different to any home she had ever been in before. It didn't really feel homely, it certainly didn't look homely. It felt like a luxury squat; unclean and dank yet dotted with pieces of expensive electrical equipment and unusual art mounted wherever there was an opportunity. Some pieces were just hand-scribbled doodles, but there were many quite striking pieces in oil and spray paint on prominent, boxy canvases. In comparison, Mrs. Burrows' house next door had contained a linear display of black and white, vignette-ridden, framed photos spanning the previous century, cataloguing an orderly collection of people in formal embraces all staged for a photographer. In the hallway there was a small, square piece depicting some kind of creature with pipes for legs, security cameras for eyes and a chest emblazoned with skull and cross bones in a pallet of neon and sparkly pastels. A few inches along hung a much larger piece that appeared to be made from layered black and white photocopies of various trainer classics from the 1980's entirely held together with blobs of *papier mache*, tinsel and Rizla papers . How bizarre. Standard Bristol.

The ceiling in the hall was covered in bellowing draped fabrics, like a field of gravity-drawn Bedouin tents. Camouflage netting ran up the wall in the reception area near the front door and a set of rainbow coloured Nepalese Buddhist prayer flags crowned the doorway. Each piece of fabric or art alone looked cheap and ridiculous in Tabitha's eyes, however collectively, the house felt like she was part of a travelling circus or new age festival which drew her up the stairs like a child in a toyshop.

Creeping up the staircase, Tabitha traced along the rickety banister with her index finger, collecting and pushing along a reem of thick, grey dust. She wondered if they'd notice if she did a spot of cleaning... surely it couldn't be hygienic to live in such a condition? She resisted, after all, she was to leave no trace of her visit other than the totally defunct sound system that she hoped they'd presume had died of natural causes. Tabitha shook the dust from her hand and followed the wide beam of light her torch cast on the stairs. Arriving at the top, she scanned the hallway slowly and pondered excitedly over which path to take next. It reminded her of an old role-play computer game she had enjoyed as a child on her Amiga where you could click on one of many doors of a grand castle and a totally new plotline would unfold. A real life 'Choose Your Own Adventure' book. There were five doors along the hallway, one of which was a cupboard and also a narrow staircase travelling up and over her head into a loft conversion. On the furthest door, which was plastered with stickers and graffiti, she could see one bright slogan that stood out amongst the others. It read '*the only good system is a sound system*'. Tabitha etched out the word sound and replacing it with silent in her mind and cackled.

She decided to open the door closest to her to see what was inside. A little treat for her courageous actions in secretly aiding Mrs. Burrows that evening. Tabitha chose this door as interestingly, it was the only door that was not decorated in postcards, stickers and biro scrawling. It was clean and unlike the others, fitted with a shiny, new Yale lock. How intriguing. Even though this was a shared student property, it wasn't halls of residence. It looked like a communal, friendly, albeit weird home and she wondered why this room had been made lockable. Luckily, the door was ajar so she shone her light through the gap cautiously, whilst nestling up more closely and trying to peep in before opening it any further. It was so dark she couldn't see anything except for a slice of green and yellow dots, all blinking at her like a faulty traffic light. Seeing that no one was in the room, she surreptitiously pushed the door further open and took a step inside unchartered territory for the second time that night.

It was not what she had expected at all. Not that she was sure she knew what she was expecting. The room was small, tidy and full. Full of equipment, full of books, full of framed and unframed pictures, but it was so tidy, almost business-like. The room also released a soporific hum due to the many computing devices buzzing away like a field of happy crickets, busily processing incredibly important information. Tabitha walked over to the bed, perched on the end of it and took a panoramic look around her. She felt like she was sat inside the brain of a super intelligent life-form or was single-handedly manning the controls aboard Starship Enterprise. It certainly felt like an alternate dimension in contrast to the aesthetic headache that was the rest of the house. The blinds were drawn and the room appeared to be painted slate grey, coordinated with the dark coloured bedding and carpets. What a strange bedroom. Far from cosy, yet strangely enchanting. She resisted the urge to recline and uncoil Goldilocks style on the single bed and deciding that she needed extra light to have a proper snoop. Knowing the students would be out for hours yet, she switched on the large desk lamp. The heavy black-out blinds ensuring no one outside would be able to see she was there.

Whoever lived in this room was a fastidious creature, and she wondered if the drawers and cupboards were organised with the same degree of precision and care. Tabitha approached the large wooden desk, the helm of the spaceship which was crowned with not one but three PC screens. Tabitha had no interest in the computing equipment, she generally felt more out of her depth with 'IT' than she would if cornered by a tribe of Yanomami people in their birthday suits. She opened the top drawer first. Each subsequent drawer slid open with ease, and each, to her disappointment contained nothing of interest to her. Cables. Neatly coiled cables of various lengths and colours, a huge collection of external hard-drives and some jewel cases full of discs, all very neatly arranged and labelled.

The chest of drawers yielded nothing but tiny clothing in various shades of black, grey and leopard print and there were few cosmetics or trinkets to fondle. Looking up to an over loaded bookshelf on the wall, she ran her finger along the spines of the books which were tidily presented as if on show and sighed. Dull sci-fi and computing manuals seemed to be the order of the day.

A wave of transient depression blew over her as the disappointment of what the room contained or did not contain hit home. The thought of returning to her sleeping partner and child with nothing but the television and a stack of marking as company for the weekend ran through her mind. Tabitha sighed and slumped back onto the bed.

As she lay down to sulk, she glanced down at her toes. Her vision trickled past her toes and zoned out slightly, staring blankly at the huge stack of flashing lights surrounding the desk. Suddenly her eye was drawn to a large metal box. It looked like a posh, family sized tin of disappointing shortbread that you might receive at Christmas from your old aunt and re-gift to the other half of your family. It had been pushed deep underneath the bottom draw. She tapped at it with her foot and slowly jimmied it out. Bending down excitedly, picking it up with both hands, Tabitha sat back down again and quickly pulled off the lid.

At first, she thought the box was full of beads; some kind of, frankly out of place, haberdashery stockpile, squirreled away. There must have been well over a hundred individual small, re-sealable bags squashed in tightly, each full of something brightly coloured and arranged like a rainbow. About a quarter of the tin was full of various shades of white. She pulled out a deep emerald coloured bag and brought it up close to her eyes, squinting and moved it towards the lamp. She drew in a sharp breath as she realised what she had discovered. They weren't beads at all. They were drugs. She had discovered a massive treasure trove crammed to the brim with the widest selection of illicit street drugs that she had ever seen in her life.

What she'd thought had been a packet of pea-green, glass threading beads was actually a bag of pills. She slipped her gloves back on and carefully tapped one of the tablets out onto the desk. On closer inspection it carried an image - an indented picture of a crown, similar to the Rolex logo.

Ecstasy.

The closest Tabitha had come to drugs before other than the strange concoction she'd been knocked out with in childbirth was paracetamol for period cramps. The nitrous oxide she'd had during the middle of her labour was like nothing she had ever felt before and she struggled to describe it to her family members when the birth was over. Her husband had laughed hard as she'd described how gloriously ethereal the brief moments between agonising contractions were. Soon after the birth, he had told Tabitha heartlessly that she may have felt like she was in La-La Land but she looked like she was having some kind of hideous seizure; writhing in the hospital bed like a claustrophobic python, eyes rolling like a bucket full of marbles.

Tabitha stroked the packet against the side of her cheek, lost in her drifting thoughts when a loud whooshing noise came from one of the computer stacks, bring her back round. She wanted to somehow document her experience. What was she going to do? She certainly wasn't going to take any of the drugs. There were so many different shaped and sized tablets – some were triangular, hexagonal - there were even a few red ones shaped like tiny Lego bricks. Probably something evil dealers did to get young kids interested in taking drugs. It certainly wasn't a government funded initiative to increase the number of youths interested in joining the construction industry. She still had a good half hour before she needed to think about returning home. Taking a few of the pretty coloured bags out from the metal tin, she laid them in a circle and took photos of them with her phone camera. She took a guess at what some of them were but for the majority of the pills in plastic bags and powders wrapped carefully in folded origami paper pouches she had no clue. Some were neatly labelled; cocaine, amphetamine and MDMA she had heard of. A lot of the other names seemed more like car number plates. 2C-i, 2C-b, N-bomb, S-isomer ket, MDPV...

She took some more photos of the drugs and the strange bedroom then decided she should explore the rest of the house, fearing she may run short of time. It was a junky's equivalent of Quality Street except dabbling with these treats was probably a little bit more risqué than chomping on a toffee penny with a loose filling. Placing her phone down on the table top and starting to push the variety of bits and bobs back into the tin, she feeling disheartened that she still hadn't found what she was looking for.

Suddenly, a banging at the front door startled her. They were back... early! Or someone was visiting. She panicked. At the same time, her phone lit up. The display screen flashed on and off. Incoming call. She quickly swiped down and dismissed it, but within seconds it started to light up for a second time, 'withheld number' flashing and throbbing for her attention on the screen. Tabitha turned her phone off and slid it into her bum bag. The knocking at the door repeated, this time louder and longer. She needed to get out of there quickly. She frantically piled the drugs back into the tin as they were, rammed it back under the drawers, descended the stairs at a rate of knots and ran out through the back door, leaving all exactly as it was found – well, all except for the sound system.

CHAPTER TWO --THREE MONTHS EARLIER.

Tabitha placed her hand firmly over her tender belly button and probed for any lumps. A sign in the waiting room of her GP surgery said that females under the age of 50 had a 0.3% chance of developing colon cancer. That was three in every thousand women. She knew the odds were stacked in her favour but she also knew 357 people on Facebook and most of them were ladies. None of them had intestinal malignancies as far as she was aware. Why not her? She'd asked Dr. Meaker to examine her a few weeks ago due to some trouble with her bowel movements. On self examination, she'd detected a hard mass where her left ovary surely belonged. It had turned out to be 'faecal impaction' this time and he'd sent her away with a prescription for some gentle laxatives.

She'd checked her breasts already that morning whilst lying in bed squeezing her way through three sets of Kegals. If it wasn't cancer, then what were these flutters she could feel in her stomach? It resembled a baby kicking but she definitely wasn't pregnant - she hadn't had sex with her husband for months. Up until recently however, this unnerving feeling had felt more like sluggish caterpillars, albeit very hungry ones, constantly needing to feed; one red apple, two green pears, three purple plums.

'Jack. Jack. Can you get up please? It's 7.30,' she yelled up the stairs as politely as she could for the fourth time that morning.

Tabitha lifted the lid of her kitchen bin and pulled out a plastic wrapper. She carefully examined the list of ingredients more closely. It was the third sugar-free sports nutrition bar that she'd eaten that morning for breakfast.

'Excessive consumption may cause laxative effect.'

But what is deemed excessive? If there's any risk, surely a maximum dosage should be clearly stated on the box? Three small bars couldn't possibly be too much could it? As she bent down to return the wrapper to its stinking grave atop the remains of last night's spaghetti bolognaise, something seemed to shift forward in her colon; a blockage seemed to clear and in an instant, her discomfort had passed.

Unfortunately, within minutes, the bubbling sensation built again. Clearly these visceral, winged mini-beasts wanted out. They needed to break free from the protection and boredom of the chrysalis. She needed an outlet like a kettle needed a spout. Tabitha Fox wanted to make a massive change to her humdrum life, but she wasn't quite sure what it was or how it would be actioned. She twisted around to check the time on her phone and passed wind so loudly that her angelic two year old boy, Oscar, who was sat playing by her feet started to giggle hysterically. She scooped him up and rubbed his nose against hers and smiled. Her pain stopped instantly.

'Oh no! Now, Oscar? Really?'

A steaming trickle of straw-coloured fluid gushed down from her waist to her leg, dripping onto the kitchen floor.

'Not my linen dress.'

It collected in a small, shiny puddle that, as she crouched down to remove her son from her hip, reflected a solitary ceiling light into her eyes. It was too early for this. Oscar pressed his sticky palm over his mother's mouth, squeezed her nose with his other hand and then smirked like a gleeful Bond villain. Pulling out a handful of wet wipes from the packet on the scribble-covered kitchen table, she started to mop herself down and then applied a fresh nappy to the youngster before placing him into his high chair; the 'isolation zone'. Thank God for five point harnesses.

She could cope. She'd been conditioned by several years of sleep deprivation and her survival skills were polished with finesse. It was easier to continue with the slog than it was to strike, so those butterflies would have to wait a little longer to be released. She ran upstairs to get changed into yet another selection of clean work wear then dashed back down into the kitchen, took a sip from her lukewarm earl grey and packed her bag for the day. Phone, purse, planner, a selection of neatly folded supermarket discount coupons stacked in chronological order by expiry date, pencil case and memory stick all tidily slotted into the correct compartments of her faux leather, over-engineered handbag.

She sighed slowly, gazing into the space her exhaled breath hung before swigging on the cold dregs from her 'Best Teacher' mug; a mug given to her funnily enough by one of her 'Worst Pupils'. The ceramic mug featured a small mouse giving a large bear a hug which was a scene that had as much chance of occurring in nature as the student that gave her this gift had of passing his GCSE's. Mice sighed over 40 times an hour. This was a fact she had learnt not from her many years studying science and working within the education system but from a Saturday night quiz show. What on earth did they have to sigh about? At least they didn't have to get up at 5am every day, pick mushy Cheerios out of the carpet, mark a stack of BTEC coursework that would easily pass the height restrictions for The Oblivion at Alton Towers and scrub someone else's skid tracks out of the toilet bowl all before the sun had fully risen.

The sloppy thump of her partner's footsteps across the landing and down the wooden stairs signalled that Jack had finally risen. How had he managed to sleep through five episodes of Peppa Pig, mild screaming of discontent (from her son, not her) as said programme was turned off and the forceful repetitive clunking of a spoon against a cereal bowl?

'Croissants?' he grunted.

'Nope. I've worked more hours than you this week. You pass the Co-op every day on your way home. Maybe pick some up for yourself tomorrow?' She smiled civilly whilst scrubbing the urine from the floor.

'Parking.'

His monosyllabic mumbling was typical. Since having moved in together several years ago, Jack, a grown man of 42 years, had managed to successfully regress to full blown teenager. His ability to sort and fold clothes, carry out basic washing up (plates and bowls, not the cheese grater or garlic crusher as he'd never quite mastered those) and flush the toilet after a wee had completely disintegrated.

Tabitha hadn't spoken to another adult in nearly 24 hours. Despite his flaws, the main one unfortunately being showing absolutely no interest in anything she ever said, he would have to do.

She needed to run through the events of yesterday with someone before facing the kids she taught again that morning.

'So yesterday, Zac, the dopey one in Year 13, picked up his scalpel. He managed to sever a minor artery in his hand!' Tabitha started to dab at the tide mark the urine had left with a sodden dish cloth, moving warm liquid around the floor. 'Blood sprayed across the lab, all over my year nine books and all over his white lab coat. Becky fainted. She's haemophobic. Leila had to take Zac to casualty or 'A and E' or whatever it's called nowadays in her own time,' she said, pausing for breath.

'Mmm,' Jack murmured.

'That reminds me. I have the doctors after work today. Can you pick Oscar up from Izzy's at five please?' Tabs stood up and started subconsciously poking at her stomach again.

Tabitha glanced up at her husband of nearly nine years, realising that was probably a bit too much information for him to take in, bearing in mind he wasn't the best of listeners even after his coffee and morning ablutions ritual. He'd developed a severe case of selective hearing and Tabitha was growing weary of working, having to run the family home and do the lion's share of the childcare. In nature, it was the lioness that did the majority of the hunting and rearing of the young whilst the males lolled about in the sunshine or shade, occasionally rising to feed or fight. She'd frequently wondered why the lioness didn't just fuck off and go solo or pair up with another female lion for a more peaceful, manageable life.

All she could see of her husband, who was now sat facing away from her at the dining area in their kitchen, was the back of his mop of straight, originally black now slightly salt-and-peppered hair. It was swept over slightly to one side in some kind of vague attempt to disguise his marginally receding hairline. Jack nodded briefly without turning around but remained otherwise silent, vehemently engrossed in whatever bumf he was looking at on his phone, infinitely scrolling.

'What on earth are you staring at anyway? What's so engrossing?'

'Huh?'

At last he had looked up. It has taken a few extra decibels and a pitch change, but he was looking, almost focussing solely on her.

'What is that you're reading on your phone?'

'Oh, some kid died near Dorchester. The doctors can't work out what happened, said they've seen nothing like it before. He was 'drained of colour' apparently. 'White as a ghost.' Waving his arms and legs about like a drunk... then his hair went grey whilst he was in hospital as they tried to sort him out. Then it just all fell out the following day. Only sixteen. Sad, really sad. Really odd. Some drug or something the cops reckon.' Jack was stroking his own hair whilst paraphrasing the article to his wife. Tabitha wasn't sure whether he had found the article sad because a child had died or because said child had lost all of its hair.

'And this is relevant how?' She huffed.

'I don't know, just came up in my news feed. It's near Dad's I guess.'

His eyes and index finger returned to the small screen on his phone. Tabitha could feel herself getting wound up internally, fists clenching and the muscles between her shoulder blades had voluntarily taken on some kind of Insanity Challenge pulse. She heaped another half spoon of sugar into an inch of earl grey before throwing it down her neck like a shot of Tequila. That's an extra 15 calories she'd have to enter into My Fitness Pal later on and she didn't even really want it any sweeter. She let the sweet, cold tea trickle down her throat and counted to ten slowly in her head.

'Jack,' she barked, still strung like a new tennis racket, 'Oscar. Today. From Izzy's. Can you pick him up please as I have the doctors?'

'Uh-huh,' came the reply, although still not accompanied by any visual interaction. He put down the bowl of baby food on top of his own empty plate, slung his phone in his back pocket and went to the front door to find his shoes.

'Uh-huh? So that's OK? You can finish work a little early to get him?'

Tabitha crouched down next to her partner, surrounded by piles of shoes that Oscar had flung from the rack an hour earlier and addressed him at eye level. She made sure he was looking directly at her, with a slight Vulcan grip on his shoulder and waited for a nod to ascertain that he had actually taken in what she had told him. This was a technique she had picked up on a training course for dealing with children displaying challenging behaviour. Except for the gentle Vulcan death grip – that was her own special touch just for her vacant husband.

'Uh-huh.'

She stood up, stretched out her back and walked away, shaking her head in a clearly disgruntled manner before continuing to clean up the post-breakfast annihilation. Who would have thought two and a half people could make so much mess in less than twenty minutes of grazing?!

Wiping her two-year-old's face with a lick of her fingers and kissing him on the top of his beautiful, blond curly locks, she lifted him down from his high chair to get him ready for his day ahead with the child-minder so her and Jack could go to work.

'Shoes on, Pickle,' she smiled as she hoofed his Thomas the Tank Engine trainers onto his feet and helped him zip up his chunky coat. He smelt of biscuits. She wished she could bottle up his scent and carry it with her. She took the coat off again, having second thoughts about it. It was the tail end of summer after all and still quite mild.

Had she packed him a change of clothing?

Where was his elephant rag?

He couldn't go the day without his favourite comforter. She entered the lounge at the front of the house and started rummaging down the back of the slightly worn, corduroy sofa, frantically searching for his precious piece of smelly, frayed fabric. Three pieces of Lego and several husks of old toast later, she had found it and tucked it into his day bag. She returned to the hallway and helped Oscar put on his shoes for the second time.

'Now, please keep them on!' she said gently, 'Jack? Are you ready yet? Oscar is waiting.'

She picked up her phone with the intention of double checking the weather forecast, and there, in her own news feed, as if her phone had been eavesdropping was the gruesome story that Jack had been telling her about. The death toll in the South West now having risen to three.

She kissed them both goodbye as Jack left with Oscar on his shoulders, and after closing the front door she felt once again the familiar tug on her heart strings watching Oscar get whisked off to childcare so she could go off to teach other people's children. Still, at least she wouldn't have to clear up wee or worse for a few hours or pretend to enjoy hiding and finding a small plastic lizard again and again and again.

She wondered to herself that even though she was so incredibly busy all of the time why she still sensed a sort of emptiness and ennui deep down inside as she pummelled her stomach fat whilst striding up the stairs.

Jack's dirty socks and underpants were in a small, stinky pile several inches from the laundry basket in the bathroom. So many times she had asked him to put his dirties in the basket or even better, take them down and put them by the machine himself. She could feel a tiny, frustrated wheel spinning in her stomach like the start of a catastrophic tornado spiralling faster and faster, collecting momentum and force on its path of destruction. Her sacral chakra was totally off-roading. She sharply scooped up his dirty underpants, folded them carelessly and slopped them back in his top drawer. Overwhelmed with guilt, she took them back out and hurled them down the stairs towards the growing mountain of filthy kid's clothes, wondering if her passive aggressive laundry behaviour bore similarities to the career path of a serial killer; a cruel murderer that starts out by mutilating stray cats before working their way up to mass homicide.

Tabitha cleaned her teeth then placed her withered toothbrush back into the brush pot and began to clean the white smudges from the mirrored cabinet doors that she had noticed whilst examining her surroundings for jobs to do with her spare hand. Who on earth manages to spray stringy spittle everywhere every bloody day? Mid swipe, she caught sight of her reflection. The lines were deepening. Where had the years gone? She was going to be 36 next year.

As she took her final wipe of the cabinet mirror with the grubby jay cloth, her eyes were drawn to the black wisp poking out from a small mole near her chin, like a bourbon amongst a splayed packet of custard creams. At least she still only had one chin. She fished out her tweezers and yanked the culprit out.

After a quick check that none of the other blemishes on her face and neck had also decided to sprout their own hairstyle she followed this brief encounter with her appearance with a quick smear of moisturiser and a few lashes of mascara. Bourbons. Custard creams. Why a mole hair had made her think of biscuits she didn't know, but now her stomach was rumbling. She panicked slightly, her thoughts running away with her. Was she premenopausal? She did feel a little warm. An increased appetite was one of the symptoms of the gradual drop in oestrogen that accompanied 'the Change'. She wasn't quite ready for brittle bones, Velcro shoes and loose-fitting, polyester, tailored classics available by postal order from The Telegraph insert just yet. She'd grab a smoked salmon and cream cheese bagel or even better a lovely 350 cal prawn salad from the school cafeteria at breakfast club.

Taking a step back in her bathroom, bottom touching the radiator, she squinted slightly and inspected her brunette bun for loose strands in the now clean mirror. She winked at herself with her dark green eyes. Not so bad for a 35 year old. Not that anyone would ever notice. Would they? She set off for work.

Tabitha quickly finished off the third and final raspberry jam filled donut from the multipack. Technically, the raspberry flavouring was made from beetroot juice so it contributed to one of her five a day. She gulped down her coffee as the second bell of the day rang, signalling that registration was over and period one was about to start. Grabbing her notes and memory stick, she dashed down the panelled corridor from her desk to the teaching lab which was at the far end. Some of her students, well the ones she expected to actually pass the course, were queued up outside the lab chatting about pretty much everything except Biology.

She held the door open with her body and stood straining, creating a human archway allowing the class to flow in like the river of noisy pheromones they were.

Today they were going to be learning about the structure of DNA and also extracting it from their own bodies. She rubbed her tummy gently with her free hand, pondering whether the discomfort that had just flared up was due to the three donuts she had scoffed or the onset of colon cancer.

'How are you today Shelly?'

'Lovely thanks Miss. I got my certificate for dance which is going to look great on my university application,' Shelly replied.

'Congrats, but I thought you were applying to study Economics?'

'Yeah but it shows I'm well rounded, doesn't it?'

'I suppose so. You could do the caterpillar down Wall Street.' Her attempt at 'banter', as usual, had received a blank stare.

'Solomon. How are you?' Tabitha asked apprehensively. Solly was the class clown. There was always one, and if you were particularly unlucky when the classes were allocated, or hadn't signed up for enough 'voluntary' break duties, sometimes there were several. He was definitely it. He was an affable character on the whole, but needed firm guidelines as he could sometimes push the boundaries. His older brother, Jon, had also attended the school but had been asked to leave for a collection of reasons.

'Yeah not bad, Miss. I managed to do a flob from the top of the outside staircase and land it in Bryce's rucksack. Stupid twat. He should have zipped it up.'

'Thank you, Solly. I don't think that's an appropriate way for a seventeen year old to behave at all actually and I'd really rather not hear that language again or I will have to send you to the library for some time out.'

'Nah, Miss it's Okay. We were doing it to each other. It's a game. All bants, Miss,' Bryce shouted from half way up the corridor nearly five minutes late, leisurely strolling along with more swagger than a Premier league football player rolling out of Stringfellow's.

'Oh dear God,' Tabitha muttered under her breath. 'Move forward please Solly. Bryce do you think you could move a little faster please? When you're in, please clean yourself up. Get your notes out and your lab coat on. It's practical this morning.'

Solly ambled past her and plonked his massive camouflage Super Dry back pack down at his place. It was huge. She had made the mistake of asking him what he was lugging around a few months ago, to be shown that he had 3 two litre bottle of full fat Coca Cola and a couple of cans of ludicrously over-caffeinated energy Monster drinks in there that he'd bought with his lunch money on the way into school. No books or pens. Just diabetes-inducing liquids which he imbibed entirely over the six hours he spent at school each day. Tabitha had joked that the contents of his bag were perhaps more 'Super Wet' than 'Super Dry' and she had again been met with a vacant glare.

'Any more silly behaviour and I will have to have a chat with your mum again.'

'Ouch – owned.' Becky chipped in. The old call-your-parents trick usually worked a treat, even though these students were young adults themselves. After registration and introductions, Tabitha explained what they were going to do that morning.

'What does every cell in every organ in your body have in common?' she asked. They were going to take some tissue from their own cheek lining in order to break open the cells and nuclei within them so that they could see their own DNA.

'I don't know, Miss, but I bet Solly wants to show Ruby his organ.' Ruby blushed and sank down in her chair as the class blew up into hysterics.

'Thank you Bryce. You have just earned yourself one phone call home. Congratulations.'

They were using a very simplified procedure used across the globe to get DNA from plant or animal tissue. Once you had the DNA out you could see what genes it contains. Tabitha explained how genes are the instructions your body contains so that each cell knows what to make, what to do and what to be. Before launching into the practical, the group talked about genetic modification of food, possible cures for genetically-triggered cancers, treatments for inherited diseases such as cystic fibrosis and haemophilia, designer babies, how Jeremy Kyle's paternity tests worked and even the dubious cloning that happened in Jurassic Park.

'Solly, Liam and Bryce, come close to the front as I may need some glamorous assistants for this demonstration. I'm going to quickly talk you through the procedure that you will be doing this morning and show you how to do a few of the trickier parts, however all of the instructions are on the laminated sheet at your desk. Please follow each step carefully and read through the whole method before you even so much as pick up a test tube or pipette.'

She gathered them all around the front of the modern teaching lab, still amazed and proud that the flashy cupboards and desk space hadn't been vandalised yet. She had felt a little out of the loop with the teenage gossip however, as that is where she often found out key info about who was sleeping with who and which delightful member of the sixth form was currently the student that the others got their booze and fags from. The old laboratories, with their spray of biro and key-etched comments kept the staff up to date with vital information on which students to watch out for. There was still the old students' toilet block though which yielded such delightful clues. Although that was the last place any sane adult would want to enter unless they were cloth-touchingly desperate for a number two or had a defunct olfactory system.

Tabitha brought down her safety specs from where they were perched on top of her head and picked up a sterile, glass media bottle, skilfully unscrewing its blue lid with the same hand she was holding it with.

'So, after mixing the salt with the sterilised water, you are going to gargle with it for as long as you can bare then spit it out into the bottle. You can also use the sterile cotton bud to scrape gently on the sides of your cheeks and mix that into the bottle too.'

'What, so our cells come off then?'

'Yes, along with whatever debris you missed when cleaning your teeth this morning Solly'.

'What you saying Miss. – I didn't clean my teeth?' the hostility in his voice had risen.

'No Solly. I meant generally, anything else in a person's mouth from their last meal will probably come out too.'

'I get you. Glad I had cheesy Nik Naks and Lucozade for breakfast then.'

'The diet of an athletic champion, no doubt,' Tabs sarcastically replied with a cheeky wink.

There was a shriek of cackles from the corner from a trio of girls that had more make-up on between them than a parade of clowns. Orange clowns.

These girls, Lucy, Ruby and Danielle were known as the Witches of Eastwick in the staffroom. They were like clones of each other; the way they dressed, the way they spoke, and on most occasions, the way they worded their homework. All three had ridiculously straightened hair, Lucy and Danielle were naturally brunettes and Ruby had bright ginger curls in Year 7 but now had opted for black hair dye and GHD straighteners, to try and conform to some unrealistic media-pushed Kardasian image.

'Girls. What seems to be so funny?' said Tabitha.

'Sorry Miss. We did something similar in Year 8 and we looked at the cells from our mouth under a microscope. It was after lunch break and Meikka Stebbings had been behind the cricket hut with Dempsy. Turbot projected her microscope up on the screen and there were sperm in it.' A cacophony of laughter erupted for a second time.

'That's not true. The magnification wouldn't be powerful enough on a standard sixth form light microscope,' Tabitha stated, 'and it's also utterly disgusting'. The class filled with laughter once more and Tabitha couldn't help but chuckle along with them.

The triplet of trouble continued with their guffawing in the corner, snorting and crying like a stable of horses in a thunder storm. She regained her focus and coaxed the students through the remainder of the practical work until the majority of them managed to get their very own DNA in a tube. Crimestoppers would probably have benefited from some of the genetic information. She'd placed a wager with her colleague, John Turbot, that one of Year 13 would either end up in prison or pregnant before the year was through. Shame she couldn't preserve these samples as they could come in use.

As the students peered into their final test-tubes of gunk with perplexed looks upon their faces, she could hear a few of them whispering with uncertainty that their end result didn't look like the textbook twisted ladder of DNA that they had been taught to learn but more like a load of spit or snot suspended on the top of the liquid in the tube. Bit of an anticlimax after an hour or so of careful measurements, fiddly filtrations and teacher-driven hype. Especially considering it started off as a bit of spit in a tube.

'Looks like jizz, Miss. I bet Ruby would know,' had been the final comment from Liam as he tumbled out through the door in a flurry of testosterone and E numbers at the end of the lesson.

'That's two phone calls home I'll be making at lunch time then, Liam – thanks for taking away the five minutes I needed to eat my lunch in with your foul mouth.'

After work, Tabitha got into her mechanically sound if aesthetically flawed Corsa and drove over to her doctor's surgery. She settled into her seat in the waiting area. The whole place looked like it needed a good spruce up and possibly a steam clean too. A pile of germ-ridden, ripped magazines, several years out of date, were on offer on a small side table next to the signing-in desk, along with a box of vintage (but not in a good way) plastic toys. It seemed liked the surgery had spent the entirety of its entertainment budget on the prominent electronic notification sign above reception and a small television screen permanently tuned into an American channel churning out twenty four hour news.

After a twenty minute uneventful wait, intermittently probing her stomach, checking her phone and picking the dirt out from underneath her fingernails, Tabitha got out of her seat to stretch her legs and wondered over to the television screen. White text on a red ribbon was streaming across the bottom of the screen and the content had caught her eye. The American news channel was reporting four more deaths in the South West of England linked to a strange reaction to an unknown substance. Seven people dead in under a week. All the victims had lost colouring in their eyes, hair and skin before having violent seizures and dying. Tabitha moved to the reception desk cautiously and squirted a generous slug of hand sanitizer onto her palms and rubbed it in fervently. After waiting for a good half an hour, her name flashed up on the LED screen along with the room number she needed to go to.

She knew the building inside out by now having had so many appointments. After correcting her skirt and shirt, brushing off imaginary debris from her shoulders and wiping the corners of her eyes with her finger tips for that sleepy collection of black mascara that seemed to consistently pool there, she headed towards room four and Dr. Meaker.

'Well Tabitha, take a seat. How can I help?'

'I've come for a follow up appointment. I had some tests done a few weeks ago,' she replied.

'The bloods are back and everything is fine, as we had expected. Looking at your notes, I can see you have had a wide range of tests. Chest X-rays, ECG's, repeat bloods and several specialist referrals to Urology, Neurology, Respiratory and Sleep Disorders, Oncology and Haematology to name a few and all to no avail. We have had a letter back from your most recent referral to the Physiology Department and they have said there is nothing of any clinical significance apparent. Would you be happy to complete a mood evaluation quiz for me now?'

She knew there wouldn't be anything wrong and that she was probably just a little run down. Teaching and motherhood were hard work and visiting the doctors had almost become part of her fortnightly relaxation ritual; almost like free therapy. She usually quite enjoyed the half an hour of staring into space in the waiting room, eyeing up the other patients and trying to guess what was wrong with them like a medical detective. Although now, all she could think about was the families of those poor people she'd just read about on the news that had died, wondering if it had been anybody she knew. The most recent two deaths had been from Bristol, where she lived.

'Tabitha. Tabitha? Did you hear me?'

She looked at the notes on the doctor's computer screen and panicked, wondering what the doctor might see and think as he scrawled through page after page after page of unnecessary test and procedures that she had insisted on over the last few years. He looked at Tabitha's hands and as she followed his line of vision, she realised that she'd been prodding around her belly button quite firmly for the past minute. The butterflies were back. She realised he was waiting for her to speak and so she politely asked him to repeat what he had said, his brown eyes stared caringly at her as he spoke. Or were they full of concern?

'I'd like you to complete this short survey for me. We've pretty much ruled out all physical illness and I'd like to investigate your emotional wellbeing,' the doctor said after he'd finished mulling over her elaborate notes.

Her husband didn't believe in 'mental health'. Whenever Tabitha felt emotional, he told her to go upstairs and sort herself out and that he didn't want his son to witness her lack of self control.

'Oh, erm sure,' Tabitha replied, a little disappointed that nothing sinister had been found but also relieved that he hadn't seen everything on her file. A proper diagnosis of some sorts might surely help her justify why she had been feeling so anxious and strange. Out of sorts. Lost even. She had progressed from one minor medical complaint to another.

She quickly filled in the paper questionnaire that the doctor had slid over the desk. Nine multiple choice questions entitled 'PHQ-9'. She filled them in honestly and handed it back to the doctor. Several minutes passed as he looked at her responses whilst Tabitha's thoughts wobbled between the scary news story and a fairly backseat argument about whether to cook a curry or chilli for dinner that evening.

'Well Tabitha, you have scored 4 which means we can say with some confidence you do not have clinical depression or anxiety. How do you feel about your mood?'

'Well I guess I can be a little anxious at times, but that's just one of the joys of motherhood I suppose.'

'It could well be,' replied the doctor, skipping back through her onscreen notes, as if he was looking for something but not sure what, eventually appearing to give up. 'Look, I feel unhappy letting you leave without offering some advice and treatment as I feel despite the test results there may be some underlying anxiety issues here. There's an NHS website called '*Living Life to the Full*' where you can access some free cognitive behavioural therapy. I'm also going to give you one month's prescription for an SSRI. It's used for mild cases of depression and anxiety. I'd like you to come back and speak with me or another doctor in a month to see how you're getting along.' He handed her a note with a website on and the names of several NHS free apps to aid with anxiety: 'Calm Harm', 'Catch It' and 'Big White Wall.'

'But I'm not depressed,' Tabitha replied. 'I certainly don't feel depressed, I only cry occasionally. I'm exceptionally good at suppressing emotions. Except for laughing at the kids at school sometimes when I probably shouldn't. In fact, other than watching Watership Down last Christmas, I can't remember the last time I cried. If anything, I feel numb mostly. Will it be you I see next time?'

'Yes certainly. Let's book you in now so we can pick up where we left off. I'm not saying you're depressed Tabitha… I think you just need a little nudge back on track. It may be possible that you're just… well… a little bored?'

CHAPTER THREE -- MRS. BURROWS

That night whilst putting Oscar to bed in his room dimly lit from the corner by a small Tiffany style 1930's stained glass lamp, Tabitha went through the same slow, peaceful ritual of helping him get into his digger pyjamas, brushing his teeth and gently tickling him all over.

She lay down next to him and passed him his warmed bottle of milk – he glugged on it, forcefully at first then slowing down for the last few drops as his eyes closed. She gave her gorgeous son a long hug, caressed his cheeks and forehead then stroked his curly locks for what felt like hours, all the while staring at her most marvellous creation and feeling blissfully lost in the moment. He had folded himself into the foetal position. He had always been a side-sleeper, and was facing Tabitha. Their breathing was synced and Tabitha found herself momentarily resting the heavy lids of her green eyes. She could still see his gorgeous sleeping face, permanently imprinted on the inside of her eyelids. She didn't care if this was the last thing she ever saw. The love she felt for her son was so deep it floored her. He was perfect.

Oscar's generally trance-inducing gentle snores were broken by a loud snuffle and Tabitha regained awareness of her surroundings. She realised that he was asleep and probably had been for nearly half an hour. With her eyes now open, but her nose pressed against his, she tried to inhale as he exhaled; their faces so close that she felt at one again with him, just as she had felt when he was inside of her. In all truth though, that feeling of being bound together almost physically with love had never left her and hopefully never would.

'You're perfect. Never change,' She whispered to her sleeping infant.

She slowly pulled away from Oscar and got off the bed, tiptoeing along the narrow gap between the side and the window. She noticed the curtains were not drawn fully and as she stood, facing out over her back garden softly yanking the metal rings along the pole, she took a quick peak outside. She realised that although it was now getting dark, she could clearly see into several of the houses opposite on the quiet road behind hers, the other side of the muddy access-only track. Most of the houses belonged to families, and she could see many of her familiar neighbours sat in front of the TV or having a meal gathered around a table. She only knew several of her neighbours by name, and the one she spoke with the most was Mrs. Burrows who lived directly opposite. They often shared pleasantries in the summer as they both pottered around in their gardens. Mrs. Burrows seemed to know her way around a flower bed and Tabitha found her garden hours split between trying to keep freshly sun-creamed skin away from the sand pit and reducing the amount of daisies Oscar ingested.

Mrs. Burrows lived alone, a lady of God. She'd been married at seventeen and widowed young and seemed to have a busier social life than Tabitha, out most evenings of the week. The last time they had chatted, Oscar was having a tantrum and Tabitha had been tired. She had opened up to Mrs. Burrows, who had sensed the desperation of a struggling mother and listened compassionately.

'The church provides many opportunities for socialising and being involved with the local community, you know dear – I am sure you would find something to get involved with,' she'd said something along those lines several times to Tabitha even though Tabitha had never asked for advice.

The Vineyard was their local church and was an uneventful ten minute walk from where Tabitha lived. It was a traditional, gothic building with large, stained glass window and an adjacent hut fitted with toilets and a simple kitchen to be used by the local community. It had been carried and rebuilt brick by brick in the 1800's, with over 100 coffins and chests of human remains being reburied elsewhere in Bristol in the process. Its original site was deconsecrated in the late 1980's and converted into a climbing centre like a modern-day Tower of Babel.

As Tabitha stared vacantly at Mrs Burrow's back garden, the words of the unrequested advice echoed in her mind. Oscar wasn't going to be small forever and perhaps it was time for her to have a bit of a life again. Maybe she could help out with Scouts? But so much of that was outside activities, campfires, insects and mud. Maybe not for her.

Mrs. Burrows had lived in the house directly opposite Tabitha for as long as Tabs and Jack had been there, in fact, Tabs was pretty sure that Mrs. Burrows had lived there her entire adult life, although Tabitha had never been invited in. The interior decoration from what Tabitha could see from her own home looked like a museum exhibition. Tabitha looked in through Mrs. Burrows back window. She was folding laundry downstairs in her front room. Her laundry basket was overflowing with grey and white linen. Mrs. Burrows stood slightly hunched with one eye on her old-fashioned, black and white television set and the other on the task in hand. Tabitha wondered why one little old lady would have so much laundry. Suddenly, Mrs. Burrows looked up as if startled or distracted by a movement from her garden, perhaps a bird or urban fox and in doing so, caught Tabitha's eye. Tabitha realised she looked like she was spying, she was of course merely browsing the horizon, so she raised a hand and smiled at her neighbour whilst continuing to shuffle with the curtains. Mrs. Burrows, a kindly soul, smiled and waved back before returning focus to her house work.

Tabitha had lost her own parents and grandparents and Mrs. Burrows reminded her of her own grandmother. Although they chatted quite often and lived so close, neither of them had invited the other over for tea and cake. Perhaps it was time to. Did she have children? Grandchildren? She certainly had never mentioned them to Tabitha and no one other than other old biddies from church ever came to visit her but she did go out to a lot, probably to church related activities. Perhaps she led a secret life as a professional escort? A niche market but a market none the less. Or maybe she was an ardent taxidermist, collecting road kill at dusk and taking it down to add to a dungeon of strange stuffed animals in her cellar? Tabitha giggled at her own strange mind and went downstairs to start work on her own massive pile of laundry.

Jack was home and playing some kind of game on his console that involved shouting commands at his friends via his 'internet-linked headset' whilst moving block-shaped objects around a virtual field.

'Alright, love?' he asked without moving his neck.

'Yes thanks. Pretty tired but I'm going to finish the laundry, make the packed lunches for tomorrow then I really need to give the hallway a quick hoover. Someone seems to have brought a lot of mud in with them,' she replied, rubbing her tired eyes. 'Did you hear more people died today from that drug you were reading about this morning? A couple in Bristol as well.'

'Huh? Oh yeah. Weird. Bloody druggies.' He battered the buttons on his controller with one hand, took a big swig from his third can of lager with the other and started to swear in jest through his headset.

'When I've finished my hoovering, I have some preparation for work to do so please don't keep resetting the router like you did the other night. I lost a lot of my reports.'

'But my game went glitchy. It had to be done, love. I'll give you a heads up next time OK?'

What appeared to be a cube-shaped pig was bouncing around the bottom left corner of the TV screen and Jack was laughing hysterically at this whilst suggesting that they needed to build a pen for it to his online mates. Tabitha sighed and headed out into the kitchen.

Before embarking on the laundry, she decided to indulge in one last cuppa of the day and sat down to do some ever so important swiping on her smart phone. She Googled 'The Vineyard' and discovered that Monday night was Salsa evening, Thursday night held a Women's Institute gathering, 7 until 10pm, and Friday evening was book club. She couldn't dance and didn't have time to actually read a proper book so other than the remaining bible study sessions, W.I. seemed her only option. She had been pretty good at sewing when she was a girl and she liked a cup of tea and a biscuit as much as anyone. It was really just like the Scouts without all the nasty, outside stuff. She would ask Jack if he would mind doing bath and bedtime on Thursday so she could check it out.

Mrs. Burrows always went to W.I. and Tabitha occasionally saw her walking slowly towards the old church building when she was driving late back from work after the various compulsory after-school meetings and parents' evenings she had to attend. She often noticed that her lights, bar the ever-lit hallway pendant, were all off each Wednesday, Thursday and Sunday evening. Maybe they could become closer friends, take the short walk each week together, share gardening tips and swap recipes?

Had Tabitha inadvertently been stalking an OAP? Tabitha heard the Doctor's words in her head again. Bored? How on earth could she be bored?

'*W.I 7pm,*' she scrawled in her diary slot for Thursday that week. The blue ink popped against an otherwise clear week-per-view spread. She leafed through the month ahead and stared sadly at her blank diary. Her vacant diary stared back at her. At least she had something in it to look forward to now.

CHAPTER FOUR -- STAY AND PLAY, STEVE and the RAT

'So, my little Arlo took his first steps today! He's definitely advanced according to the Little Bear app. We were having our breakfast around the island, eggs Benedict, smashed avocado, and he made it from his deluxe sheepskin play rug to the Brio train set. We were so proud. He sleeps through too.'

'Chester simply adores his new amber teething necklace. I haven't had a squeak of a problem from him since he's been wearing it,' another perfect-mum-clone piped in without even acknowledging perfect-mum-clone-mark-one's self absorbed comment. Tabitha could feel herself do a little sick in her mouth whilst involuntarily eavesdropping the yummy mummy group sat by the window at the stay and play group she had taken Oscar to that morning. It was Tuesday, her day off, and as much as she despised the cliquey groups and one-up-mum-ship conversations that happened here, she knew her boy loved it, and the cake was good.

They weren't even listening to each other. And how on earth had they managed to be out at 9.30am with a full face of make up on, and such colour coordinated, trendy outfits? She had given up on coloured clothes, opting for stretchable black leggings and sweaters on her days off which meant no ironing and she could just sling on whatever was on the top of her clothing pile without worrying too much about looking a state. At least now Oscar was that bit older she didn't have to worry about puke covered shoulders, sodden nursing bras and taking an ancillary of wet wipes and clean clothes out with her each day. It had only been a fortnight but he was dry through the day now - hallelujah! Poo-magedon eruptions which reached the back of his neck were hopefully passed now too. Yes babies were cute, well some of them anyway, some looked like Phil Mitchell or that bold guy from Master Chef – but Tabitha was well and truly glad that Oscar was now able to communicate a little and occasionally entertain himself and was 90% of the way along the path to continence. In fact, they were probably at the interesting cross-over point at which, after a very long, natural, vaginal birth, her son was more continent than she was.

Glancing over at Oscar, she could feel a smile of pure adoration creeping across her face. She hoped she didn't look smug, and tried to hold the inner glow back but in doing so, she started to worry that she might look like she had a facial tick so she released the grin anyway – no-one was looking. No-one looks at women over the age of 35 with babies in their arms or toddlers wrapped around their ankles anyway, unless they're under nine years old and lost in a supermarket or you've just run over their dog.

She watched him sifting through the piles and piles of immunity triggering, BPA-rich, often broken toy tat, searching again for the same collection of cars and trains. He did the same thing every time she took him to Rainbow Sprogs' stay and play. Oscar wouldn't settle until he had all eighteen of the vehicles cradled tightly in his clenched arms and hands. He'd then carry them over to the same spot on the toxic-green and city-grey transport-themed kids' rug. Next he would push them back and forth, making all the correct sound effects, then line them up in order to then slide them down a plastic car park ramp before lobbing them at the wall. He was a creature of habit she thought to herself. Like a puppy, never tiring of the same games. At least this recently new habit didn't involve pooping in the bath and smearing it all over the shower screen.

'We're going to baby sensory next Tuesday,' perfect-mummy-mark-one said.

'Have you seen the new plaster of Paris foot imprint kits they're doing in Mothercare?' the second replied. Tabitha had accidentally tuned into the mums by the window again and she could hear they were now bragging about the new range of organic children's clothing that they had been spending their money on. She grimaced at the thought of how much money they were spending on clothing their babies – babies probably really don't care what they are wearing – even Jean Paul Gautier was happy rolling about naked as an infant, immersing his arms in his porridge just to see what it felt like.

There were mountains of used, clean baby and toddler clothes at all the charity shops she had ever visited, all worn by several babies previously; none of which had cared about what shade of midnight mocha and honey they were wearing or whether their sailor cap and tally matched their striped Breton. Even better, maybe not breeding at all would have reduced their carbon footprints even more. She held back. Realising that this anger was ridiculous and they were actually just really caring ladies wrapped up in the hormones and opiate-like blanket of early motherhood.

Her mind had successfully taken her from full blown livid to a zen-like state of calm within minutes but even though she had been sat in the same spot she could feel herself breaking out in a heavy sweat. Panicking that maybe she was experiencing some accelerated form of peri-menopause, she glanced down and realised she was sat right next to the radiator which was on full blast, in the middle of summer. Ridiculous. But she was relieved. She got up and moved to a different seat. Some of her mummy friends that she had known from her ante-natal classes had come into the hall and joined her.

Tabitha joined them and they all got a coffee together and started moaning about their partners and how much washing they had to look forward to when they got home.

'Would anyone be able to check up on the house, water the plants, feed the cats et cetera?' asked Laura. Laura and her family were off to Lanzarote the following day.

'Sure, no problem... anything to get out of the house in the evenings. Jack could do Oscar's bath and bedtime and I could get some fresh air,' Tabitha said, as she found herself volunteering. 'Maybe I could even jog over? Best order another piece of cake if I'm going to be doing exercise this week then.'

Laura only lived a few roads behind Tabitha anyway so it really wouldn't be any problem at all. She did bloody hate cats though. Scratchy buggers. The irony of her name being synonymous with cats had been a standing joke between her and her mother as she was growing up. They were possibly her least favourite of animals, bar giant African land snails. They'd had a load of snails at school a few years ago and the hermaphrodite molluscs kept reproducing. They moved ridiculously slowly but they bred like rabbits and the Science department ended up with an epidemic. They were everywhere; in old jam jars, Tupperware boxes, 2 litre ice cream tubs… Eventually they had to start freezing them to get rid of them. It was a monstrous act of mass molluscicide.

Laura gave Tabitha the spare key for her back door then gave her brief instructions on how to feed and water the cats and plants. Tabitha was sure it wouldn't be that much of a challenge, but she listened carefully as she didn't want to end up pouring Baby Bio in the cat bowl and freeze-dried meaty nuggets on the cheese plant.

A heavily pregnant lady entered the hall. She was rubbing the small of her back with one hand and pushing a battered, overloaded buggy containing a snotty, screaming toddler with the other. An overfilled, green rucksack hung on her back bursting at the zip, spilling out contents like a vomiting tortoise. The clearly stressed lady made her way to the nearest chair to deal with her little girl's outburst.

All four ladies faced each other with the same knowing look. A look which was a mixture of fear and nostalgia. Tabitha was so glad the early days were past her and so it seemed, were her friends. The Disneyfication of pregnancy had fooled all of them. Tabitha had expected swarms of cute, fluffy, forest animals to follow her everywhere as she skipped about singing with happiness when pregnant, but it had actually been quite the opposite. All she really wanted to do after teaching all day long up until 36 weeks when pregnant was eat carbohydrates by the bucket load, lie on the sofa watching This Morning and sleep. The 'joy of pregnancy' scheme should be dolling out more paybacks than the 'mis-sold PPI' scandal.

The next day, Oscar at Izzy's and Jack out selling doors, Tabitha arrived at work just in time to prepare for her first lesson. Out of the printer in the Science office streamed twenty five warm A4 copies of a worksheet. On each sheet, a picture of a rat, supine and spread-eagled, paws pinned down with its abdominal cavity neatly sliced from throat to genitals. Each rat spread open so that the innards were all on display. She entered her teaching lab and quickly checked the back of her lab coat for drawings of penises (always better to be safe than sorry) before swinging it on and donning a pair of disposable gloves. Leila the lab technician was also in the class helping to set up the equipment for the first teaching session of the day.

Bam, bam, bam came the sound of the dissection boards as the science technician slammed them down around the otherwise silent room. In the centre of each cluster of tables she placed a glass beaker of disinfectant and a plastic beaker with scalpels, sharp tweezers, surgical scissors, long pins and a mallet ready for the class.

She left a stack of old newspapers donated by the staff to be used to protect the desks from guts at the front of the class next to Tabitha's computer. Having a quick browse at the pile together before distributing the sheets out to the desk clusters, Tabitha and Leila shared a smile at the collection of trashy tabloids that the staff had brought in over the past few weeks, removing the page 3 ladies from the various dailies so as not to cause offense to the students.

'Nice to see the teachers read such high brow materials hey Tabs?' Leila joked. 'Rats are in the bucket. Make sure they go back in the bucket at the end please. Oh, and please count back in the sharps. We've had a few go missing recently which is a bit of a concern.'

'Sure. Will do, thanks Lei,' Tabitha chirped. She always did anyway. Couldn't help it, it was in her nature to be thorough. She always tidied away her practical equipment in the same way she always made sure that a box of Celebrations was never returned to the larder with just one sweet left in the bottom.

Leila trotted off to the sanctity of her prep room before the students arrived and the noise escalated to somewhere between eleven and sonic hell.

The second bell of the morning went off in the hall and she could distantly hear her A-Level students ambling along the corridor, the noise and banging of their shoes building up to a fairly intimidating approach akin to the late nineties advert for Guinness where a row of huge, watery stallions rise from the sea, breaking onto the shore with the crashing surf. She went to greet them at the door, quickly hiding the bucket of rats under her teacher's desk at the front beforehand to delay any inevitable hysteria or feinting. She wondered if anyone else in the world had ever had to hide a bucket of dead, formaldehyde-filled rats of a morning other than perhaps Damien Hurst from his parents in his bedroom as a strange teenager.

She welcomed the class in.

'Coats off, lab coats on and get out your notes please.'

On the front wall, she projected the image of a splayed rat and started to talk through the procedure, letting them know how to carefully slice away the furry, top layer then peel back the epidermal tissue below, holding it down in place using the mallet and pins. They would hear the sound of tiny bones snapping but not to be alarmed as the rat was well and truly unaware of what they were doing to it. After gently cracking open the fragile, tiny ribcage, the class were to investigate the digestive system first, starting with the sharp rodent teeth, all the way down to the large intestine, gently squeezing out any impacted faeces with the a gentle, gloved finger. The class all groaned and a couple of the boys made pretend vomiting sounds. If they were exceptionally careful they could prise away the connective tissue and unravel the entire digestive tract from oesophagus to anus and stretch it out around the outside of their dissection board to measure. What a time to be alive. Or dead... in the case of the rat.

The students tucked into their practical work with enthusiasm and only a few further shrieks of disgust were made, even at faeces time. Solly was reading one of the newspaper articles and paying no attention to the task in hand. Tabitha pulled him up on this quietly, moving him and his rat to a different seat where she could see him more easily and took the very out-of-date sports spread from him. She could see a few other students also browsing some of the news features but as they were also working concordantly she chose to let it go. Pick your battles. That's one of the first actually useful things you learn on the job as a new science teacher, chose what to challenge and what to ignore. Alongside always turn the mains gas off when not in use to avoid some pyromaniac Year 8 trying to create a blow torch with orange Bunsen tubing, never smile until the first term is over and always check for fresh cock and ball drawings on the back of your lab coat before putting it on.

'Oi Miss, is it true you're never more than 3 feet from a rat in London?'

'Firstly Bryce, my name is Mrs. Fox not 'Oi Miss' and secondly, it's rude to wave your cutlery around whilst you're eating. Please keep your scalpel below waist height for safety.' She pointed at the knife that Bryce was brandishing in the air as he spoke.

'What about rats though, Miss. Are they everywhere in London?'

'I believe so Bryce; lots of food everywhere and a fabulous sewerage system. I'm pretty sure that there are plenty of rats in all cities actually. I'm sure you'll discover some when you start cooking and cleaning for yourself in student accommodation next year.'

'Eeeeeewwww!,' squealed one of the witches, 'not in my gaff thanks.'

'Did you hear about that guy Miss? The one in London?' Solly chipped in, taking some invisible prompt to now take over as lead clown whilst Bryce stepped down to contemplate how close he might be to a rat, forgetting that he was elbow deep in a fine specimen.

'A little vague, Solly – and is this relevant?' Tabitha responded with a slightly jaded expression. She could see the eyes of some of the other students rolling back. Solly loved the red herring game. He knew Miss was easily led off topic but it sometimes backfired and she often ran over the bell into the start of their break time retelling hilarious stories from her university days.

'Can't remember his name. Some homeless dude. Broke into the Queen's house?' continued Solly.

'The Queen's house?! Buckingham Palace you mean, you moron!' quipped Liam. Liam was one of Solly's sidekicks. Nowhere near as affable as Solly and Bryce, in fact Liam's personality was borderline sly with an offensive glare in his eye at times. He had the sort of face that made him look like he suffocated animals for fun.

'Yeah. Off his face ha ha ha. London sounds crazy.'

'Yes bro. I've just seen an article about it on one of these newspaper bits… hang on let me just scrape the blood off it,' Bryce joined in.

'Look, here... *Steven, 45, of no fixed abode was arrested in the early hours of Sunday morning earlier this month after trying to get into bed with the Queen. He was sentenced to 28 days in jail for trespassing on the site of the 775 room royal palace, and 21 days for criminal damage.*'

'Yes bro! Nice one Steven. Ha ha ha. Absolute jokes bro. What's a homeless guy got to lose hey? Got to be worth a shot. It's a win-win situation for him, init Miss? Was he trying to touch up Queenie's crusty old vag or nick her crown? Now he's got a few months with a comfy bed and hot meals every day too. Winner winner homeless dude's got a free chicken dinner.' It was Solly's turn again.

'Thank you Solly. That is quite enough of that kind of language.' Tabitha interrupted disdainfully, trying to hold back the giggles. How on earth had the conversation led to this? It was only 9.30am and the class had moved from learning the intricacies of a rat's innards to laughing hysterically at a bodged attempt to touch up her Majesty. After managing to suppress her laughter and re-adjusting her professional mask, Tabitha marched over to the cluster of lads and spoke again with a more orderly tone.

'OK boys, back to work now please. This is a conversation you can continue at break time if you wish... by yourselves... in your own time. Look, let me show you its omnivorous dentition.'

After settling the class she meandered over to a quiet group sat in the far corner who had been diligently continuing with their practical task the whole time and showered them with praise. At the back of her mind however she was still thinking about what the lads had been joking about. She wondered why the homeless chap had tried to break in. It was possible he'd been high on drugs? But surely no one could believe they would be able to break into the actual palace itself and steal treasure? Then again, he probably was in a position where he really did have nothing to lose so why not give it a try?

At break time Tabitha quickly pulled together her resources for Year 7 who she was teaching next. They were eleven years old and still fresh from primary and mainly unscathed by hormones, local gang signs and designer sportswear. With her lesson prepared, Tabitha let herself have a few minutes browsing the internet whilst sipping on an earl grey before the bell. She found herself Googling the news sorry that Solly and company had been chirping on about earlier. She had so many more important things to do but felt oddly drawn to the strange tale the boys had spun. Apparently the poor tramp already had 56 previous convictions and had only broken in to find somewhere safe away from the road to sleep for the night. He'd vandalised a display cabinet and bench to make an area to sleep on in one of many palatial gateways. The courts had let him off on unconditional bail initially but he had thrown faeces at the prison guards, so he was pulled back before the judge for indecent assault and put inside for several months. Maybe he wanted to be locked up. How sad that being detained was more attractive than his alternative option. Still, he can probably access drink and drugs on the inside and may even have had Sky TV, a daily shower and hot meals. Apparently he'd been asleep in his homemade bed for several hours on the palace grounds before being discovered. She was not really one for politics but Tabitha new that the austerity measures due to the current government was having a direct effect on policing but surely the palace still had exceptional security? If they hadn't then she bet they sure did now. The bell signalling end of break rang and Tabs trundled off to class feeling slightly glum. Ah well, she could always sling the rat poo from the previous lesson at her Year 7's and then maybe she'd get sent home early.

CHAPTER FIVE -- CATS, DILDOS AND WOMEN'S INSTITUTE.

Tabitha sprang from the sofa, slid back on her slippers and walked to the front door, a uPVC double-panelled 40's imitation classic if you're interested. It swung towards her as she turned the key and gave it a gentle pull with the handle. Jack was home.

'Evening. You're back late. Busy day at the office? How is business anyway? I took a different route home yesterday and noticed that Gainsborough Road could do with flyering. There's a lot of potential work for you there. It's over in Redfield – house prices are creeping up. Gentrification I suppose.' Tabitha said.

Jack entered, gently pushing past his wife without even looking up from his phone which he was glaring at and swiping. It started to ring and glow like an angry supernova and he answered it gruffly, taking himself back outside. The reception was atrocious in BS5, yet mysteriously telesales agencies always managed to have perfectly clear lines when they called either of the Fox's mobiles. She could hear him chatting about business. He seemed to be doing reasonably well. They'd been into Curry's and bought an oversized television the thickness of a paperback on black Friday last year, and Jack had treated her to a new microwave at the same time. Oh the fun she had had with it watching the jacket potatoes rotating on its internal glass plinth as he zapped zombies on his new screen at full volume of an evening. Who'd have thought that selling doors could be so profitable?

He rounded up his call with what seemed to be an agreement to have another meeting the following day at 8am.

'Hey Tabs,' Jack called up from the sofa and screen to which he plonked himself. He was grinning like a child. She knew a joke was coming. Something that Dan from work had told him on the phone. He looked proud of himself. The exact same expression was on his face that Oscar had after managing to successfully do a poo on the toilet and not in his pants.

'Yes dear?' Tabitha answered, stood in the archway of the lounge door, tea towel in one hand, a selection of Tupperware boxes she was trying to match up with their lids held precariously in the other

'I knocked on Stephen Hawkins door today, but nobody answered...' he said, taking the time out from starting up '*Death Zombies from Hell 4*' on the games console to indulge her.

'Uh huh.' Tabitha had dropped the lids on the floor and was on all fours trying to scope them up.

'All I got was '*error 404 page not found*'! Get it? Error 404? It's what computers say when they can't find a website. He's got a computer voice hasn't he?'

'Yes. He DID have. He has died now sadly. Quite a distasteful joke, did you hear that from Dan or a customer?' Tabitha tried to feign interest.

'Yeah, Dan of course. He's hilarious. Should have his own show on TV. I knew he was a winner when I took him on.'

'It is quite distasteful though – he has only just passed.'

Jack looked annoyed that she had not found the gag as hilarious as the boys at work. He puffed out his chest like a humiliated ape and clicked 'Start' on his controller forcefully.

'Not as distasteful as your cooking. That ratatouille the other night was vile,' said Jack bitterly.

'It was a risotto,' Tabitha muttered under her breath as she returned to the kitchen.

Jack got up from the couch, threw the controlled down and followed her out to the kitchen.

'Bloody internet. Virgo Intacta are rip off merchants.'

Whilst looking at her partner as he strolled past her, who was still not making any form of eye contact and moving straight to the American style fridge, she struggled to remind herself of what exactly it was that brought the two of them together. It was 6pm. Her legs were tired, her heart felt jaded and she had just noticed that Oscar had sneakily managed to twang a huge, sloppy spoonful of orange gunk from his high chair earlier all over the floor. She'd been watching the news and several more people, one of them only sixteen had died from this strange new chemical that had flooded the South West causing to irrationally fear for the future her son would have.

Tabitha glanced at the mess which now appeared to have taken up semi-permanent residence as it had dried on and fought off some strong overbearing urge to automatically clean it up. Jack could do it. She threw the Tupperware back in the bottom drawer and tossed the tea towel towards the washing machine. She was going out. He could tidy up for once. She sat on the bottom of the stairs to don her trainers.

'Oh dear, I guess you'll have to clean that up. Tonight's the night I need to nip over to Laura's house to feed her cats remember? I did tell you about it yesterday. Oscar needs a bath, the washing-up needs doing in the sink, the duvet covers need putting on in the spare room too as I simply didn't get round to doing it this afternoon.' She was shocked at her own assertiveness although also fairly sure her instructions were falling on deaf ears.

'Yeah, yeah. Whatever.'

'Maybe you could play with Oscar for a bit first too? He hasn't really seen much of you this week.'

'But he's not very good at this game. He keeps getting us killed by chewing on the controllers. He can't even hold it properly. His hands are too small.'

She wasn't sure if he was joking and she certainly didn't think that the zombie shoot-em-up was appropriate for a two year old and she shot him a very concerned, slightly angry glare.

'I'm kidding. I'm kidding. I'll do something with him in a minute.'

'There's some post for you on the table in the kitchen. I think it's just a bill though and... oh... that needs cleaning up,' she said rapidly, pointing at the sloppy floor mess again, aware that repetition was perhaps the only way to break through his recalcitrance.

'Yes yes whatever, stop nagging,' he retorted. The router had reset and he had picked up his controller once more. Oscar was rolling cars down a slope.

'I'm not nagging...' Was she nagging? She was questioning herself now. She finished lacing up her trainers, grabbed her key and skipped out of the front door without giving him the chance to speak back. She would bet her left arm that next to none of these chores would have been done by the time she got back, but as long as he had put Oscar to bed before she returned that would suffice.

Although Tabitha was still pretty trim for her years, it had been a while since she had put on her Lycra sports tights and bra. It felt good though. She liked the idea of becoming a runner. She'd often watched men and women jog past her front window from the comfort of her sofa thinking that could be her new hobby. They all looked so fit and sporty. She could get one of those bottles with the holes through the middle to hold as she ran and an mp3 player to listen to music or podcasts. It could be her thing. Dr Meaker had said she was bored. Maybe fitness could be her new '*joie de vivre*'?

After adjusting her knickers she put one foot in front and headed off along the pavement, down the busy main road out of the front of her house.

Thud thud thud thud. Pound pound pound. Pant pant pant.

Thus thud thud thud. Pound pound pound. Pant pant pant.

It was early evening and the traffic congestion was starting to ease up as most people other than residents left the area straight after work. They lived quite close to the centre of Bristol and during rush hour, the road outside the front of their house was always busy but after these peak traffic times, it was exceptionally quiet. She plodded along the main road and then turned left and left again to go down a muddy track which ran behind the long row of terraced and semi-detached homes of which her house was part. She could see into her back garden, and also into the back gardens of all of the other houses that hadn't chosen to erect garages or sheds. It was surprising that the area hadn't suffered from more fly tipping or crime really as it was a sheltered, muddy lane, big enough to get a car down but supposedly access only for residents. On the left she saw her back garden and she looked in stopping to stretch out her tight calf muscles. She could see an outline of Jack lifting Oscar up and onto the large double bed in the back room of their two point five bedroom home. She smiled and waved hoping to catch either of their eyes. Jack saw her first and waved but she had a change of heart and pushed forwards; Oscar may get upset if he saw her actually out of the house in the evening.

The 'run' had turned into more of a fast walk and Tabitha had to stop again a few houses along when out of Oscar's field of view. She pulled her phone out of the zipper pocket on the back of her leggings whilst panting fast and hard. She looked on a maps app that she had downloaded earlier in preparation to see how far she had come. Must be at least 2 miles she thought to herself. At least a Cadbury's cream egg worth of calories surely.

257 metres the screen informed her.

257 measly metres and she could barely breathe. Sweat was pouring from every square inch of her surface and she was pretty sure she might have pulled a muscle in her knee. She put her phone away grouchily and continued to walk over to Laura's house which was on another long road of terraced houses parallel to the busy road she lived on and also up hill. No way she was going to risk this running malarkey any further. If she injured her knee, how would she manage at work and looking after Oscar? No, running was not for her. What a shame. She would have to find another hobby. One less risky and less dangerous. How on God's earth do people run marathons? There clearly must be something wrong with them. They must really not care about their knees.

She bent over forwards, her clammy hands on the top of her Lycra-clad thighs, legs and back straight, panting, wiping and flicking off the beads of sweat that were queued up on her forehead. As she looked up she pondered whether to carry on running or simply to maintain the kind of strange motion in between running and walking that she had slipped into. 'Joggling'. She noticed Mrs. Burrows across the other side of the road. She waved at her neighbour and called out.

'Off to church Mrs. B? Lovely evening isn't it?' It was a fairly standard evening by all accounts but when one spends the majority of one's evenings inside, one probably would have found it lovely.

Mrs. Burrows politely responded. 'Yes dear, glorious evening. I'm off to the Vineyard, as always, God is good. It's my women's meeting this evening.'

'Sounds a treat.'

'We have a wonderful chap in to show us how to make macramé light pulls for the bathroom. Then we've got a chap in with his Bonsai tree collection. You be careful now with exercising at your age dear – running incorrectly can cause all sorts of injuries you know.' Mrs. Burrows pulled up her lilac skirt to thigh-level, revealing to Tabitha that she was wearing royal blue knee support wraps and elasticated ankle bandages on each of her skinny and bony legs. She had the lower half of a Mumm-ra/Skeletor hybrid.

'Have a lovely evening yourself,' Tabitha replied. At her age? Cheeky old bag. Tabitha forced a smile through gritted teeth and summoned the Power of Grayskull to provide her with just enough strength to jog at her fastest speed yet further up the road until out of Mrs. Burrows' sight. Even if the ligaments in both her knees were instantaneously severed by a flying Power Sword she would have continued to push through the pain and run after such a comment.

Tabitha made it around the corner. Every muscle and joint in her body was throbbing with pain. It almost felt good but not in a way that she would ever want to repeat. She took a seat on low brick wall surrounding another distant neighbour's back garden and whilst waiting for her heart rate to drop anyway back close to normal, she looked around, still reeling slightly at Mrs. Burrows' comment, also, had she just been flashed at by an old aged pensioner? Looking around her, taking slow, deep breaths, she noticed she could see straight into a kitchen-diner through the double glass patio doors (a rather naff, composite choice - she could hear Jack's voice in her head) of the particular house she was resting next to. Number one hundred and something, Dormer Road.

She stood up, brushed the grit from her bottom and had a good peer into the house. Lovely oak top kitchen surfaces, a shelf filled with books whose spines had been organised into the colours of the rainbow and beautiful hanging baskets with tropical looking plants draping down that seemed to be thriving (unlike the black-tipped-leaf, droopy Basil plant she had on her windowsill at home). What a tidy house. Beautiful Monet prints in matching wooden frames on the walls too. She could see they even had one of those fancy remote controlled corner sofas with the extending leg rests. Certainly didn't look like they had any children, which explained why it was so tidy and clean. No one seemed to be at home. She placed her foot on top of the wall and started to do some kind of impromptu calf stretch so she could prolong her snooping without causing alarm. Then, when realising no one was around, she jumped over the wall and pressed her sweaty, cupped hands and eyes up to the glass for a better look in their front room.

All of a sudden a small, yappy dog, some kind of miniature bug-eyed Pomeranian or Chihuahua, sprung out of nowhere. Barking and growling at her, it ran up to the glass patio doors angrily. It was a digestive biscuit coloured dog that looked like its head had been squeezed through a hole in a sieve, forcing its facial features to pop out like a cartoon character. As it exposed its set of ridiculously small yet still threatening gnashers at Tabitha, it started to chase its tail and then jumped up and down recklessly. It made enough noise to scare Tabitha onwards even though it was trapped behind glass. She walked off, limping slightly, hoping that she hadn't been seen. No one was around so hopefully she wasn't about to be labelled as the local busybody.

Continuing on her journey to Laura's house, Tabitha regularly checked that the front door key she'd been given was still safely in the little zipper pocket on the back of her jogging tights. She'd settled for more of a brisk walk with pumping arms for the rest of the 10 minute venture. Her trainers took her along Dormer Road which went up to number 164, then she branched off to the right up a flight of steps. It was definitely starting to feel a little cooler and darker in the evenings and she could feel summer was drawing to a close. It was still light enough to see clearly though, allowing her to skip over the dog poop that was spread over several steps. Surely the owner could have stopped and let the dog finish its work in one place? She pictured somebody clearly in a rush dragging their pooping pup up or down the steep steps as it was trying to curl one out.

She got to the top of the path and turned left then continued on her walk. So many of the houses looked the same with two point five bedrooms, downstairs kitchen-diner set-ups and small, additional lounge spaces at the front. She could see into every single one of the terraced houses along Forest Road. Some had built loft conversions with one or two Velux windows, perhaps to room additional family members, or as office space or simply to add value to their property in this area on the boundary between the 'up-and coming' Bristol districts of St. Werburgh's and Eastville. The house prices in the area perhaps suggested that whatever was up and coming and already been and gone, with Tabitha's own house nearly doubling in value over three years.

All of the young professionals who had moved into the area to experience a multicultural existence, to fully immerse themselves in all that the amazing city of Bristol had to offer had since found themselves surrounded by people exactly the same as themselves,

Ultra-Bland-Ville. The influx of wealth, property developers and young professionals had forced the original inhabitants out of the area. Many of these privileged, middle class families had built single or double ground floor extensions into the back garden space which Tabitha kept a mental tally of as she walked along. These affluent people in their thirties and forties were flooding the area, searching for culture yet displacing it at a rate faster than their gin and Dubonnet ice cubes melting on a sunny day. Once they had pounced on a house that a greedy landlord had put up for sale, a landlord who had treated the existing rental tenant that could no longer afford the monthly increments like an unwanted infection, they invested in their own properties as their own families expanded, contributing to the sky high rises in home prices in the area. Tabitha was fully aware she was part of this process, instigated by greedy estate agents and the banks, which she felt helpless over yet still sickened her somewhat. Gentrification was spreading over Bristol like a bacterial colony on a Petri dish.

She passed several family homes, where older children were up and playing on desk top computers and handheld tablets or chatting to their parents in the kitchen around the table after their evening meal. Some houses were owned by very elderly people; couples or widowers, like Mrs. Burrows who had lived on this road their whole adult life. Bait for property sharks - just waiting for them to pop their clogs so their homes could be modernised and flogged for a hefty profit.

A few of the properties were student properties, rented out from September through to June, then often hollow for the Summer whilst redecorated and prepared for a fresh batch of youngsters with student loan money to blow, mainly on rent. Bristol was blessed with two superb universities and Tabitha had links with both of them as part of her teaching career and really enjoyed visiting both for various promotional events or open days with her sixth formers. The student properties were generally pretty easy to spot. Like in most built up busy cities, they usually had both extensions and loft conversions so that whoever owned them could claw back as much rental income from them as possible and often, were fairly poorly maintained. On bin day, a lot of the student properties – if they remembered to put out their recycling and waste –could usually be spotted a mile off as their waste overflowed all of the council-provided containers into the roads; empty beer and cider cans, cheap bottles of wine, fast food packaging et cetera pouring out onto the pavements. The curtains of such student properties often remained closed until midday and loud music pumped out of them well into the night. The student gardens were usually just places to store bikes, where, due to the temporary nature of the occupants, very little pride was taken in maintaining beautiful flowers, ornaments or nice furniture. In fact one back garden Tabitha passed on her way to Laura's was just a thick blanket of mud edged with wooden pallets instead of grass or concrete. It was further garnished with a large, chipped, clay plant pot full to the brim with hand rolled cigarette butts, a display of various up-ended traffic cones, 5 large, empty cable bobbins (that had presumably been used as make-shift tables and chairs), cardboard packaging and a rusty shopping trolley tipped on its side. It reminded her of a Tracey Emin piece; a late nineties grunge-era installation art statement.

The contrast was extreme as the house next door had a delightful multi-levelled rock garden with a fairy-themed water feature and hanging baskets along the fence filled with what looked like had been climbing strawberry plants. She scaled up another flight of steps and came to Timber Road which was the third road behind and parallel to the road on which she lived and the road on which Laura lived.

She tipped the lever to open the back gate; a tall, wooden affair preventing anyone from seeing into the back garden. Great idea. Tabs wondered why other inhabitants on this street had not built such fences. It gave Laura's back garden much more privacy. It would certainly keep out any nosy busy bodies or potential burglars. Tabitha couldn't stand it when people peered into her lounge window whilst stuck in a traffic jam out the front. She realised that Laura and her family had probably had these tall fences built not just for privacy but also as added protection for their pets. Laura had struggled to conceive and her and her partner, Theo, whom Tabs had never actually met, had all but given up trying when they fell pregnant with baby Charlie. They were both in their early forties and had filled their child-shaped void up until the point of successful conception with feline affection.

Tabitha put the key in the back door lock, turned it to the left until she heard the bolt move out of its socket and she slowly opened the door. She didn't want to scare the cats and she also didn't want them to escape. Laura had told her that they did occasionally go outside into the fenced garden when supervised but they were not allowed off the premises as they were extremely expensive pedigrees. She had called them her 'coon babies' which was a term Tabitha was pretty sure had some heavy racist connotations to it but was too polite to mention this. She had conjured up an image of some kind of strange racoon-slash-moggy creatures with striped tails and bandits' eyes, standing assertively on hind legs discussing how to avoid the evil Cyril Sneer. Her imagination at play again. What on earth was Cyril Sneer anyway? Some kind of pink, hairless, miniature elephant?

They were just cats. Maine Coones. To the untrained eye, basically quite big cats, easily fill a pillowcase but still space for a brick sized cats, with really fluffy manes. Tabitha was not a fan. They were almost lion-like in appearance and stature. There were three altogether: Sheba, Aslan and Simba. Simba was the most recent addition and was one of a litter born to Sheba and Aslan. Sheba was a graceful, proud female cat and the first of the trio to come over and greet Tabitha with a shin-dance, Tabitha let the cat weave in between her slightly sweaty leggings and it did so in a slightly hypnotic, figure of eight pattern. Sheba then became shy suddenly (all cats are turncoats at heart aren't they?) and retreated to a different room – out of sight, somewhat nebulous in nature just like the real Queen of Sheba.

Tabitha was definitely more of a dog person. It's wrong to categorize and stereotype but, if people had to be categorized, then it should definitely be based on their preferred choice between the two common house pets. Dog people were, in her mind, generally loyal, kind, thoughtful hard working people, with a tendency towards overeating, becoming mildly anxious and flighty when left alone for long periods of time or overtired, but such behavioural problems easily solved with more food. Cats, well, cats weren't meant to be stored in houses for starters. Cats were vain, powerful, selfish creatures of the night. Cats were scratchy little buggers. These guys seemed standoffish and aloof, stereotypical cat behaviour really. Cat people certainly didn't care about gentrification – they would have pretended to, to their fellow cat people, but in their hearts, cat people only cared about themselves. Cat people would build an extension that blocked out their neighbour's afternoon sun completely so they could bask in it in front of them.

Tabitha scanned the kitchen area and nodded her approval to no-one of their tasteful, neutral décor choice. She instantly spotted the cupboard next to the dishwasher that Laura had said she would find the food for the animals. She grabbed from it an 'exquisite salmon flakes' re-sealable food pouch and using a clean spoon from the draining board spooned some into each of the three metal bowls by the back door.

God it stank. The only animal she disliked more than cats and giant African land snails was fish. Well, dead fish anyway. She had often reflected on the irony of being named Tabitha which was to all purposes a cat's name when she couldn't stand the rhinitis-inducing scratchy monsters. At least she hadn't been named after a fish. That would be worse. A lot worse. Poor Mr. Turbot featured heavily in much of the semi-illiterate graffiti at school, even though he was actually quite a nice guy. Pervert-Turbot, Master-Fish-Bait, Mr. Fishy Fingers... The level of creativity that teenagers applied to insults was outstanding – it's a shame Ofsted didn't fully appreciate it in the way Tabitha did.

She popped the spoon in the sink and put the food pouch in the fridge to be finished off next time she was there. She emptied and filled up the water bowl which the trio shared – apparently cats liked fresh water daily and wouldn't sip from it at all if it was more than two days old. Typical feline standards. Oscar would happily glug juice on the turn from an old sippy cup he had stashed down the back of the sofa maybe a month earlier. He had also eaten a handful of maggots out of the brown food recycling bin just after his first birthday too so perhaps his standards were fairly low by comparison. Kids were much easier on the food and drink department than these fancy cats. She was glad she had been blessed with a baby over a cat, even though having a baby was undoubtedly the hardest thing she had ever done. Also, Oscar didn't crap all over her garden and dig up the marigolds. Well he hadn't yet anyway, although there was still time for this. The two remaining cats who had been eyeing her up with ultimate suspicion were still staring at her from afar.

Dogs would have been straight over, but these cats weren't giving anything away in this lifelong battle of power between human and feline. One of them, Simba, the kitten, she guessed by his slightly smaller size, eventually came over for a sniff of the fishy dish but had the cheek to turn his nose up and walk away into the other room. They'd eat it when they got hungry she thought tersely and went about looking for the indoor watering can Laura had mentioned with which to hydrate her greenery.

Tabitha had a quick look through the kitchen cupboards for the watering can. Everything was so neatly put away. Lovely crockery too. She inspected the base of a saucer to see where it was from before placing it carefully back. Then she took it out again, along with a tea cup and made herself an earl grey. Why not? It's the least they could do; provide her with a lovely cuppa to rehydrate herself with after the exertion in getting there. She inspected her trainers and wondered whether they would be passable as new if she tried to take them back to the sports shop later in the week. Perhaps not, too much mud on them already and she had pulled the laces a little too aggressively in her rush to leave the house earlier, puckering the holes slightly. She slipped them off to avoid marking the beige carpets and lined them up by the back door.

Whilst she sipped on her courtesy-drink, she roamed around, opening and closing the wall-mounted cupboards and found a few biscuits to accompany her tea. Tabitha found she quite enjoyed looking through the cupboards, each time she opened a different door, not knowing what she was going to find. It gave her a slight pleasure, a bit like opening your Christmas advent calendar window as a child. What would the picture be today? Was there chocolate behind it?

In a cupboard, she found a shoe box containing loads of pens: biros, felt tips, indelible markers, some pencils, a few rubbers and a pencil sharpener shaped like a small (politically incorrect) globe. She loved writing materials, especially smart sets of colour-coordinated markers. Sometimes Tabitha wondered if her love of all things stationary related was the main reason she had become a teacher. Good job she hadn't mentioned her adoration of WH Smiths as her *raison d'être* in her PGCE interview though. It probably wouldn't have clenched the deal.

Tabitha, munching on biscuits, tipped the box of stationary goodies out onto a work surface and spread the pens out and started to match loose lids with stray pen shafts. How satisfying. She managed to match them all up except for one spare lid with no pen to call its home. She debated briefly whether to put the lid back in the box or throw it in the bin. What if the rest of the pen turned up later? What if it never did and the spare lid spent the rest of its days floating around the old shoe box bumping into other complete, coupled up felt tips? What if this made it feel low and useless, incomplete? What if it felt free, liberated and single, laughing at all the other set-in-their ways miserable couples?

She finally decided to bin it. Chances are the pen it belonged to would have dried out anyway. Perhaps it was even already in the bin, waiting for its hat back. She shoved another two Jammy Dodgers into her mouth at once, put the organised stationary box back into the cupboard from whence it came and decided to have a look around the front room. She took the watering can with her, which she had found in the cupboard under the stairs, balanced on top of a Henry hoover and a bag of tools which were exceptionally well organised.

There were several plants in the front room. An aloe vera that clearly needed potting on (she could do that tomorrow evening), two spider plants in handsome matching red and yellow Mexican style ceramic pots and a cacti which looked like it was soon to flower.

Tabitha wasn't a big cacti fan. She saw them as a pointless investment, worse than cats in some ways. You can't stroke them, they bloody hurt if you try and catch one as it falls from the windowsill (personal experience) and they only flower once a year. So typical of it to chose to do that spitefully whilst its owners were away. She would try and get a photo of it if it happened that week and at least she could show it to Laura.

She sighed a woeful sigh as she moved the plants so that they were equidistant and much more aesthetically pleasing. Is this really what her life had become? Getting excited about taking photos of other people house plants rather than spending time with her husband? Yep. But pottering around in someone else's house seemed to be making her feel a tiny bit happy, liberated at least anyhow. A life in someone else's shoes. Someone who had chosen a different path, made different life choices, chosen different colour combinations of soft furnishings. She made a note in her phone to write a note in her diary to remember to take a photo of said plant and then gave them each a splash of water.

Tabitha pulled off a few dead leaves from the spider plants and gave the windowsill a little dust with her sleeve before noticing the well organised book shelves either side of the fireplace. Tabitha couldn't remember the last time she had actually finished reading a book. Any reading she did tended to be work from her students when she was marking it or Todd the Little Tractor 'lift-my-flaps'. She picked up 'The Alchemist' by Paulo Coehlo. It had such a lovely cover, and added it to the list on her phone of things she'd love to read when she got some time to herself. She placed it back in the same place she took it from then moved across the tightly packed collection of spines, feeling each with her finger from left to right. She was absorbing the texture and noting the strange 'kdkdkdkdkd' sound that it made than actually paying further attention to the names and authors of the novels. She came to the end of the row and found three large photo albums. Tabitha decided this called for more tea, which she made, and then looked through the photographs, all 540 of them in the comfort and peace of Laura's well-furnished lounge.

She relaxed back into the velour sofa and put her feet up on the poof. She said the word 'poof' out aloud several times, fairly loudly just because she could, and as she did this whilst looking at herself in the standard above-the-fireplace-mantelpiece mirror, she enjoyed the way the 'ooooo' sound felt to her cheeks and jaw, making her face look younger and slimmer. She paused mid poof as if she had been caught pinching penny sweets from the post office and wondered if she was even allowed to still say the word poof or was it now deemed offensive, even if used in context of a foot rest.

On finishing the assortment of family snaps, she bounced up from the sofa and placed the albums back on the shelf. She realised that the poof on which her sweaty feet had been resting was in fact of the storage variety and she couldn't help but lift up the smooth 'Majestic Mauve' coloured velour lid to have a look inside. It was full of toys. What a fabulous idea. No wonder their house looked so tidy, they had simply shoved everything into this huge poof. Out of sight out of mind. The whole house looked immaculate, almost like a show home but this was why... everything was just shoved into cupboards. Some might call this tidying, others cheating. Tabitha, by her very nature, would have loved to live in a house as tidy and barren as an IKEA showroom, but Oscar was at such a busy age. In the newborn days she'd told herself it was a waste of precious time which could otherwise be spent carrying out her two favourite hobbies of sleeping or eating, and as long as there was a clear path from the bottom of the staircase to her kettle for her morning coffee, she tried to not let the huge sea of plastic toy cars and building blocks that littered her humble abode bother her too much.

She rummaged through the designer toys and found confirmation that no one, no mother, was perfect and every mum had to deal with piles of kid-junk that just somehow swam like a lethal undercurrent from one part of the house to the other, slowly spreading and filling every void like plastic cancer.

Laura had birthed one of those sleepy babies; one of those ones that did twelve hours straight from day three. One of those ones you read about in the guide books for expectant parents. One of those ones that were about as rare as a rocking horse shit.

What would she find upstairs? Laura hadn't mentioned any plants upstairs, but there maybe one or two up there she had forgotten about that would have needed a watering. Laura would be so upset to come home to wilted foliage wouldn't she? Tabitha convinced herself that it wasn't so much prying as going above and beyond the call of her role of house sitter as she skipped up the stairs with the watering can and pushed open the polished wood door of the first of two bedrooms. She jumped onto Laura's bed like a child on a sleepover and pulled her phone out to check for any missed calls or messages and then, finding nothing of interest, leapt up again and opened the large, mirrored built-in wardrobe doors in the master bedroom. Laura always looked smart and she seemed to have lots of stylish clothes. Tabitha took out a particularly stunning sequinned number and checked the size label. Yup, size twelve. She could probably just about squeeze into it.

So she did.

Sort of.

As long as getting the zip done all the way up didn't count. Along with not being able to open her legs apart far enough to take a normal looking step.

Tabitha, remembering that she may still be a little bit sweaty from her 'run', whipped the cocktail frock off, accidentally making a slight tear in the process.

'Oh crabsticks,' Tabitha muttered out loud to an audience of no-one except for the arching pile of hissing fluff that had been hiding in the corner - bloody cat. As it lowered its whiskery snout to the ground and stretched out its clawed arms, Tabitha threw the dress at the cat more through sheer frustration at herself for having ripped it than to deliberately hurt the creature. Luckily the cat escaped unscathed, slinking off half way down the stairs. That one definitely wouldn't be greeting her with purrs and smiles tomorrow. Damn it.

She pulled her running gear back on, bent forwards to collect the discarded dress and carefully edged the outfit back onto its hanger. After slotting it back into its place in the depths of the wardrobe, Tabitha closed the mirrored door, reflecting back at her the guilt of the damage that she had just done from every angle, and heard the cat creep back up the stairs for a second round. Bloody good job that they couldn't speak or she'd have been up the proverbial creak without a paddle. A total cat-astrophe.

The furious feline was sat on the landing, making sure it had the final say in the dispute and it just glared at Tabs, throwing her a look as if to say '*dah-ling, you are most definitely not a size twelve anymore. Who are you trying to kid*' before scampering off once again down the stairs.

Tabitha reassured herself that Laura would never find out about the tear. When would she ever get to wear a dress like that? It wouldn't at least be until Christmas party season or New Year's Eve and that was months away. By then she'll have long forgotten that she ever invited Tabitha into her home. She could say one of the cats must have done it if she ever got challenged. Tabitha crept over furtively to the chest of drawers, carefully looking out for more felines as she went, paranoid that she may step on a furry tail and all levels of hell might break loose. The chest of drawers was very pretty; solid wood, possibly maple and definitely not the cheap, laminated type. On the top rested a large baroque-style mirror, a family photo of the three of them slid under its frame and several other framed photos of the cats. A small trinket box containing a few odd earrings and rings lay on a lace doily. Tabitha tried a ring on and took it off straight away. She had never been one for jewellery and only wore her wedding ring as she had to. Rings got in the way when she was teaching, dissecting rats or frogs or sheep eyeballs anyway. The chest of drawers itself had four wide drawers and the top section was split into two. The knobs had beautiful enamel flowers on in shades of aubergine, reds and greens. Tabs pulled the left hand side top drawer slightly ajar, slowly and cautiously to sneak a peak without releasing the genie from its lamp. As she released it, she could see it was stuffed full of underwear like most people's top drawers. She pulled the drawer with more gusto and once fully opened, she started to sift through the pants, bras and socks with her hands.

She enjoyed the feeling of the different textures against her skin; soft satin and sexy knickers right at the back in a range of sexual shades, opal greens, lusty reds, lots of silky, skimpy numbers, untouched for months probably if Laura's baby experience had been anything like Tabitha's, and at the front, the coarse feeling of sensible, bobbled, high rise and tummy control pants. Proper passion killers. Apple catchers. Under-crackers. Granny-pants that leave everything to the imagination. The imagination where nightmares were formed. Knickers that when pulled on, spanned from the top of the knee to well over the belly button, sucking everything in, acting as supporting infrastructure for the soft, sagging body parts left behind from nurturing a baby inside. Underwear that didn't so much suck-in and slim but merely pushed the excess flesh to its rims, leaving the wearer with a flabby frill. The rough binding and cold metallic catches of rigid, functional nursing bras she also felt and saw at the front of the drawer. The daily essentials; used and washed and used and washed until grey and eroded. The contents were very similar to her own top drawer, yet it still felt exciting and novel, rummaging through someone else's smalls.

She excitedly opened the drawer to the right, expecting more of the same and she wasn't disappointed as once again, she could see the brightly coloured, 'practical yet fun' socks of motherhood at the front, a hilarious collection of cartoon character themed hosiery, bright stripes, the occasional sock with ears and smiley faces on them – one pair bright pink complete with curly pigs tails at the back. As she frivolously dug to the back depths of the drawer with her cupped fingers, scooping frantically at fabric like a mole in a tunnel, the socks became replaced with black tights, a jewel encrusted thong, and even a suspender belt with clips and stockings.

Tabitha pulled a pair of frilly French knickers out and looked at the size label. There was no way these would still fit Laura she thought smugly, almost vindictively wallowing in the fact that she wasn't the only mother in the world to still be clinging on to a few extra pounds after giving birth... two and half years ago. She made out like she didn't care, as was the trendy feminist way, but she secretly did, of course she did; as did the majority of all of the other mothers whose bodies had been ravaged by childbirth and breastfeeding. Only would men and women be truly equal when science had developed a way for men to give birth through their penis.

She stuffed the fishnet stocking that she had been twirling around in the air like a majorette's baton back in and in doing so, felt something cold and smooth, plastic possibly. It felt long, familiar yet alien, cylindrical in fact and was getting wider the further along it her hand moved. All of sudden, it started to move. It buzzed and started to move in an orbital motion. She pulled her hand out and away from the sex toy in disgust suddenly realising what she had stumbled upon. It continued to whizz and whirr in the drawer. She forced her hand back in, laughing loudly and switched off the Rampant Rabbit. How would she ever be able to look Laura straight in the face now, after having had an illicit rummage through her underwear and an accidental grope of her vibrator? She went straight into the bathroom and washed her hands thoroughly before heading back in to close up the drawers properly, feeling confident that as long as she left no trace no one would be none the wiser.

There were no plants upstairs and Tabitha realised that it was now totally dark outside whilst drawing the curtains in the second bedroom so she decided to lock up and head home.

Like most other people in the area and many further afield, Tabitha was following the news closely. Each evening on her walk over to Laura's she strolled along, face in her phone, reading about the gradual increase in deaths linked to what the media were now referring to as 'Bleach'. Tabitha had never taken drugs and never would. She had too much to lose, but she knew it wouldn't be long before whatever this monstrous chemical was impacted on her school community. Students were often caught with pot, smoking or selling it to each other at the bottom of the playing fields. How long would it be before they started messing about with this nasty new substance? She found her visits to Laura's house to be a little pocket of escapism. Each evening, letting herself in, helping herself to Laura's tea, drinking it uninterrupted on a different sofa; it was a chance to get away from the stress of her job, the doom and prophetic misery the media was pushing, the constant demands of her toddler and the chasm of a relationship with Jack.

Along with watering the plants and feeding the pesky cats, she also inspected and vetted pretty much every other single drawer, cupboard, nook and cranny that she could find, always making sure to return everything to its original state. When her hands were in someone else's woolly jumper drawer pulling out someone else's favourite cardigan or holding someone else's shower gel whilst in someone else's shower, she felt strangely liberated. She didn't have to think about her own life and how unhappy she was at home or how young people all over the South of England were so misguided and so lost that they were continuing to risk taking a drug that was killing so many in such a horrible manner purely for something to do on the weekend.

She saw her chance to fumble around as her reward for being there; for turning up each evening and spending time with the cats. There was nothing else particularly exciting to reveal at Laura's though, the encounter with the dildo had been the peak of excitement and Tabitha felt a veil of disappointment fall over her as she stepped out into Laura's back garden and locked the front door for the final time before the cat lovers were to return from their holiday.

She placed the spare key back carefully under a large stone toadstool in their front garden as agreed and as she turned her back on the house and the slightly ghastly garden ornament, she wondered to herself just how safe that key really was. Looking all around her to double check no-one had seen her put it there, she marched on reassured that it would be fine but wondered how many other people thought they were being crazily original in hiding a spare key in their garden somewhere for emergencies. Her gran and mother used to do exactly the same thing.

Her grandmother had also often told her how things were much better in the olden days where people would often leave their entire houses unlocked and if a neighbour needed to nip in for a tea bag or two then they would just take what they needed and then leave again. Things were so much better in the past her gran would say. Yes, except '*a person could die from a broken arm and citrus fruits were luxury items,*' Tabitha had often heard her own mother replying, tongue in cheek. There was nothing worth pinching back then either. Thy neighbour had nothing worth coveting.

When Tabs got home that evening, Jack was sat upright on the sofa, with a bean bag bottomed tray acting as an improvised desk, scanning through various images of front doors on his laptop. He must have been working, or playing a ludicrously boring game of virtual Knock Knock Ginger. The TV was blaring out and she could see huge giants shaped like ice cream cones lifting up parts of cars.

The World's Strongest Man or some kind of sports competition. Jack was oblivious to whatever it was it seemed as he continued to scan the door catalogue, eventually clicking on a delightful egg shell blue reinforced composite number for a closer look.

Finding it hard to understand the ecstatic grin that had now spread over Jack's slightly stubbly face, she felt a tad sad yet relieved that she would never truly appreciate doors in quite the same way that he did. Tabitha slipped off her muddy trainers and nipped straight up the wooden stairs to check on her son. Oscar was fast asleep, on his side curled up into a tiny ball; perpendicular to the conventional direction one takes in bed as an adult. He generally did several 360 degree rotations over the course of an evening like a slow motion Catherine wheel before settling for one final position at around midnight where he usually remained until the early hours of the morning when for some reason, frustratingly unbeknown to Tabs, he would start rotating and fidgeting again restlessly until dawn. She had often watched him boxing imaginary monsters in his sleep and he would occasionally sleep talk too, letting out a deep belly chuckle or repeating the names of his current favourite toys and cartoon characters. Oh to be two years old. She kissed him gently on his forehead and pulled the eiderdown-filled duvet up and tucked it underneath his chubby chin. The room smelt of biscuits. She sniffed his neck and kissed him on his forehead. The curtains were slightly ajar again so she crept around the outside of the bed to readjust them, poking her head out in between just to have a quick glance up at the crescent moon before cascading downstairs to find her slippers and open a bottle of Merlot.

She had seen the gorgeous moon and she had also glanced incidentally at the row of houses immediately behind hers, noticing once again that Mrs Burrows lights, bar the ever-lit hallway bulb, were all off. Of course they were. It was Thursday. She would still be at her WI meeting. Tabitha sat down with her glass of red and sank into the comfort of her soft, all encompassing sofa. Yes, it was smattered with the odd stain, badges of Cow and Gate, Ella's Kitchen and something dark blue, possibly blueberries, it definitely wasn't as luxurious as Laura's but it was so homely and comfortable. Plus, they hadn't finished paying for it yet so it would have to do for the foreseeable. Beds and sofas – the two things that you should never skimp on; although Jack would have also added front and rear doors to this universal list.

The wine tasted delicious.

Jack scanned through the evenings offerings hoping to find something that the two of them could enjoy together on TV, and they eventually settled for a wildlife documentary about the accumulation of plastic in the Atlantic. Neither of them were particularly satisfied by this and by ten minutes in, they were both foraging for their mobiles. On her small handheld screen, she took a quick, desperate look into what the upcoming timetable programme was at WI. She had sadly missed a talk on re-potting succulents that evening but next week, an introduction to crochet was on offer with the captivating subtitle of '*How to hook your own dishcloths.*'

Wow. At least she'd still get to sit down if she did attend, and they probably had a good supply of tea and cake.

'Jack dear,' she spoke, gaining enough attention from her husband to make his index finger freeze on his phone screen yet not quite enough to consider his wife worthy of eye contact. She'd settle for this, he was possibly partially listening. 'I'll be nipping out next Thurs evening between 7 and 10 if you don't mind. I'd like to try a new club if that's OK? I am going to learn how to crochet down at WI'.

'Uh huh,' came the predictable response. Tabitha stood up, feeling proud she had made a step, albeit a small one, in the right direction to enhancing her somewhat stale life and salubriously polished off the drips of wine from the bottom of her glass. She patted her other half on the shoulder twice before walking to the kitchen to write down the WI meeting in her red diary. He may not have heard her but she had said it out loud and he hadn't said he was busy so she was blooming well going to go to it. What did she have to lose? At worst she could always leave the WI session early by pretending the baby was ill or something, at best maybe she might learn a new skill and would be able to refurnish the whole house with elegant crocheted doilies. What a time to be alive. She looked at the time. It was 10.35pm. Tabitha considered catching up on the latest on the Bleach situation, but decided to try and stay focused on more positive things. The news was starting to make her feel a little edgy. She yawned, stretched out her arms above her head, arching her lower back and plodded up the stairs to get herself ready for bed.

CHAPTER SIX -- CROCHET IS NOT FOR ME

'Alright Miss? Miss, are we cutting up rats again today Miss? He's dead Miss.'

Tabitha could hear Solly, short for Solomon (a name of Hebrew origin meaning 'peace'. Oh the irony) shouting down the corridor towards the Science office. It was Wednesday lunch time and with five minutes to go until the bell for her afternoon lesson with her upper sixth, Tabitha wasn't really feeling up for an existential banter session with one of her most affable yet most hoodlum-esque students. Soon enough his spotty, asymmetrical face poked around the office door. Tabitha looked up from her desk nonchalantly, lacking some of the enthusiasm she usually had for her students. She was feeling a little tired after her boy had woken up to be comforted several times in the night. Why does he always do that after she's had to stay up until midnight marking homework assignments? She saved her Word Document before making eye contact with Solly who had a shocked, yet keen look on his face.

'He's dead. He's dead, Miss.'

'I'm pretty certain that we made sure the rats were dead before we wrapped them in cling film and put them in individual plastic bags for you last week Solly. Some people deem it cruel enough that 25 rats are bred and killed, albeit as humanely as possible, for each class of students to cut up anyway. I think dissecting living mammals would be a significant animal welfare issue,' she sharply replied. She didn't have time for this nonsense that morning. A pile of Year 7 projects on the uses of magnets was toppling out of her in-tray plus she had 120 reports to write and several lessons to prepare for the following day.

'Nah, Miss. That tramp from London. The one who tried to shag the Queen.'

'A-hem, Solly, wash your mouth out with soap and water. One does not speak like that, especially in the presence of the gracious Science Team,' Tabitha gyrated her wrist and forefinger in a mock-royal manner signalling his attention to the industriousness of the Science staff room. Mr Turbot looked up at Tabitha from his desk across the room, glared at Solly and then deliberately made a point of looking up at the sweepstake the science staff had written on the communal staff whiteboard, obviously encoded, reminding Tabs of their wager. He had good odds on Solly gaining at least one of the attributions by the end of the school year, probably starting a fire by accident or trying to vape ethanol he'd pinch from the Chemistry flammables cupboard. Tabitha couldn't hold back a giggle but then forcing a stern look back on her face she looked at Solly and thanked him for sharing such vital information before asking him to leave and wait outside of the lab with the other students.

'But don't you want to know what happened, Miss? It's well weird. He was found dead in his cell with white eyeballs Miss. All the colour from his pupils gone, and his whole body had turned grey. Gross. Liam reckons he'd been on the Bleach. It's this new drug. Sounds awesome. Except maybe he did a bit too much if he died so maybe not so awesome. It makes you see heaven though. You put it in your eye and it makes you see heaven. He was my idol Miss and he's dead Miss. Dead.'

Tabitha was slightly taken aback by this monologue; her initial response was to correct him on the science in his statements. Iris. He had obviously meant iris as the pupil was actually a hole and appeared black in order to let light in to the eye. Newton actually proved it was a hole by sticking a sharp bodkin needle through his own pupil in the 1600's. She sensed that Solly was joking and playing the fool slightly by the tone of his voice but she wasn't sure if he was lying and if he was why would he make up such a strange, gruesome story? She looked across at Mr. Turbot who was rolling his eyes and mouthing *dropped on his head at birth, Tabs* behind the palm of his hand so that only she could see. She felt a mixture of shock, disbelief and a fit of the giggles rising up from the root of her spine. She looked directly at Solly and once again thanked him for the information. This was truly quite horrific and once again an excellent reason to steer clear of illicit street drugs. He scampered off back down the corridor whistling a repetitively annoying tune and she could hear him greet his mates with voracious high fives and fist bumps. The bell went and she followed him towards the lab slowly and thoughtfully. Poor man she thought to herself. That drug sounds hideous.

The following day, Tabitha woke up after a much more restful night's sleep. She had gotten all of her reports and planning done and was looking forward to a quick morning at work and the afternoon with her precious son. She also had the evening off. Jack was doing bedtime and she remembered on scanning her diary whilst drinking her second morning tea from her Best Teacher mug that she was going to nip down to The Vineyard at seven to check out the WI meeting. She'd probably be the youngest person there so at least that would be a nice feeling.

Her and Oscar were off to soft play that afternoon. Ah, the glorious world of over-stimulating colours, textures and noise. So much noise. A true nightmare for anyone with Asperger's, a propensity for migraines or fully functioning ears. Kids loved it though, and it meant she had a chance to put her feet up and sip hot drinks whilst trying to avoid hearing any more news on the Bleach death count. She might even look at some crochet websites on her phone whilst relaxing alone. Hopefully no one would try and make small talk with her.

On entering, a young child, perhaps 4 or 5 who probably should have been at school was having some existential crisis at the entrance resulting in Tabitha and a very eager Oscar having to wait a good ten minutes to get into the Padded Warehouse of Joy. As the grizzly, spoilt youngster who was flailing around an industrial sized packet of Skittles, sweets falling to the floor like a rainbow shower and her father who had the dishevelled, shifty appearance of a down-trodden drugs mule, pedalling sugar no doubt finally moved through the one-way gate, Tabitha got caught staring at them, accidentally catching the father's eye and gave him the most reassuring of fake smiles as if to say 'I feel your pain, I understand. Kids. Who'd have 'um hey?' but inside she was slightly revolted by the pair of them. She wasn't that fond of children she didn't know. She was pretty sure this was true of many other teachers too. One of the best forms of contraception in the world would be spending a week with Year 9.

She had remembered observing one of Mr. Turbot's lessons where a cocky, lanky fourteen year old had openly accused him of favouritism, and confronted him in front of the other 29 kids, asking him whom he liked the best. Turbot had replied, tongue in cheek: '*I don't have any favourites, I hate you all equally*'. The teen went silent after that. Put in his place. Fifty percent of teaching was acting anyway.

Cushioned walls, bouncy floors, wipe clean surfaces, massive foam rocking horses and defunct speakers blasting out hits from the nineties (that should have been left there) at ridiculously high decibels, punctuated with the occasional harsh hiss of high pitched feedback. At least the cups of tea were adequate to taste and a reasonable price. Although, it was essential to check the cleanliness of the edge of the mug and teaspoon before stirring and indulging. The food was atrocious as standard at such 'Boutique Bounce' establishments and Tabitha was sure that she was not alone in sneaking in a bunch of sterilising hand wipes, a couple of Wagon Wheels and a banana for emergency rations to be scoffed in the least filthy of the toilets. When was heavily-processed food and lots of jumping ever a good idea anyway? She dreaded to think about the amount of vomit the staff here would have to deal with on a weekly basis. Nonetheless, a delightful environment to spend the afternoon in when it was looking very wet and grey outside – when the Wifi worked. Summer was definitely trailing to a finish now and late September was bringing with it many symptoms of the Autumnal era ahead.

She released Oscar who ran off like a rat up a drainpipe into the jungle of small plastic balls, netting and slides and she headed for the counter to order a hot drink. So many choices of coffee. Tabitha wasn't actually sure what all the different types of coffee were and she found herself quickly Googling 'Americano' and 'espresso macchiato' whilst queuing. Could their internet be any slower? She was now front of the queue and still none the clearer. The options were too confusing yet simultaneously all sounding exactly the same according to their internet definitions. Tabitha didn't have a degree in Italian she had a degree in Biology. If the drinks menu had been written using the Linnean binomial classification system she would have coped much better, but all these different coffees… she was sure ordering a hot drink wasn't this hard ten years ago. She settled on an earl grey. Why couldn't they just list '*one teaspoon of instant coffee with water from the kettle and good, old fashioned green-top milk from the fridge?*' She felt a little angry at the world for making things so complicated and also ashamed at her own lack of knowledge and sophistication. With her mug of failsafe tea in hand, she headed for a large fabric sofa and thought about sitting on it. It did look comfortable but then again it could also be full of head lice so she opted for a firm plastic upright chair and sipped her drink, daydreaming about her evening plans.

That evening at quarter to seven, Tabitha kissed Oscar on the head and waved goodbye whilst he sat in the bath belting out Twinkle Twinkle Little Star to Jack. Cute, but very off key.

'Definitely room for improvement on the vocal front!' she joked to her husband as she left for her outing to the WI meeting up the road. She felt startled slightly by the volume of cars that were whizzing past and decided to get off the main road as soon as she could.

Tabitha fully appreciated her proximity to the M32, but at times it was noisy. The M32, being such a short motorway, perhaps 7 miles tops, was a Godsend when Oscar was a baby. It was the perfect distance to drive up and back down again in order to get her little baby to sleep. Tabitha was walking this evening though. As soon as she had left soft play, the sun had come out. She could still feel the sunlight on the back of her neck as she headed down the road towards the Vineyard Hall. She thought about calling on Mrs. Burrows on the way and had decided against it. Too keen. Not cool.

Pitching up five minutes early, Tabitha filled in the new member form on the door and headed in. There were a few other ladies there, not all as old as perhaps she had expected, but she was still the most youthful by approximately 15 years.

A lady called Jill, perhaps mid sixties, who was almost quite as wide as she was tall came over to say hello and they had a brief chat about the weather. Jill reminded Tabitha of a small, friendly dragon; her nostrils flared each time she started a sentence and each sentence ended with a long, slow sigh that wouldn't have looked out of place accompanying an exhalation of smoke. Half of her grey hair was piled up on the top of her head in 1940's sweetheart pinup curls and the rest of it tumbled down the back of her neck like spikes. She also had some hideous overgrown big toenails that were curling over and around her feet proudly on display in her built-for-comfort,

Velcro-fastening sandals. The only reason someone would allow such disgusting keratinous outshoots, Tabitha thought, would be to distract from the huge, yellow bunions pointing East and West on the outside of each of their feet.

Jill introduced Tabs to the other ladies that were there and explained that this evening's session was an introduction to crochet by another lady called Pat who was turning 83 that winter. Pat apparently had the 'constitution and figure of a teenager', a 'young pup' she was. Tabitha loved the way that these ladies seemed to boost each other's self-esteem, supporting each other by offering genuine love and companionship at a time in their lives when the number of their male counterparts was perhaps dwindling in comparison. The kind reward that the average woman earns for the pain of periods, childbirth and putting up with men is a few extra years over the opposite sex when they hit their eighth decade. Many of the kind, elderly ladies were widowed or divorced and a few spinsters had simply chosen never to marry. Pat took centre stage, circled by brown plastic chairs with holes in the back. The very same chairs that were also found in schools up and down the country, each with a perfect sized opening at the back for poking someone or placing rude post-it notes onto an unsuspecting child during a dull assembly. Tabitha thought the benevolent description of Pat was stretching the truth slightly though, as Pat, although she did have a youthful glint in her eye that suggested she might still enjoy one too many sherries at Christmas time more closely resembled an arthritic Shar Pei dog than a 'spring chicken'.

The session commenced, all the ladies were full of tea and cake and apparently there was to be more tea and cake during the two intervals that evening, as standard. Good Lord, haven't these ladies heard about adult-onset diabetes? When the mention of more cake was made however, Tabitha unsure up until this point felt like she may have finally found her people. Multiple cake breaks would always get her vote. Pat demonstrated the triple and double crochet basic stitches and how to create a neat edge when casting off. She also showed them how to make a colourful granny square from their scraps and how to switch yarns. The ladies all got their own crochet needles, current projects and balls of pastel wool out at the end of Pat's talk and continued to crochet or knit at intergalactic speed whilst nattering to each other about the price of milk at the local corner shop and the Royal Wedding – wasn't it delightful, but didn't she have too much make up on? There were some world class cable stitch creations in every shade of purple imaginable flowing from the elderly ladies' laps .Tabitha felt that Pat may well have been preaching to the converted.

Mrs. Burrows was serving tea and coffee from behind the hatch and Tabitha was pretty sure that she had seen her there but Mrs. Burrows made no conscious effort to come and chat with Tabitha. Perhaps she felt Tabitha was encroaching on her territory, her extended family or maybe she was just too absorbed in gossip and serving hot drinks? Jill carried over a cup of tea in the most delicate of teacups on a saucer with three biscuits arranged around the outside, stopping every few steps to catch her breath and make a strange huffle puffle sound with simultaneous nostril flaring. Tabitha was slightly concerned that Jill might not make it over to her before the break was over or before the tea went cold as she seemed to be struggling. Poor lady. Time can take its toll on the physical form.

Tabitha decided to meet Jill half way and started to walk over to the hatch, collecting and thanking her for the cup of tea. As she stood there sipping, she listened to Jill chat with another lady about the new Lidl store that was opening on Muller Road later in the year and how she hoped there would be a suitable and direct bus link there. The other lady started reciting a fascinating tale of the several buses that she had caught that week, how polite each driver was each time, providing the trapped audience of two with full details on the specific bus numbers, their maximum carrying capacities, upholstery patterns and snacks that she had packed that she enjoyed on each journey. Tabitha could feel her focus on the pair of them fading but she continued to nod and smile without really paying attention.

Her attention drifted to Mrs. Burrows' recognisable voice coming from behind her.

'But Margaret, they're just so loud... and there seems to be so many of them. Coming and going at all hours. I've no idea who really lives there.'

'Oh dear Edith, I wish I could help. There are some advantages to having one of these after all.' Margaret, Mrs. Burrows confidant, jokingly pointed to her hearing aid and its tiny on off switch. 'I thought it was a family that lived next door to you?'

'No, there was a lovely Polish family with two small children and a cat that used to enjoy sharing my mackerel fillets but they are in the house opposite and up the hill,' Miss. Burrows replied as she nibbled on a Rich Tea Finger. Tabitha turned briefly to see that Mrs. Burrows was stood behind the hatch chatting to another small, frail looking lady named Edith who seemed to be wearing every single shade of yellow that had been discovered to date all at once. Mrs. Burrows apparently had a problem with noisy neighbours.

'The Poles moved out and another family moved in. Shame to see them go. Their cat seemed to spend more time lingering in my garden waiting for treats than it did at their house. It had started to scare the birds away.' She went on to explain that she was concerned it would stop the hedgehogs coming to greet her at dusk so she had decided to stop with the premium fish treats.

'Ah, no I meant the other family. The boy with the blonde curls,' Edith said.

'No, you mean the lovely family of three down the hill.' Tabitha's home. Her ears pricked up. 'They're a quiet family by all accounts too,' continued Mrs Burrows. 'It's my neighbours next door but one. Oh what a terrible racket they make. Loud music coming out every other evening and sometimes into the early hours of the morning.' She wasn't sure if it was music or gunshot they were listening to, but whatever it was, it was hideous and she was glad to have a reason to be out of the house as when they were home with their sounds blaring she couldn't hear herself think.

'They were playing music as I left this evening. All sat out in the back yard, must have been eight or nine of them with their tangled hair and silly clothing, smoking and drinking before the sun went down.' They must have been students, she speculated, as it was ever so quiet through August and the end of July but since mid-September, for the past week or three she had heard and sometimes even felt regular parties happening there, shaking through her walls. Mrs. Burrows was almost in tears as she divulged her story to her concerned friend.

'Why don't you use the information from the complaint letter session that Betty is about to do? Write directly to the tenants? Send a copy to the Council too. Try and get them to make them turn it down or even better, kick them out? If they are students they're probably renting anyway so hopefully they wouldn't be there for too long.'

Mrs. Burrows thanked Edith for her marvellous suggestion. Edith offered to stay on afterwards at the Vineyard with her, perhaps getting Jill to help them draft something up on one of the computers.

Tabitha felt a pang of sympathy for her elderly neighbour. Although Mrs. Burrows was quite a ballsy, chirpy character generally, Tabs could see the tears pooling in the corners of her eyes when she turned around and hated to think of her suffering so much. If it was her own grandmother, she'd be up in arms. She didn't think that Mrs. Burrows had the gusto to approach the students directly. Maybe she was even a bit scared which was a sad state really, as no one deserved to feel unhappy in their own home, especially in their twilight years.

Tabitha was surprised to see that they could all already crochet and knit quite proficiently, and many were clearly operating at supreme Shaolin Master level. Why did they need the teaching talk? Perhaps they had run out of other things to have meetings about or perhaps it had been done purely for her benefit to welcome her and other potential newbies into the crinkly cult? Whatever the case, Tabitha had decided that after 45 minutes of listening to them yarning on about yarn that she maybe hadn't found her people after all and after helping herself to another piece of complimentary carrot cake, decided that maybe she would make her excuses and leave quietly.

As she sneaked out, she heard Jill announce to the other ladies whom were all waving sweetly at her as she left, that the following session was going to be run by Betty and was about how to effectively write a letter of complaint to the council with a focus on the inadequate collection of waste and recycling. Tabitha was doubly reassured that she had made the right decision to leave at this moment. She had a packet of custard creams in the cupboard and an evening in front of the TV eating biscuits by herself suddenly felt all the more appealing. The letter writing session sounded rubbish.

CHAPTER SEVEN –- MAKE YOURSELF AT HOME

On her amble home from W.I., kicking stones from the pavement as she walked slowly, she gazed at the moon which had popped out to start its night shift. The sun was still just about visible above the row of houses running along the top of the large slope trimming the borough of St. Werburghs. It scraped the horizon line like a shiny two pence coin - half in, half - out of a beachfront arcade slot machine. The sky around it was deep red and blue, almost purple in places. Dusk. It was dusk and Tabitha felt free and happy on the outskirts of the city. She didn't want to go home, yet she definitely didn't want to be at Women's Institute. She had another two hours of freedom until she needed to go home and get to bed and she didn't want to waste it. Crochet did look mildly fun though, perhaps something she could do on her evenings in, but she was seeking something a little more exciting to fill her rare evening off parental duties each week. She strolled along racking her brain for things to do.

She decided to pop into the local library which was only a five minute walk from where she was. It was open for another half hour or so until 8.30pm. Maybe she could find a book on crochet to talk her through the basics which she could follow step by step in the comfort of her own home and in front of something exciting on the TV. Anything would be more exciting than hearing a detailed account about how succinct Bristol South's bus service was or whether the standard of Marks and Spencer's ready meals had gone downhill. As she moved through the automatic door of the cosy, dimly lit library, she was passed a large notice board on her left which was full of an assortment of colourful posters of things to do;

local businesses offering various services and employment opportunities, services and support groups. She stood browsing the board for several minutes. Leaflets and posters for tree surgeons, roofers, Pilates lessons in your home, music tuition, willow weaving courses, Tai chi and yoga by the bucket load, sustainable gardening courses, making peace with your womb and various other diverse opportunities and business numbers were pinned chaotically, overlapping each other like a ruffled, feathered wing. Tabitha picked up a small card with information about the *'Healing Power of the Nepalese Gong Bath'* and chuckled out loud before carefully replacing it on the ledge at the bottom of the display board. She could almost make an entertaining hobby out of reading all of the possible entertaining hobbies available to people in an area of Bristol referred to locally as the 'Muesli Triangle'.

She moved into the main space of the library, with its high ceilings, desk and resources, it felt like school only without the disruption of the pupils. Once again, Tabitha found herself running her finger along the spines of the books packed into the shelves. She found something quite nurturing and reassuring about this action. The feeling, the sound, the knowledge packed within each package of text. It felt almost as if she was absorbing the information and power held within each book as she touched them like a reverse Midas sucking up the intellectual gold through her fingertips. Tabitha didn't have time to read fiction, the odd audio book made it onto her phone of an evening, but she usually fell asleep without taking any of it in. She felt that the several hours she would need to devote to reading a novel was too self-indulgent a use of her time. She also felt it was such a shame as she was sure she used to love reading for pleasure as a child, but in her busy, structured life, she felt that there simply wasn't time for a novel.

Drawn like a magnet to the non-fiction section, she found it to be simply four rows of books, each row about a metre and a half wide. She could almost touch either end of the shelf at the same time if she were to give the book case a hug. What it lacked in quantity and girth though it made up for in terms of its organisation, and unlike the library shelves at school, each book was neatly placed, in alphabetical order, dust jacket were present, fully intact and un-ripped. There was a layer of dust over the books with the only fingerprints being where Tabitha had run her fingers along. With the invention of the internet, it wasn't surprising to her that these fact-packed books remained largely untouched by human hand for some time, much like her own body. The only people really accessing the adult section of the library were the local, elderly population of the area and many of them were so old that they would have probably already mastered any skills that they had desired mastery of. They would have no need or desire to take out a loan on '*A Beginners Guide to Lathe Work*' or, as retired and no longer seeking employment, the rather outdated '*How to complete your self-assessment and tax return, 2003*'. The children's area of the library was always busy though, with lots of bright, colourful picture books and grubby, well worn, young reader comics. She must remember to bring Oscar here next week. Along with a discrete bottle of hand sanitizer and some Dettol wipes.

The library was shaped like a cube, with shelves around the edges, toilets at one end and a computer suite in the centre next to a red slide for toddlers which was boarded up due to an accident that happened several months ago. The financial state of the country meant that the local council didn't have enough money to remove the prohibited slide even though it had caused an accident and was left as visual torture for anyone under the age of four. Tabitha sharply remembered why she no longer brought Oscar here as the last time they had come, the slide had been taped up to prevent children from using it which had resulted in a rather spectacular melt down. Why on earth they installed a slide in the centre of an establishment renowned for its institutional silence she puzzled to understand. Perhaps back when times were good there was some spare cash to splash about and some forward-thinking liberal in the expenditures department must have put forward the crazy idea, spending the last of the local Council's sports and leisure budget before the financial crisis of 2008. The destructive financial crash that had resulted in increasing austerity measures and slides-in-libraries restrictions across the country ever since.

The man sat behind the check-out desk with a Bristol City Council ID card and lanyard around his neck was quietly checking out Tabitha's actions. He could see she was staring at the abandoned, taped-off slide. It looked like a police crime scene shielding the aftermath of a Mr. Men party that had gone badly wrong.

'Bloody Tories,' he said in a gruff voice whilst shrugging and pointing at the slide. 'Now with Brexit too, that eyesore is going to be here for a lot longer.'

Tabitha smiled politely and looked away. She didn't want to hear a political tirade. Plus, he gave her the creeps. She could feel his eyes burning into her from the other side of the building. He continued none the less. He was shorter than her, had tightly curled grey hair with a small bald patch at the back, the rounded, bumpy belly of a heavily pregnant goat and a face that looked like the halitosis fairy had visited. There was only one other person in the library, a young lad with his headphones on watching Top Gear over the internet on one of the computers. As the library worker approached Tabitha and asked if she was looking for anything in particular, she could sense that he wanted to chat and she was the only person available to listen. Despite not really wanting to engage with him she didn't really have a valid reason not to. Perhaps she was being too judgemental. Tabitha patiently reminded herself of something she would often say to her students along the lines of having two ears and one mouth thus the importance of listening twice as much as you speak. It was possibly Plato, although it may equally have been Disney. Also, that common ground could be found with everyone if you give them the chance and every conversation can lead to learning something new if one remains open-minded. She turned to face Library Guy and tried to arrange her face into an 'interested yet definitely not in that sort of way interested' expression.

It turns out the library worker was a volunteer. He filled her in on how rewarding voluntary work was and that if she had any spare time she should consider it. Tabitha didn't really have much spare time and even if she did, she was way too selfish to donate time to others. Her home life role was pretty much kitchen and laundry slave-for-two anyway. It also turns out that the library worker was a local community support officer, also a voluntary role. He filled her in on how the Tory cuts had resulted in a decrease in police in the area. In fact Bath had just closed down its only police station due to a lack of funding. She had noticed a marked decrease in bobbies on the beat and she mentioned this, finding out in return that police had not been sent out to patrol the streets to ascertain community security for well over five years. She also found out that someone had spray painted 'BOOK WANKER' and drawn a detailed cock complete with balls, pubic hair and a ray of ejaculate on his retractable garage door and the police hadn't even bothered to come over and inspect it for evidence.

Tabitha politely rounded up the rather one-sided conversation and moved back to the non-fiction section. She started to browse through the titles, her eyes scanning over the choices half-heartedly. There were so few books that rather than being organised by the conventional dewy decimal library catalogue system, these books were organised alphabetically.

She decided to look for a beginner's book on crochet for her quiet evenings at home. She could easily purchase some wool and a hook from the internet or even buy one of those colourful craft magazines displayed proudly near the entrance of all supermarkets at £3.99 a pop that often come with some free bits and bobs. The section of magazines that either distracts you or your two year old on your way to grab a few bits quickly for dinner. The section of magazines that you end up spending thirty minutes in, perusing all of the choices and then leave, having completely forgotten what you entered the store in the first place for.

Nothing under 'B' for beginner. She continued to scan across until she reached the brief 'C' section. Crochet. Yes. There were three books on crochet and she drew them out and leafed through the pages. One book was clearly too advanced for her, with very elaborate patterns written in some kind of Wingdings alien language so she placed it to one side. The second contained some fairly simple instructions that she could possibly puzzle out however the items that said instructions created were hideous pieces that should never see the light of day. The other book was aimed at children and seemed to contain photos of small, cute toys using a technique called amigurumi which seemed to involve a Japanese method of tying lots of tiny knots. She felt there may be at least one pattern within that she could follow and make for Oscar so Tabitha placed it on the floor to her left and searched for her handbag for her library card. There it was, neatly in its correct compartment, so organised. The content of her purse however was a different story. As she forcefully tugged the zip open, the tightly bound contents bulged out. She definitely had a library card somewhere.

She had so many store cards, loyalty cards and various forms of identification; her driving licence, cards for the gym and also now various cards for Oscar. There was even a loyalty card for an organic health food store which she visited once a year after Christmas in order to stock up on healthy lifestyle products like acai berries and wheat bran for porridge; most of which simply ended taking up ground space in her large kitchen larder, like hidden stow-a-ways waiting to reach their expiry dates before walking the plank into the bin.

Having made a mental note to have a good sort through of her purse that evening when she got home, almost certain that she was carrying unnecessary weight, Tabitha placed her library card in her pocket for ease of access in checking out.

As she prized apart the books in the 'C' section that were either side of the crochet books, she noticed a brightly coloured paperback entitled 'Criminology' and for some reason she was drawn to it. Perhaps it was the lurid colour combination of title on background that caught her eye, unsure what exactly had attracted her and with time to kill she pulled it out from its slot. She flicked through looking for interesting pictures, of which there were few, but a section flopped open on a page entitled 'crime and the eye of the beholder'. Leila at work loved CSI and talked about it all the time. It was something that Tabitha had never given a chance really. Maybe she was a secret sleuth at heart. It certainly made a change from poorly written student essays on the structure of the eye or the Kreb's Cycle. She sat down on the floor with assertive posture, legs tucked underneath her buttocks. Following each sentence with her finger and silently sounding out some of the more challenging words, she found herself transported back to her university years a good seventeen years ago.

After reading the whole section on the different human perspectives of crime she drew the conclusion in agreement with the author that perhaps a crime wasn't truly a crime unless there was a victim. Library Guy was still at his desk, occasionally taping on his computer keyboard and frequently looking over to her perhaps hoping for a re-ignition of their earlier conversation. Even he wasn't truly a victim Tabitha thought. Yes his garage might now need a new coat of paint which was probably covered by some kind of housing insurance policy, but other than his pride, no one was really hurt were they? No real damage had been done. Was it really worth wasting police time over such a minor disruption when what limited resources there were left were surely best left in dealing with the drug dealers, rapists and murderers of the world?

The following section in the book was about gender and the extent of female crime. Tabitha had taken a comfortable position on the floor now, so involved with the book and her own thoughts that she became unaware of the continued fleeting and hopeful glares from Library Guy. How fascinating. She read that women were in fact thought to commit an equal amount of criminal activities as men however the types of crime that they were likely to commit or the way in which they carried it out was less visible to society and therefore ladies were statistically less likely to get caught. A chap called Otto Pollak had written a book called '*The Criminality of Women*' in 1950 and had concluded that due to peoples' preconceptions of women, they were less likely to be convicted of crime and if they were, they were significantly more likely to be given less harsh sentences for the same crime than if it were carried out by a man. Sexism that actually worked in a woman's favour. Still didn't make up for the women of the past with mild post natal depression or a bit of rage from discovering their partner had been sleeping with their best friend that would have been incarcerated in mental hospitals and left to rot though.

She finished the page and flipped over to the next section which was a big chapter on the legal system. No pictures. She yawned. Enough studying for one day. It was getting dark outside. The warm, orange glow of the streetlamps as they started to flicker on was unfamiliar to Tabitha who was normally snuggled up in the bedroom next to her son, stroking his blonde curls until he settled into a deep sleep. Sadly, it was exciting for her just to be out alone in the evening. What should she do next? What could she do next? She still had the best part of ninety minutes until she should really be back home and get herself ready for bed. After popping her phone back in her zip-up pocket, she slid all of the books back into the 'C' section. She had remembered that the internet existed and could probably get all of this information and more from the comfort of her armchair from her phone. Plus, Google was a lot lighter and more up-to-date than the books here. As Library Guy started to approach her, she collected her belongings with fervour, hoiked up her shoelaces a little tighter, hopped up from the floor dusting off her bottom and marched out through the automatic glass doors, disappointed with her pitstop.

Tabitha decided to take a slightly different route home, weaving in between two houses down a short dark path using the torch on her phone to spot any dog poo or broken glass. In the name of adventure she chose to take the un-surfaced, narrow 'access only' road that slinked its way to the street on which her home sat.

There were no street lamps along this track but it was still light enough to see detail and on both sides, ran a parallel continuum of dishevelled sheds and double garages blocking off the ends of many gardens. Sometimes there was a break in the out-housing where a fence or brick wall separated the rubbly path from gardens. Tabitha found herself grading the gardens on a scale of one to five stars to pass the time. Occasionally she found herself walking through mud and grass where the barely-used road had started to surrender to the powers of natural succession. It was easy as pie to tell which houses were occupied and which weren't, which houses were student-lets and which were privately owned. It was also fairly easy to see the houses where new families had moved in and started the essential middle class peacocking of extension building and loft conversion.

Tabitha started to guess what the people inside of each property might be like. Her very own 'Through the Key Hole'. Several of the houses belonged to people that she knew and about half way towards the end of this long path was Mrs. Burrows' house. Mrs. Burrows hadn't even spoken to her at the meeting that evening, which Tabs had felt a little bit offended by, after all, she was the metaphorical fish out of water there and Mrs. Burrows seemed to know everyone else at the group, weaving her way slowly around each member at cake break, greeting each person and having a good old catch up since their previous session. It was almost as if she had deliberately avoided her. Tabitha managed to talk herself around from this paranoic state of mind; maybe she genuinely hadn't seen her there. Perhaps Mrs. Burrows was actually a little shy. Sometimes people can come across as brash and even rude when in fact they are just extremely anxious inside. It's almost as if as the mind is overworking. Over-processing all of the stimulating data around them and trying to filter out all the things they shouldn't say, and then, the thing that is the most alarming accidentally slips out, unleashing an eruption of unintentional offence, hence amplifying the original anxiety.

Tabitha had been a little bit like this herself in her younger years but age had hardened her somewhat and it was now not anxiety that caused her to make the occasional rude comment but simply her diminished tolerance of fools. Her filter had been removed like an un-muzzled Rottweiler. They say patience is a virtue but unfortunately years of dealing with teenagers had emptied her reserve of restraint.

Tabitha stopped dead in her tracks. Two boys were walking towards her down the muddy path, no one else was in sight. She panicked. They didn't look familiar. Why were they walking down the back lane in the dark? She felt afraid and tucked herself into a narrow gap between two fences. They hadn't seen her yet and she wanted to hide out of harm's way until they'd passed.

The pair of young lads were stumbling about and shouting loudly. One of them had a ridiculous man-bun on the top of his head, a freshly shaven undercut along with a bushy, jet-black beard, can't of been more than 15 or 16 years old. The other, perhaps a few years older sported long, dirty, blonde dreadlocks and had a heavy looking gold, chunky chain around his neck. The shouting and shoving continued but they didn't seem to be angry, just a couple of mates - perhaps a little bit drunk. Tabitha's heart was pounding. She was tucked away and turned off her phone to avoid being spotted. She knew they wouldn't be able to see her where she was hidden so she stayed put, poking her head out occasionally to see if they were still there. She could hear them chatting as they got closer.

The boys were definitely drunk. They stopped and the tallest of the pair slumped up against the garage opposite where Tabitha was wedged. He blurted something out to his mate in a thick Welsh accent.

'I've got it, what are we waiting for, let's get bleached,' he said and then threw a small baggy of lilac-grey powder towards his chum.

The other lad, who turned out to be called Floater, drunkenly staggered to floor level next to his chum. Both were dressed in some kind of urban uniform: black Nike joggers, a smattering of other designer sports labels, smart, expensive trainers with gold laces and sovereign rings and crude, probably ridiculously over-priced t-shirts. One of them took off his backpack and opened it up, retrieving from within it a set of three small speakers and flashy smart phone.

It turns out the slightly smaller of the two was called Mick. He turned on the little circular speakers, and as he connected them up to his phone, the Minirig logo glowed up on the side of the cylindrical amplifier. Brash jungle music came blaring out. Loud enough to make it slightly harder to hear what the boys were saying but not loud enough for any residents to hear. Tabitha wished the boys would turn it up. It could've helped her to get out of this uncomfortable, slightly scary predicament perhaps - if it caused someone to come out and tell them to go away and leave the back alley. But no one came.

'Nah mate, nah. Something more chilled.' Floater took hold of the phone and selected some weird, ambient background music.

'Aphex Twin. Always good, Dude!' Floater looked up at Mick and winked, making some kind of strange slapping sound with his fingers, beating them against thin air.

Mick took the small bag of powder from his friend's fingertips, pulled out a plastic dropper and added a few drops of water to the bag from his water bottle. Pumping the powder and liquid up and down with the pipette until it had all dissolved, he sucked all of the liquid up into the pipette and squirted half of it into Floater's eye, the other half into his own.

What on earth were they doing? Were they taking acid? In an alley?

'I can't believe this stuff is made in the UK. Glad we get to support the local economy, hey?' Mick said.

'Is it like spice? What does it do?' asked Floater. Why on earth hadn't he asked that before allowing his friend to squirt it into his eye? Tabitha couldn't believe what she was seeing. She hoped to god that this didn't end up the same way that some of the cases on the news she'd heard about had.

'What does it do?! It's beautiful, man. Words Can't. You know? Course you do. Apparently once you've done this stuff you won't want to do anything else. It only lasts about ten minutes a hit but it feels like ages.'

'Sounds like Ket to me mate,' said Floater. Tabitha knew about ketamine. She'd heard about it in the staffroom. Some of the sixth formers had been found with a small bag of it last year at the leavers' ball. It was a drug designed by the government as an anaesthetic to replace the disaster that the highly addictive PCP had been in the fifties and sixties. Apparently, it worked by separating the mind from the body. How on earth could a chemical do that? Most bizarre.

'Yes bro. Maybe. We'll find out in a minute I guess,' said Mick.

When Tabitha had naively asked Mr. Turbot about ketamine in the staffroom, he'd told her that the Dalai Lama was getting annoyed that people were abusing it and cluttering up the astral planes. She had found that most peculiar to imagine. All these kids on drugs floating about like astronauts, stuck between worlds like some kind of rubbish secret level in a computer game. She still wasn't sure if he'd been pulling her leg or not.

Tabitha could see Floater starting to slump back against the wall and his arms started to gesticulate more slowly. A blank stare spread over his face.

Something had changed. Their eyes. The boys' eyes had changed.

They looked wrong. Broken.

She panicked, unsure what to do. She didn't want to wait around and see what happened to them, but as a mother and a teacher and simply as a compassionate stranger, she felt a duty of care. The boys had stopped talking completely. There was enough daylight left to make out their faces clearly as she took another peak.

Both the boys were staring into the space in front of them at nothing. Both of their bodies perfectly still, lifeless almost, except for their waving arms which were doing some kind of slow motion tai chi routine. Their backs then arched stiff as if they were about to convulse but they didn't and after a few seconds, they crumpled into a messy pile of sportswear and cheap aftershave. The colour in their eyes had vanished. Their faces and eyes had turned completely white.

All she could see in their eyes were their tiny black pupils. No colour in their eyes, their hair had started to fade and their skin had turned ashen. Tabitha could probably have performed (unqualified) knee surgery on the boys and they probably wouldn't have flinched. These boys looked like cartoon characters, skin like a piece of plain paper, eyes like frogspawn. Vacant, monotone, glazed marbles. White. Bleached.

The pair were still lying there in silence after several minutes had passed. Tabitha couldn't stay squashed behind a fence all night. She needed to do something. Adrenaline was rushing around her body. She pulled her phone out, called an ambulance and then she ran. She ran away from the boys. She ran up the muddy lane until her legs tired and she became breathless. She didn't know where she was going but she certainly didn't want to be around to watch two boys possibly die.

Her subconscious had seemingly taken Tabitha's tired feet the route home that led her past the back of Mrs. Burrows' house and as she approached the recently creosoted, shoulder height fence, Tabs could see the same view of the back of Mrs. Burrows' house that she could see from Oscar's bedroom. She stood there for several minutes and caught her breath. She was scared but she knew she had done the right thing for the boys and for herself. Why hadn't she just gone home? Why was she outside of Mrs. Burrow's house? She knew Mrs. Burrows was still at W.I. Yet she felt strangely more at ease here stood looking at her neighbours back gate than she did stood in her own home where Oscar would be fast asleep in bed and her husband would be doing anything but talking with her.

She wanted to be in Mrs. Burrows' lounge, watching Mrs Burrows' ironing, listening to Mrs. Burrows voice that had reminded her so much of her own grandmother's. She would have to open the gate in order to see the fancy hexagonal paving slab pathway that wove up the well maintained garden. Each slab with a picture of an animal engraved onto the top of it along with the National Trust emblem and '2000' around the outside.

Tabitha found herself grasping the wrought iron ring attached to the gate latch and pulling it downwards slowly so as not to make a noise. It was now getting dark quite quickly, although the light pollution in the city meant it was hard to find true darkness anywhere but in the depths of her own lonely soul and the night was silent apart from the occasional juggernaut engine loud enough to be heard from the M32 when the wind blew in the right direction.

Either side of the five star garden were raised beds with a selection of precious perennials and border shrubs. Did the skill of gardening appear with menopause? Did nature trade a lady's chaotic hormonal cycle for some super power to know your frost hardy grasses from your tubers, bulbs and corms? Mrs. Burrows kept on top of her garden and it was evident that she was very proud of its presentation. There was a stone bird bath in the centre and a long washing line, currently empty and cranked up high which ran from the entrance to the side of the house.

Suddenly, the sound of a siren pierced her ears, blue lights were bouncing off walls of buildings a few roads back. Tabitha felt exposed. She needed to be inside. She pushed opened the gate and strode up the disjointed path, bouncing from one slab to the next. Squirrel, badger, fox, hedgehog, rabbit, stoat or was it a weasel? She should really have known being a biologist and all but she didn't really care and didn't stop to study.

She came to the edge of the house, a tidy, patioed area, where several large and small potted plants were carefully placed either side of the drainpipe and backdoor. There was also a small metal bowl of bread and milk that was probably put there for hedgehogs.

Tabitha blinked twice. The next door neighbour's security light had turned on most probably due to the movements she had made bounding up Mrs. Burrows path like Bambi on a bender. She froze in the spotlight and all she could hear were sirens. She needed a wee now too. She stood up close against the house wall then squatted down and remained as still as she could for a full five minutes, unsure whether to run away or stay put. The adrenaline was flowing full throttle now and panic mode had fully kicked in. In some deep-routed, very peculiar way, once again, Tabitha seemed to be enjoy this dangerous series of events. What on earth was wrong with her? Was she a sociopath stuck up a garden path?

Another five minutes must have passed and the siren noise had stopped. Tabitha realised the stun of the security light and the drop in air temperature had made her need the toilet even more. She really needed the toilet. Just a number one, but having had a baby, her ability to hold it in was akin to the weight bearing ability of a twiglet. No-one was around. God, she hoped those two boys were OK. Tabitha's heart rate started to drop again, as she assured herself that they would be in good hands. The medics were there now. She focused on breathing in and out slowly and deeply, hands both placed on her diaphragm. She really needed a wee. She could just pop-a-squat in the garden. But what if someone did see her? She'd have to move house, move city possibly if caught urinating on a hedgehog by a passerby.

What if Mrs. Burrows had left a key out? She'd be out for at least another hour and a half. What if Tabitha was to just quickly let herself in to use the toilet? They were practically friends. They chatted about the weather at least once a month. Worst case scenario and she came home early, she'd understand wouldn't she? She was just a sweet, old lady. Plus the police wouldn't be interested. After all, if she wasn't stealing anything and wasn't harming anyone it wasn't really a crime was it?

Tabitha started to scurry around on her hands and knees, lifting the various plant pots and large pebbles that had been arranged to decorate the space between the patio and the wall like an exterior organic skirting board. Bingo. She found a key. The surge of excitement she felt was similar to how little Charlie Bucket must have felt on opening the chocolate bar to reveal the Golden Ticket, or how one of the old biddies at W.I. must have felt when they completed a knitted blanket, or how the two boys earlier must have felt purchasing the strange chemical from their dealer before it all took a turn for the worst. Placing the key into the back door lock and turning it to the left 270 degrees, she heard the lock slide out of its hole and then on pushing the handle down, the door swung inwards.

The lights were off. The house smelt like her childhood home had after a Sunday lunch. A mixture of excessive heat (didn't the elderly know how to adjust a thermostat?) and overcooked cruciferous vegetables. She could see the red light of a slow cooker bubbling away gently in the corner of what must be the kitchen. She felt around the door frame and eventually found a light switch and then changed her mind. Too much light might make her conspicuous even though there was nobody around. Taking out her phone and shaking it hard twice to activate the inbuilt torch, she at first inspected the carpet and then the walls. Very retro. The kitchen ran through to the living area through a large archway and downstairs clearly hadn't been redecorated since the mid 60's. A range of rusty orange, browns and reds with the occasional dash of delicious mustard-yellow popping out on the migraine-inducing wall paper greeted her. Her eyes were then drawn to the kitchen floor which was covered with large, pattern-clashing lino tiles that merged into acrylic carpeted tiles as the space continued under the archway. On the ceiling above the kitchen area were hideous polystyrene ceiling tiles. The sort once installed in so many homes to aid in insulation that were soon deemed to be a massive risk to health as when they melt in the case of a house fire, they drip caustic plastic all over the place, searing through clothing and scarring flesh. Nice.

The majority of the left hand side of the kitchen area was taken up by a huge Aga style farmhouse oven, presumably also from the 50's or 60's, adjacent to some cupboards and work surface space. The right hand side of the kitchen area was sparsely populated with very basic, old white goods and more storage cupboards. The kitchen area was functional and sturdy but it was so dated. Tabitha half expected to see Twiggy appear in a haze of smoke through a beaded curtain clad in a black and white mini skirt carrying through a cheese and pineapple hedgehog and a canopy of prawn *vol-au-vents*.

They don't build things like they used to; Tabitha's husband was convinced that all new kitchen appliances had some kind of life span limitation built into them as their fridge freezer had packed in the day after its guarantee had expired - although he had blamed her anyway for overfilling it. Tabitha opened the fridge, partly just out of nosiness and partly to shed a little more light into the space. Inside of the fridge in the salad drawer was a selection of slightly past their best fruit and vegetables and on the bottom shelf, some milk in a glass pint milk bottle, a block of salted butter and some kind of unidentifiable meat in a bowl. The smell was not good and there was no way that Tabitha would have eaten anything from that fridge, but the elderly had guts of steel - until they caught *Clostridium difficile* in a nursing home and shat themselves to death. Perhaps it was due to living through the war and being brought up on whatever was available, perhaps it was partially a justifiable stubbornness to not waste any scrap of leftover food. Her own grandmother had been the same, resourceful to the max, but at the start of her dementia, Tabitha had noticed her fridge was frequently full of various items from around the house. One time she found the television remote control and a pearl necklace cuddled up in the fridge door, like they'd been playing an inanimate, non-resolvable game of hide-and-seek. Her gran had been as confused as her as to how they got there. The only items present in Mrs. Burrow' refrigerator door however were a large bottle of half-drunk tonic water and several lemons.

Tabitha closed the fridge and started to browse through the overhead cupboards, not knowing what to expect nor looking for anything in particular but she seemed to be really enjoying not knowing what she would find. The experience was similar to a good rummage at a jumble sale or a charity shop; that little dopamine buzz when something of interest or value was discovered. The cupboards contained a few essentials like teabags, sugar and Oxo cubes and one cupboard contained nothing but a single bowl, dinner plate and a large bottle of gin.

She slowly edged forwards towards the large arch way which led out from the kitchen, passing by a small side room with a sink and a twin tub top loader style washing machine on her way. As she moved into the living area still hesitant to put on a light, Tabitha used her spare hand to feel out for furniture on her way, in between scoping the room with the light from her phone. Damn it. Her battery was about to die. Tabitha considered whether Mrs. Burrows would have a charger plugged in somewhere that she could use briefly and started to search for one before realising that Mrs. Burrows probably would not have the latest micro USB charger, in fact there wasn't much from the twenty first century in her home. Tabitha turned off the torch and put her phone on battery saver mode. As reckless as she was behaving this evening, she was a Brownie Sixer as a child and tried to always be prepared for any situation- she hated the thought of being out of the house with no phone battery left.

She fumbled near the edge of the archway for a light switch, where she found a solitary, small, knobbly vintage button, such a strange feeling compared to the cluster of six pewter dimmer switches in her house, and at work the lights simply came on when a motion detector was triggered in the corridors, office and lab. The single, central light in the living area came on. It gave a dull, orange glow to the room. She looked up at the lampshade which was one of those spherical paper ones that you can fold flat. Surely no one used those anymore? Surely if they did, it would only be in their bedrooms, not as a centre piece in the living room? It was so dated. She looked inside the shade at the vintage glass filament light bulb. They didn't even make those anymore, did they? This one looked as old as Edison himself. Everything was LED at her house now. This old light bulb was pumping out just enough light for Tabitha to be able to see yet hopefully not too bright to cause alarm from the neighbours, so the vintage look worked to her favour this evening.

The front room was presented like a 1950's dolls house with what looked like a black, leather three piece suite from the same era, possibly older but in immaculate condition. On the walls were photos of what Tabitha presumed were Mrs. Burrows' family, many of them in black and white. Other than the soft bubbling from the slow cooker, Tabitha was still surrounded by silence and with this security that no one was nearby, she stopped to look at the images on her way in search of the bathroom. Several were of Mrs. Burrows in her prime, possibly early sixties era. Mrs. Burrows must have been a teenager or in her early twenties. Fresh faced, slim figured, short, curly hair pinned tidily for a dash of sport. She was obviously quite a keen tennis player in her day. The majority of the photos lining the wall that led to the staircase above the wooden side cabinet were of her, dressed in sporting attire, tennis whites, racket in hand, standing on one side of a tennis court net shaking hands with various other ladies, sometimes holding trophies and sometimes medals.

At the bottom of the stairs was a display cabinet full of these awards that she had obviously collected over the years. In some of the photos Mrs. Burrows appeared to be playing mixed doubles with a man who also featured in some of the more personal photos. A handsome, tall, dark haired chap. Whoever he was he stood with good posture and a confident smile. It soon became clear that this dapper man must have been Mrs. Burrows' husband as a large framed photo of the pair of them on their wedding day was placed centre piece on the top of the sideboard presented on a delicate lace doily. Her wedding dress was gorgeous with a long, flowing frilly veil and train, trimmed with what looked like pearls, with a sheer, lacy, bateau neck line, nipped in at the waist and finished with a huge calf length, swirly, billowing poodle skirt. It reminded Tabitha of a scene from Breakfast at Tiffany's. Mrs Burrows looked besotted with this man, Mr. Burrows, staring at him all hazy-eyed, and him with her. It was a very romantic scene of the pair of them, wedding bouquet in her hands, his arm tightly around her waist pulling her in close underneath the stone arch of a gothic style church, remnants of paper confetti scattered on the floor. Tabitha recognised the arch way - it was the Vineyard. The couple must have married in the neighbourhood all those years ago and stayed local ever since.

Tabitha reflected back on her own marriage which had been in a registry office in Bournemouth, near where Jack was raised, with the party afterwards at the local Holiday Inn. She didn't even wear white as Jack had told her it didn't suit her complexion. There were several more photos of Mr. and Mrs. Burrows, the pair staring at each other lovingly in each one. Tabitha couldn't remember where her own wedding photo album was at home, or even if their wedding photo was still in the front room. The large television had left little remaining space for ornaments and nick-nacks. She vaguely remembered Jack moving the framed one of the pair of them cutting the cake into the spare room, or had he taken it into work?

Tabitha knew that Mrs Burrows had never remarried and although she hadn't discussed it with her, Tabitha presumed that she'd been widowed as she wore a wedding band. As she moved closer to the stairs, on the end of the sideboard were three urns; a large one in the middle and two slightly smaller. Tabitha realised at once that she must have lost her husband and judging by the lack of any photos of the pair of them together more recently, it must have been when they were both quite young. Perhaps she had also lost other family members too or possibly pets. Tabitha could feel tears collecting in the corner of her eyes. She took a tissue from the floral box on the sideboard and wiped them away before approaching the staircase to head upstairs in search of the toilet.

At the bottom of the stairs was a wicker basket full of folded bed linen and Tabitha looked back behind her to see the ironing board propped up against the far wall next to the small black and white television. Tabitha had often seen her watching it from Oscar's bedroom window over the last few weeks. She wanted to carry the sheets upstairs, where she thought they were heading, to help her neighbour out but decided against it as that may give the game away that an intruder had visited the house. Even if it was just to use the bathroom. Or worse, it may convince Mrs. Burrows that her home was possessed by helpful pixies, another situation that had occurred with Tabitha's grandmother when she'd done some chores for her before she was moved into a care home.

Tabitha got to the top of the stairs and entered the bathroom and took a much needed wee on the tangerine coloured toilet seat. They certainly didn't make bathroom suites like that anymore. Tabitha finished with great relief and pushed open one of the three bedroom doors for a quick sneak. Why not? She was already up there anyway. She suddenly realised she had made a mistake as the door loomed open. The small room was the room of a child's but not a child of today's times. It was so different to the brightly coloured, toy-packed bedroom belonging to her own son that Tabitha had spent months whilst pregnant decorating and filling. This bedroom was quite empty, but distinctly puerile. There were two teddies and two knitted dolls neatly arranged on a fully-dressed single child's bed. Alongside the opposite wall was a vintage wooden miniature house kitted out with furniture and several clothes peg dolls with wool for hair on the floor next to a small sheepskin rug. A pair of brown moccasin slippers in a size that must have been only a little bigger than Oscar's feet were neatly paired up and placed next to the side of the bed. There was a small wooden chest of drawers against one wall which Tabitha felt drawn to open even though there were tears forming in both of her eyes now. The drawer was stacked full tidily of the handmade, vintage clothes of a young girl and looked like they had been untouched for years. The bed was covered with the freshly laundered sheets that Tabitha had seen Mrs. Burrows ironing just days ago whilst putting Oscar to bed.

Tabitha had assumed that the second urn on the sideboard must have been her child's. A daughter possibly. A daughter who had passed but lived on in the poor woman's mind, a mind too fearful of letting go for good. Tabitha felt horrible. Mrs. Burrows had never mentioned any of this to her before. To lose the husband that you loved dearly and a child was awful. It was a secret far more sinister than Tabitha had ever imagined would be behind that bedroom door. Life had dealt Mrs. Burrows an appalling hand. She couldn't hold back her emotions anymore as she backed out of the bedroom. Tabitha ran back down the stairs, her hands pressed palm inwards on her own chest as if holding in the heartache that was set to erupt. She headed straight out of the back door, locking it quickly behind her and returning the key from where she found it. This evening had been too much. Just too much. The incident in the lane earlier and now this revelation of her neighbour's sad, sad past.

As she travelled out of the back gate and up the narrow road between the back ends of the terraces, she heard the sudden blare of loud, thumping music start from the messy student property next door. It caught Tabitha by alarm in the eerie darkness of the evening. She wiped the tears streaming from her eyes and returned her focus to getting herself home as fast as she could and getting herself far away from the sorrowful, gangrenous shadows of the haunting scenes she'd witnessed that evening.

CHAPTER EIGHT -- THE NOISY STUDENTS

'Come on, man. You're taking so long.'

'Yo. Sorry, didn't realise there was a deadline,' Sky spat back with a smirk that stretched from oversized, gold hoop earring to mismatched, oversized, gold hoop earring. As she smiled, she looked even more like an Enid Blyton character with her bazaar bundle of ice white dreadlocks piled up in some kind of knickerbocker glory fashion on top of her heart shaped face and her large, piercing blue eyes. Sky was a naturally stunning girl with artistic flair whom prided herself on her strange, creative expression of self. She glanced at Soma's reflection in the oval mirror that was suspended over the disused fireplace by a short shoelace and a lot of good luck. She could see her mate was eager to go out, yet her friend's demands made no difference whatsoever to the speed at which she slowly perfected her look for the evening ahead.

'Oi oi savaloy. I reckon I've spent about a third of my adult life waiting for you to get ready. I guess another few minutes won't hurt.'

'You cheeky bitch. It's totally worth it though - look how incredibly sexy we look.' Sky grabbed her buddy by the chops and forced their heads together to gawp at their mugs in the mirror. They both burst out giggling and hugged.

'I won't be long you muppet, promise babe.' Sky returned to looking at herself and started to apply multi-coloured false eyelashes with the precision and steady hand of a heart surgeon.

It was their first night out together back in Bristol after a long summer break of festivals, illegal raves and house parties at different ends of the country and they both had loads of people they wanted to catch up with. Soma tapped her foot impatiently and turned to face the wall. With her petite finger she started to trace over the purple and gold fractals in a large unframed print that was blue-tacked on the side of the mirror in the front room of their rented house. With the other hand, she wiped a thick layer of dust from a spooky African tribal mask that had been carved crudely out of a dark wood that was hooked randomly next to the mirror. A mask they all found slightly creepy, yet incredibly cool.

'Yuck! Look at all this dust. What is dust anyway? I'm surprised our dust doesn't have a higher glitter content.'

'Dead skin isn't it?' Sky replied.

'No way - that's gross! I refuse to believe it.' Soma picked up her phone and searched the internet to confirm what her friend had said. 'It is as well. Yuk! It's also plant pollen, animal hairs, textile fibres, soil and bits of burnt out meteorite particles too apparently.' Soma flicked the dust bunny onto the floor and wiped her fingers on her leggings. This was probably the only effort in the name of cleaning that their front room would receive that academic year. Not particularly because they were going to be busy with their studies but rather because they just didn't have any inclination to clean. Especially as the property did not belong to them and they'd probably be moving on to pastures new for their third year. Like a sneaky cuckoo laying its egg in another bird's nest, these girls lived in the moment and were decades away from the voluntary responsibility of property, hopping from one messy abode to the next.

They were both excited about finishing their studies in a few years and then more than likely trying to find somewhere to squat to avoid paying any rent at all. Plus, their current landlord who they'd never even met would probably keep their entire deposit anyway so what was the point in cleaning? Although they were both inherently bright, they were both also naturally hedonistic and lazy.

'Tonight's going to be a fat one! But then I'm definitely going to have a few nights in, maybe a couple of weeks. Make a good impression at the start of this year,' said Sky.

'What, you mean actually go to some lectures? Maybe even find out where your departmental library is?' chided Soma.

They'd agreed to buckle down a little bit more, perhaps after Winter Solstice or maybe in the New Year as they had both heard rumours from friends in the year above and mates who'd already graduated that the second year at university was a little more stretching than the first. Their end of second year finals actually counted towards their overall grade. However, they'd decided to start the year with a big night out down at Lakota, a mega club in an old brewery in Stokes Croft, the bohemian part of the city centre. Sky had told Soma that she'd heard that the building used to be the site of a gallows in the pre-Victorian era which had freaked Soma out a bit but also seemed, callously, to make the building more appealing as a place to go and party.

Sky had in fact been lying but Soma believed her and had told everyone she met there last year. The rumour had spread like wildfire. Soma was reading Performance Studies, specialising in circus skills and was a natural story teller extraordinaire and general all round loveable girl - but also extremely gullible. Sky was studying for a degree in Classics.

The girls had met whilst travelling around Peru in their gap year, putting them both a whole year older than most of their fellow classmates, except for the mature students who they didn't really mix with as the mature students were always in the library studying. This additional year of life experience gave them a super-inflated air of supremacy over those an entire year younger than themselves and they'd remained tightly connected ever since. Despite their very different upbringings – Sky was from a wealthy family of barristers and doctors, old money one might say, and Soma had grown up in a council house with her mother raising her and her sister - they still had a lot in common. Their joint love of partying, veganism, joss sticks, fire poi and sleeping in late had brought them closer along with many nights getting mashed off their pickles and sharing stories deep from within their souls whilst watching the sun set and then rise again.

Despite their seemingly alternative lifestyle, they didn't look or feel particularly out of place, as Bristol, being renowned for its plethora of cultures, acceptance and celebration of diversity, was also the home of the 'snowflake hippy'. Sky's elder brother who had practically walked into Trinity Hall at Cambridge to study Law with his amazing A-level grades and rugby skills had coined this term after visiting her once last year, much to Sky's disapproval. The girls had both somehow passed their first year at university with perhaps the bare minimum amount of effort required and had successfully so far managed to have their tofu-pie and eat it.

In the smallest of the four bedrooms lived another girl called Emma who was also a petite girl, like Sky and Soma, but sported a more conventional hair style – a short mousy brown bob with a thick heavy set fringe. She was a little bit older than the other two and was a post graduate computer science student. Emma had been in the house alone over the summer holidays and although she had enjoyed the peace and quiet of the eight week sunny break, she had missed her friends who she had met at a party at Christmas the previous year. They had been the last few huddled around a fire near Exmouth beach after an outdoor rave and had chatted away, putting the world to rights whilst watching shooting stars over the pebble-lined coast.

The three of them had done so much MDMA together than evening that they were awake for much of the rest of the next day, sharing most of their life stories with each other. They had all got on so well and Emma had promised the girls they could move into the student digs she was living in when they came out of first year halls.

In Emma, still waters ran deep. Although she was studious and quiet, her mind was a constant whirl of questions and data and she probably consumed more booze and drugs than the rest of the household together. Her room looked like a set from Red Dwarf - an underground, clinical cubicle; walls painted dark grey, with her horizontal black blinds permanently drawn and an artificial daylight desk lamp permanently switched on over her worn keyboard and triple computer screen set up. With flashing lights of hard drives and plug-in devices from floor to desk height to the side of her bed, and strange, rare, framed comic strips nailed to the wall in a precise line, Emma was a fan of structure and order. One wall was almost entirely covered, neatly so, with black and white flyers with images of speaker stacks and trucks from techno nights that she had been to over the years. A wide bookshelf filled with non-fiction books on anything and everything arranged in decreasing height from left to right lay above the display. Against the other long wall was her decks, set up for the occasional mix when she got the chance and her vinyl collection which was filed away tidily underneath. She had switched to MP3 and WAV a long time ago but her records were like her children and, unlike children, worth keeping alone for their amazing artwork. Order out of the chaos. She liked her room to be an organised sanctum as the rest of the house was generally carnage.

Emma enjoyed going out and partying with the other two girls and the fourth and final housemate, Casper, yet she also enjoyed her own company.

The fourth and final house mate was peculiarly handsome Casper, with his straggly bob of black dreadlocks, chestnut-green eyes and all year round tan. He was a final year Graphic Design student at UWE who had also been there throughout the summer splitting his time between sleeping, working on his tan, adding to his art portfolio and tight rope walking in St. Andrews Park. There was always an element of flirtation and ribbing between the bunch, with Casper bearing the brunt of many jokes about how he hadn't got into Bristol University and had to go to UWE instead, yet secretly the girls had all fallen a little bit in love with him – just a little bit- and were all very envious of his artistic talent from which he was already fairly well known for in the local area. He lived in the loft conversion, which he'd filled with fresh pieces of his own spray paint work and lots of green plants. It looked a bit like an exquisite graffiti jungle yet smelt like a solvent factory.

Sky continued to carefully apply small pearlescent jewels above her eyebrows with eyelash glue and an old pair of needle-head tweezers; she was going full Coachella Valley this evening. Neither of the girls had properly unpacked their bags into their rooms yet but that could wait, there was a big line-up tonight and they both fully intended to have a good time. The only element of predictability about their average evening out is that it would guaranteed be the sort of night that became morning and then afternoon of the following day in the blink of a fun filled, hedonistic, carefully bejewelled eye. Sky hadn't seen a lot of her Bristol crew for weeks as she'd just got back from Indonesia where she'd been helping to rebuild a village library that had been destroyed by a tsunami. Her father had paid for the flights and she'd paid a charity several thousand pounds for the experience, of which she had spent about two hours each day serving out food supplies to many of the locals who had lost their homes and living in tents whilst she returned to a hotel near the airport each evening to cleanse and realign her chakras before stretching out in the spa to catch up on some reading for the new academic year. It had been such a spiritual experience for her and she couldn't wait to start planning her future exploration with her friends. She felt she needed to do something a little less altruistic next time though, something more for herself. They hadn't decided where to go next yet but she felt that she deserved more of a holiday this time. Witnessing all those poor people in so much need - the trip to Palu had been exhausting.

Soma let out a jovial, sarcastic sigh and sat back down again on the dusty, well-loved sofa in their communal area. It was covered with a sizeable cotton throw with a beautiful pattern and Indian elephants in circles all over it. Unfortunately it was also covered with blim burns from where people had dropped hot hash rocks all over it over the years of its life in student accommodation. Soma unlaced and kicked her clumpy New Rock stacked boots off, tugged and teased her rainbow leg warmers into a slumped yet aesthetically-pleasing position, and thought about putting her Peruvian, hand woven slippers back on even though she was ready to go out. She'd bounced down the stairs and put her boots on in the hallway, expecting that Sky would surely be ready to leave. She'd been getting ready for hours, however it appeared not. Although her feet were a dainty size four, when on, her chunky boots made her diminutive feet look a bit like robot hooves but they were extremely useful for being able to stomp about in the mud at outdoor parties and also helped her to see above other people's heads at whoever or whatever was performing on stage. With shoes off and bare toes wiggling out of the end of her leg warmers like worms peeping from the ground, Soma stretched her arms up into the air and waved them around like imaginary butterfly wings for absolutely no reason before flopping back into the immersive sofa. She put her feet up onto the mango wood table in the centre of the room and in so doing, she pushed a nearly full ashtray out of the way with her foot. She chuckled to herself, remembering a sign she had sign over a bar on her travels: 'if the floor is full, please feel free to use the ashtray' and thought she'd make one for the house next week.

'Ah man, this table is getting full,' she shouted above the repetitive beats and picked up several of the ash trays before tiptoeing out into the back yard to pour the contents into the bin. She swung open the back door, and as it was still warm and dry, she crept on her toes like a tiger stalking its prey, weaving her way past the three or four industrial cable bobbins that had been used at the end of the summer term as garden furniture. She decided that rather than bothering to walk to the end of the back yard she would just tip the contents of the ashtrays into the huge, chipped terracotta plant pot that had become one of many outside ashtrays instead. The sun had set but her neighbour's security light came on and startled her. Looking back down at the disgusting pile of ash and butts that had accumulated in just a few days in their back yard, Soma backed away from the broken terracotta pot and tiptoed back inside the kitchen. She could hear that Sky had cranked up the jungle music pumping out of their ridiculously oversized front room sound system and drawn like a moth to a flame, like an alcoholic to a free wine tasting event, she decided to dance her way into the lounge backwards, looking out at the scrubby lawn as she moved. It was fair to say that the scrubby lawn, despite its littering of empty beer cans was probably the cleanest floor space of the property.

As she headed back inside, placing the empty ashtrays back onto the coffee table, she went back into the kitchen, pulled the cleanest dinner plate out of the cupboard that she could find and went into the front room again where Sky was still applying sparkles to her forehead. She pulled out a small, rectangular paper wrap from her bra, took her student ID out from her purse. She proceeded to pour out a small amount of white crystals onto the plate. After grinding it for a few seconds with the scuffed edge of her card, she racked up two inch long lines of white powder for her and her friend.

'This'll help you get a wiggle on matey,' she chuckled, bopping her head in time to the beats whilst rolling up a fiver and snorting the chalky dust. She sat bolt upright, put her boots back on properly and rummaged through her friend's bag of jewels choosing two purple raindrop shaped sticky gems and started to apply them. She placed one under the bottom row of lashes on each of her green eyes. The purple really popped against her frizz of bright ginger hair and stood out nicely against the scattering of orange and brown freckles that not only sprinkled over her nose but all over most visible parts of her body.

Emma and Casper came bounding down the stairs, each with a bottle of cheap wine in their hand.

'Guys are you lot ready? Let's head out to the Duke first. I said we'd meet Wispa there. And Ozzy,' hollered Casper, clearly semi inebriated already.

'Yeah yeah, easy now, just waiting for Sky to finish making herself look like a Christmas tree,' replied Soma. Emma smirked. She'd never seen the point in make-up and thought it was just a waste of materials that would all end up in the oceans polluting the planet. Yeah, Sky looked cool but true beauty came from within.

'Fuck off, Ginge,' replied Sky cruelly.

'Racist,' quipped Casper in retaliation. Soma poked him firmly in the ribs with a mischievous grin on her face.

'Right who wants a gurner before we leave then? I've just got some lovely Lego pills in from Holland. They're actually shaped like little Lego bricks. Look,' said Emma, pulling a bag from the buttoned suede pocket on her belt. She handed each of them a tiny building block made from, apparently, ninety percent MDMA. She wasn't sure what the other 10% was, probably some kind of red colouring and a cutting agent like caffeine. Whatever it was she had heard that these pills were good. She'd had bad pills from Holland before, cut with ketamine and some other amphetamine that just made her spin out and sweat all night, nearly putting her and her friends in A&E, but she'd done a bit more research this time. She'd made sure to carefully read all of the reviews on the Silk Road website, which had given these pills from this supplier 5 out of 5 stars and a selection of positive feedback. It proved to be a very reliable service.

'God bless the Dark Net,' they all chanted one after another, tongue in cheek, saluting each other with their beverages and downing the cheeky tablets.

'Come on you bunch of numpties,' Casper cheered, 'Let's get down the pub before last orders.'

'It's only nine o'clock, dude,' replied Sky.

'Yeah, but I want to finish off a piece on the way and I need you lot to keep watch for me down in the bear pit,' he said, pulling out a can of spray paint from the woven fabric rucksack he seemed to permanently carry on his back and grinned.

The bunch of numpties left the house, letting the front door slam behind them. It locked automatically and it would only be a matter of days before one of them left the house, forgetting this and got locked out. Casper and the previous tenants always left the window out the back ajar so they could get in by reaching around and unlocking the back door. Well, all of them except for Emma. Casper and the other kids that had lived in the girls' rooms last term had started this bad habit and she'd kept on at them to stop doing it as she was the only one with anything of any value in her room. Her computer set up alone was worth several thousands of pounds and she also had a drugs stash in there that Pablo Escobar himself would be jealous of. Emma pulled out her key from another pocket on her suede pixie belt and let herself back in, ran through the house closing the back door and securing the window before pegging it back through the narrow ground floor hallway, hopping over scattered footwear and discarded items of clothing in her path to the others who were lingering out the front, teasing each other and sharing swigs from the cheap wine bottles.

The motley crew practically skipped down the street and through the park. They stopped briefly for a compulsory go on the roundabout and swings like giant babies then chased each other up and down the slide, laughing loudly all the way. They stopped at the pub on the way and meet up with their friends, shared stories from their summers and took swigs from each other's drinks for several hours. It was pretty safe to say if one of them had had the cold sore virus, then by the end of this evening alone, the rest of them would too. As the bell for last orders rung, Casper looked around him to see where his friends might've been in the rammed pub. He spotted Soma a few feet away, her voluminous bubble of bright red hair stood out like a high-lux torch. She was laughing and dancing with some of her friends from her course. He grabbed her by the wrist and dragged her away, laughing and stumbling and whispering in her ear that he wanted to go with her outside to the beer garden for a quick smoke before they got booted out. They both occasionally smoked rollies too but tonight they'd bought some new vape liquid to try and even though several other people just vaped inside of the pub, they found it hard to break the habit of ducking out into the fresh air to smoke their vaporizer. Also, it was just nicer to be outside anyway. The joyously drunken echoes of the beer garden beckoned and without the piercingly loud ska music that was being pumped out from inside the venue, they could actually hear each other's voices to catch up properly. After stumbling over to a spare table, Casper plonked himself down on a long wooden bench, straddling it like a horse and Soma did the same, falling onto the hard seat with an attack of the giggles. Sitting opposite each other they grabbed each other's forearms with false seriousness and looked each other straight in the face before putting their hands into their pockets to retrieve their vaping paraphernalia.

'Man, your eyes are blown dude,' Casper bleated, whilst he tried to keep a straight face yet clearly he had also started to come up on his pill, as he tried unsuccessfully to repress more giggles.

'Yeah, yours too C-Unit. Massive black holes mate,' Soma replied hysterically. They both flung themselves back, lying horizontally on the long bench and started giggling again before slowly sitting back up and filling their immediate vicinity with a thick cloud of rhubarb and custard.

'What time is it? Come on, let's go find the others out the front. We've got to get down the bear pit. I want to finish tagging a piece I did last week before we head to Lakota.'

'Yeah. Sure. Okay. Just nipping to the loo. Meet me out the front by the bike racks. Grab the others if you see them, yeah?'

Casper dashed around the pub, roamed upstairs and downstairs and eventually found Emma and Sky. They'd bumped into Ozzy and Wispa. After last orders, the whole bunch of them sprawled out of the pub jabbering to each other incoherently like a group of nursery school children and met with Soma by the bike stands. They headed off to the nightclub via the bear pit. Casper got his friends to stand guard on the entrances to the large underground pass to watch out for the police or security, oblivious to the fact there were probably more cameras on him and his friends than there were on the red carpet at the Oscars. He managed to somehow successfully finish his art and stashed his bag of spray paints in a bush in the underpass safely so that he could retrieve it on his way home. The security on the door at Lakota were pretty harsh. He didn't want them to confiscate his paints as they'd just lob them in the bin - he'd never get them back. Despite the strict door staff at the club, there still always managed to be more than enough drugs in the venue to take down a small army. The girls usually just shoved their drugs down their bras and most clubs didn't bother getting in female bouncers as it cost more and they were harder to find. So, unless they had sniffer dogs on the gates it was so easy for illicit substances to get through. Casper usually had to tape stuff to his thigh or his shoe or sometimes he wore a hoody made by a mate that had a special little stash pocket stitched into it. He had one friend who insisted on wrapping his supplies in cling film and shoving them up inside of his rectum. Needless to say, he didn't buy much from him. Gross. Emma used her multi-pocketed, suede pixie-belt as a decoy, often stalling the bouncers for several minutes whilst they searched through every nook and cranny. Her drugs were never there.

The bunch of wayward students arrived at the venue, considerably more rambunctious than when they had left the pub.

The grey-brown bricks of the old Victorian building stretched skyward. It wasn't a visually pleasing piece of architecture, although it was massive and despite attracting hundreds if not thousands of young people each weekend, it still never appeared to reach full capacity. Along its street-facing side was a huge mural of a beautiful Apache Indian lady, her face slightly larger than one of the many beat-up hatchbacks parked along the street. She glared down with a welcoming Mona Lisa style smile on the queue of reprobates that frequently stretched along the painted side of the building and around the corner, spilling in to the road at places where alcohol had got the better of the hedonistic revellers. The night air was filled with a constant, almost chant-like level of banter and chat, creating a hum that rose and fell with the gentle breeze that evening. The waves of sound were carried along with the thumping baseline emanating from the speakers to the furthest pockets of Stokes Croft and beyond. Occasionally the melodic drone would be interrupted by the sound of sirens or loud impromptu cheers as someone fell over or puked whilst the revellers built up a significant level of drink and drug fuelled hype whilst waiting to enter the disused brewery.

Casper started to run, lightened somewhat after having ditched his spray bag in a hedge around the corner on Turbo Island and jumped up on the back of a friend, almost knocking him down like a bowling pin. The girls were laughing loudly, uninhibited by the shielding cloak of the night and the ecstasy they had taken earlier as they joined the back of the queue. Sometimes they had more fun in the queue than when they got inside, at least they could hear themselves talking there. After they all managed to get past the security- it was just one bloke tonight, built like Optimus Prime though- and handed their tenners into the pretty girls behind the cash holes, they bumbled past the coat cupboard and flooded into the main room. On entering the main room which was filled with UV decorations that looked like massive viruses dangling from the high ceilings and strobe lights shooting randomly in all directions akin to a drunken cowboy taking shots at a bottle, the gang split up, and began their search high and wide for the bar with the shortest queue, bumping into old and new friends along their way. The club was huge, dark and dank and smelt badly of spilt alcohol and cigarettes, where the floor and walls had been permeated over decades of exposure to some extreme nightlife.

As the night progressed and the earliest of dawn birds could be heard waking in their nests, the club continued pounding out bangers. Emma, Sky and Soma usually found themselves huddled up outside, sat on an old tractor tyre and some dangerously stacked wooden pallets chatting with other smokers whilst Emma and Sky smoked and Soma vaped anyway under the light-polluted city sky. Casper was usually to be found still stood in front of a large speaker stack in one of the many side rooms, fully immersed in the repetitive beats, destroying whatever was left of his top and bottom end hearing range, with an iridescent ice-white polo ring of powder around each of his nostrils. He often wore this Bristol nose fashion statement - a crusty mixture of ketamine and cheap cocaine. He would be stood there, amongst his people, almost entranced like a zombie, feet pasted to the floor due to his intoxication and also possibly the swamp of mess leaking from the toilets, searching for his field of vision, following the jungle music with the nodding of his chin.

'Sky, I'm going to the loo to do a line. Want to come?' challenged Soma as she grabbed her friend drunkenly by the edge of her camo tank top. Sky's mountain of icy dreadlocks was now decorated with several tiny paper cocktail umbrellas and the glitter that she had applied earlier had now disappeared.

'Yea sure. Let's stop by the bar on the way, I need a can of cider. Got a proper sweat-on from dancing. Skaggsy did a banging barnyard breakcore set.'

'OK – good idea I think they're still serving.' It was nearly 5am and the club seemed to be getting away with still selling cans of Red Stripe and Thatcher's Gold from one small bar right at the top on what felt like the fifth or sixth floor, alongside a stall selling nitrous oxide packaged inside of silver and gold balloons from medical grade canisters strapped to the wall like giant optics. One of the guys selling the balloons was shouting out 'balloons – three for a tenner or £2 a pop'. He was definitely taxing those bad at maths or in a state of inebriation far beyond carrying out simple mental calculations and laughing all the way to the bank.

The girls, holding hands, wove their way to the top of the building which seemed to narrow and darken, and became increasingly humid as they climbed the narrow staircases. The tricky journey involved following tightly the person, or the person's arse, in front, shifting to the side to allow a stream of other ravers to move down the stairs in the opposing direction to avoid some hideous Hillsborough type death toll. The stair cases and the bars were the only places that felt overpopulated in Lakota, there was always space on the dance floor. By the time they reached the top bar, the girls weren't sure if the moisture on their skin was their own or from the sweat dripping from the ceiling.

'Look, there's Emma,' shouted Soma, as she pointed to a small bench just behind the speakers. Emma was sat there with some friends slowly inhaling and exhaling into a golden balloon, eyes closed, gently rocking back and forth with each breath. As the balloon emptied, Emma slowly exhaled, eyes still firmly shut and she laid back giggling in a pile of leopard print Lycra, neon leggings and homemade leg warmers with her friends all in hysterics looking at the ceiling. She had seen the most beautiful colours oscillating and spiralling in her mind's eye and in her ears had heard an imaginary, initially loud tinging sound that somehow impossibly outcompeted the club's music but eventually faded to nothing, leaving her with a lustful feeling that she was on the edge of discovering the secrets of the universe but in fact on coming to, was still no clearer on why she was on planet earth and ten quid down.

Hippy crack.

So moreish.

She nudged her buddies and stood up wonkily as if to go and purchase some more of this gaseous pseudo-elixir. In doing so she saw her housemates and bumbled over to them, arms akimbo, all embracing. The girls together stumbled to the bar, arms linked and grabbed a can each to see them home. Then they decided to find Casper before setting off. Casper, as always, was one of the last few standing, and was in front of the Jigsore Rig in a side room that was separated from the main area at the start of the night by a floor length, glittery, tinsel door like the ones bakeries have to stop flies from entering. As it was now the early hours of the following day, the glittery door was strewn across the floor and staircase, encased in mud, Rizla papers and discarded empty wraps, tangled around crushed, long-empty cans of Red Stripe and now looked like a huge, ugly Christmas tree decoration made by a toddler. The music appeared to be stopping and starting, creating a paroxysm of sound, each time louder and more obtrusive than the last. The dozen or so hard-core fans were still stood in front of the powerful sound system and moved each time a beat dropped like a convulsive Mexican wave. The girls eventually found him, and pulled him away from the aural fireworks. Despite being barely able to string a sentence together, he somehow managed to entice them to go a friend's house for an after party. As the bunch left the club, curving down the staircase, arm in arm, hand in hand - a feral caterpillar of delinquents, the girls all received a visual slap around the face as suddenly two lads, possibly late teens or early twenties collapsed in front of them into a pile on the floor near the downstairs toilets. The girls' bodies stiffened instantly at the sight and they all felt cold shivers pass down their spines in unison. The two boys, still conscious and smiling, were sat next to each other now in a dark pile resembling a pair of neglected trouser suits that had fallen from their coat hangers and sunken to the bottom of a cupboard. The boys were slightly floppy, yet their hands were gesticulating slowly, making circular motions in the air around them, shifting and squashing imaginary organic shapes through the atmosphere.

The boys didn't look that out of place as people began spilling out of the club onto the dawn-lit streets. Ketamine regularly seemed to turn fully upright, functioning people into piles of laughable, vacant jelly and the girls had first-hand experience of this. This was different though. These boys had their eyes wide open, yet their eyes no longer looked human. The colour had drained from their cheeks, leaving their skin ashen, their eyes were bulging slightly and their eyes were also white.

White, absolutely achromatic.

As fresh snow that settles on dry concrete, bar tiny, black pinpricks.

Irises were fully receded, bleached, long gone and the huge glare from these albino discs had scared the girls. This wasn't coloured contacts like they'd seen at the annual zombie walks in the city centre, this was freaky; sterile and hollow. They'd never seen anything like it before.

'Bleach,' shouted Casper, he'd come around from his K hole after taking a rather large toot of coke that Soma had given him to bring him round so he could walk. 'They're on Bleach. It's a new research drug apparently. It looks well fucked doesn't it? Wonder what it's like. I've seen a few people on it tonight. It only lasts about twenty minutes. You drop it in your actual eye man. It bleaches your eyes while you're on it. Not sure I'm down with that. It's meant to be amazing though.'

'That's so weird. They look so pale. Possessed like zombies or something,' said Soma.

'Yeah right. It takes you to heaven. Makes you look like you're in a massive K hole but their minds aren't there at the mo. Trust. They're projecting. Some proper mad shit. To heaven whatever that is. Must get some actually. I've talked myself round to it. Sounds like DMT or something. Fuck knows what it is made from. The stuff they're coming out with at the moment. Kids are basically lab rats but I'd risk it. Wouldn't you?' He paused and drew a breath. 'Em? Reckon you can get us some?'

Casper shuffled the girls towards the exit of the club protectively. The cocaine had kicked in and he continued to talk at them. They all kept looking back at the boys slumped by the wall who seemed to be human shells; their eyes still bright white, staring off into and over an imaginary horizon, arms waving gently.

'Erm. Yeah for sure, Casp. Looks… incredulous...'

'Dez did some over the summer apparently. His folks are Hindu. He says he went to some other plane, 'swarga loka' or something like that. Said he saw a god. It was all white though, no colours at all, yet he could see everything in so much more detail like, 'fuck your 3D - it was 5D'. Or did he say 5G? I can't remember exactly He said you could see nacreous white and the absence of colour but nothing else, yet you could see everything you've ever heard about in heaven. It's all there. He said it was all around him and in him. Couldn't touch or move anything and he didn't have a body. Never taken anything like it; DMT, Ket, 2Ci, 2Cb, nothing. He said he wasn't even that sure he believed in God... Brahman, Samsara whatever, yet he felt like he'd been reborn and was everything at once. Timeless. Beautiful man beautiful.'

'F'king hell, man, sounds ethereal. Not sure I'd be down with doing it in Lakota of all places, sounds like the sort of thing you'd want to do in nature, like acid,' Sky said, with an air of fear and cynicism in her voice as she pulled a cocktail umbrella out of her hair and started to twirl it in front of her as she walked, like she was drilling through the crowd to get out faster.

Emma looked back one more time before they left the club, her eyes were filled with a mixture of fear and questioning and her heart was filled with a longing more powerful than she had experienced after her nitrous trip. What was this bleach? She was definitely going to find out more about it.

'I'm not sure I'm up for a house party actually,' Emma said, realising she had done all of her drugs that she had brought out and wanted to head home and do some research. Plus she had some new tunes she wanted to listen to.

The others headed off towards St. Werburghs, making sure Emma got home safely before they headed on to continue their day time partying. The sound of the birds' tweeting and the rays of autumnal sunshine emerging over the rows of brightly coloured houses as they walked back the scenic way, via the mound would for most have been a clear signal to get oneself to bed. The night was over and the hangover was shortly due. However, for these party goers, the day was just beginning and between them all they had enough cash on them to get some rum and coke from the corner shop and head to a party where there would certainly be more fun times ahead.

Emma made herself a spliff in her living room and tried to switch on the sound system. She wanted something classical on to try and unwind from the crazy evening. How strange. It didn't work. None of the lights were coming on. Perhaps it was a fuse? She smoked her spliff in silence, too tired to search for her screwdriver to see if a fuse needed changing. She lolloped up the stairs and rolled into bed, switched on her laptop and waited for the familiar password prompt page to pop up. Before she popped a valium, she was going to find out more about this new drug and then she was going to go on the Dark Web and buy some. Later in the term, in between working on her post-grad project at home and on campus, she was going to persuade her housemates to take some with her, maybe at the winter solstice teknival.

CHAPTER NINE -- RUBY WICKER

Tabitha made a rapid exit from the student house, fleeing as the knock at the front door grew louder and more insistent. She felt satisfied that what she'd done to their sound system would keep their noise limited for at least a few weeks until they figured out what the problem was. Hopefully this would give poor Mrs Burrows some much needed respite. After getting back in her car, her heart still racing from the close call, Tabitha drove around the block several times. She eventually pulled up behind a green truck and sat still so that she could think, watching and listening to a pair of cats fighting on a fence top. No-one had seen her. She'd gotten away with it. Had she? What a rush. Much more exciting and enjoyable than her last experience in Mrs. Burrows' abode which had left her feeling solemn for days. She switched her phone back on to see several more missed calls and a voice message. There was a text from Jack that she had missed earlier asking her to iron his shirts better as the collars weren't neat enough. She deleted it instantly. Then she had a quick flick through the photos she'd taken inside the student household and smiled as she swiped through several selfies of her holding up a rainbow of different bags of drugs. Her little secret. What would the staff at school think if they ever knew? She half-heartedly listened to the voice message, expecting it to be a sales call, hoping also to be able to delete it from her phone straight away.

'Tabitha? Hi. It's Penny from the school office. If you could, please would you give me a call back in the next half hour on the school line, if not I'll try again first thing in the morning. It's important. Sorry to disturb your evening.'

Tabitha paused and looked back up at the cats that had retreated to separate fence posts, licking their wounds. She glanced back down at her phone and started to bite at the skin around her thumb nail, it was red raw already. A tiny drop of blood appeared which trickled along her cuticle. Tabitha found it amazing how one small droplet of blood could create such a red mess. She watched it slowly spread, flooding around the edges of dried skin cells, giving them crimson borders. She wiped it on her thigh then dialled Penny back on the school office number with one hand and started pummelling her stomach with the other. What on earth did school want?

'Penny. Hi. It's Tabitha from Science. Is everything okay?'

'Tabitha. Thank you for calling me back. I hope now is a good time to chat, are you at home? Is your partner there?'

'Just on my way home now. Yes, Jack's home... with Oscar I hope. What's the problem? Has there been a break into the lab again?'

Tabitha's mind was struggling to process why Penny would be calling her on Saturday evening. Perhaps someone had got into the science department again. A few years back, before she'd had Oscar, a group of lads, one of them an ex-student, Solly's older brother if she recollected correctly, had broken in and tried to steal some chemicals. God knows what they thought they'd find in the school chemical store cupboard. Some magnesium ribbon and a bunch of matches was probably the most alluring steal there and that definitely wasn't worth a criminal record. The alarms had been set off anyway and Tabitha and Leila the technician had been called in to go and start tidying up the mess as they were the only two that had picked their phones up. That had taught her not to be so hasty when school called. It wasn't ever to let her know what a first-rate job she was doing or to offer her an extra week off, on the house. She'd promised herself whilst sweeping up broken glass into a dustpan on her hands and knees on that hot, summer Saturday morning that she would screen her calls from work after that.

'No. No, Tabitha. It's a little more serious than that I'm afraid. I wanted to check you were with Jack just in case you feel you need support with this sad info. It's Ruby Wicker from your Biology class. There's no easy way to say this I'm afraid and I hate to be the bearer of bad news, but she's dead. She passed away a few hours ago in Southmead Hospital. I've been on the phone with the police and her family. There are some suspicious circumstances around her death and the press already seem to be sticking their noses in. This is just a courtesy call really to give you the heads up. We didn't want staff to find out via the press so we're letting all of her teachers and close friends know this evening.'

'Oh my god. What on earth happened?' said Tabitha. Her adrenaline resources were dwindling from the events of the evening and she suddenly felt absolutely shattered. Her hands were shaking and she could feel an element of panic seeping in. 'What happened Penny? Is there anything I can do?'

Tabitha offered her help, hoping that Penny would realise this was a rhetorical offer. Really, what could she do? The girl was dead.

'No, no. Not at the moment. There may be questions later and I'm sure the police will want to speak with you at some point as you were the last teacher that saw her last week. Obviously just for information, you are not in any way implicated with the death.'

'How did it happen?'

'At the moment, the doctors are still unsure what exactly caused it, but she'd been drinking quite heavily and had possibly taken something. Some new street drug, Bleach I think it's called.' Tabitha could hear the distress in Penny's voice mounting. The school was large and even though they were a large inner-city comprehensive, the staff all really cared about the students and it had a strong sense of community.

'She was drunk with some friends, some others from your Biology class were there too and a few of them had seen her take something at the park. A few of them were doing it too and were fine, but she reacted badly so they took her to hospital in the early hours this morning as she started convulsing. Her body, her beautiful red hair, her eyes, everything just faded. Hospital staff said there's been a few others like it over the past few months, each time it's just horrific. They don't know how to treat it. She just wouldn't stop having seizures then her blood, her arms and legs everything just faded to white. Her breathing shut down and then her heart stopped. Someone saw her dropping chemicals into her eyes with Lucy and Danielle. The police will investigate further no doubt. We're not asking questions at the moment. It's all too raw. We're leaving the police to do their bit first. Apparently someone at school sold the drugs to her.

'Dear lord. What are these kids doing to each other? To themselves? I knew it wouldn't be long until it affected Farefield.'

'I'm sorry, Tabitha, I've got to go. I've more teachers to try and contact before the press do. I'm sure you will anyway, but the Head is asking staff to remain professional and make no comments at all at this stage until more is known about what's gone on. There will be a staff briefing about it first thing on Monday and the morning timetable is going to be changed so the Head and police can talk to staff and students. Please try not to worry and try not to speak about the case with anyone outside of your immediate family for the time being. Night, Tabitha.'

'Thanks for letting me know. It's truly awful. I don't know what to say. Her parents must be devastated. See you Monday.'

Tabitha gently tapped the red phone icon on the screen and ended the call. She felt strange, in shock perhaps. What an evening. First she was nearly rumbled at Mrs. Burrows where she was just trying to do a good deed, now this. Ruby's poor parents. What on earth must they be feeling right now? Losing a child was no doubt the greatest emotional pain a human could feel. She pulled out a small black and white ultrasound print from inside of her phone case and brought it close to her face, gently smoothing down its slightly infolded corners. She could feel tears pooling in the corners of her eyes which she dabbed away with the hem of her sleeve before starting the engine and heading home to see Oscar.

CHAPTER TEN -- MAKING PLANS

To do before Friday list:
1. *Finish BTEC marking and Year 10 reports.*
2. *Write article for Ruby's memory book.*
3. *Book Doctors appointment -potential ingrown toenail.*
4. *Oscar's Xmas presents – see separate list.*
5. *Xmas decorations – put up.*

Tabitha was sat at her desk at work, staring at her current to do list pummeling her aching belly. She put a smooth black line through numbers one, three and five. She'd finished all of the teaching work she had to do before the Christmas break which would normally make her feel quite smug; knowing that she could now let her hair down and enjoy her favourite of the school holidays with her son. Yet she felt glum. She needed to complete her article for Ruby's memory book and was hoping to get it done with the last twenty minutes of her free period that morning before facing her A-Level class. Most of them had not been in this week as they were off school with anxiety or busy speaking with one of the school counsellors or the police about Ruby.

Although stressful, school was normally a place that felt safe and comforting to her, yet since the death of her student, it had felt anything but. Police and other investigative professionals had been in and out all week, in her class, interviewing her, her students and her teaching colleagues. The press had hounded her most mornings and evenings on her way to and from work, probing for any details that she might let slip – not that she had anything to offer. She felt as lost and confused as the rest of the community. She was thankful that none of the press had turned up at her house though, as that would have been a nightmare. No escape. No respite. The school had been very strict about privacy and the release of staff data, thankfully. Even the thought of Christmas shopping for Oscar left her feeling slightly null and void. Glancing up at the bucketful of red curls and piercing green eyes in a school photo of Ruby Wicker taken in year seven that had been printed and distributed to all staff as some kind of suggestive inspiration, Tabitha re-read the memo requesting prose. The school had asked each teacher for a short paragraph for a memory book that would be given to Ruby's parents at the funeral. She double clicked apprehensively on the Word document entitled 'Ruby Wicker' that she'd tried to start yesterday and then closed it down taking a deep sigh. She didn't know where to start. Not only was the school in a state of mass grief, but the scent of suspicion and worry instead of Christmas dinner and mince pies filled the corridors.

Partially giving up for the morning, Tabitha allowed herself to lose focus on her school tasks and as her mind wondered, battling to gently escape from the present torture of her desk, she drifted back to the box of delights she had stumbled on whilst nosing around the student house a few weeks earlier. Her stomach filled with adrenaline and her back straightened abruptly and her head lifted up. Thinking about her mysterious double life as a secret explorer slash doer of good deeds gave her mind a break from the depressing state of being at school and thinking about Ruby. She picked up her pen and added on an extra bullet point to her to do list:

6. *Number 41.*

She hadn't been out in the evening since her trip to the student house and had decided that it was time for a visit to the next house along. Number forty-one. She didn't have a reason just yet, but why should she? She needed to explore first and have a good look around for ideas. She liked the idea of having visited all three houses in a row opposite her own. It would feel like getting a full house in Bingo.

From the outside, number 41 seemed like such a quiet, shabby, tired house. It was if it had retired from its function of providing occupation almost, sandwiching the student house with Mrs. Burrows' merely for a purpose to justify its existence. She'd been watching it from the safety of her home for a few days now, in between work and caring for her son, and hadn't seen anyone come or go. Subconsciously she'd been considering it as her next project and was keeping an eye on it to get a feel for the place. She knew an old man lived there, Donald, and that he liked a drink apparently. Spent most of his life in the pub according to the ladies she'd seen mouthing at the corner shop months ago who were in front of her and behind him in the queue as he'd plonked two four packs of special brew up on the counter whilst pointing at the tobacco section with a grunt. Tabitha started to day dream at her desk about what she might find inside his, by all means, fairly humble looking abode. Slightly derelict from the outside, the front wall was clearly in need of re-rendering and several tiles appeared to be cracked and missing from the roof. It must've been leaking at least a bit on the inside with such damage. It'd been like this for a long time though. Perhaps he didn't care or wasn't even aware. Maybe she could fix it if it was easy to get to. She'd mastered stereo destruction, breaking and entering and had even gone as far as to order some crochet hooks online. How much harder could a bit of roofing be? The internet had all the answers.

She'd convinced herself that Don's was to be next. It may look bleak from the outside, but sometimes the shabbiest of treasure chests can hold the most precious of gems. Never one to judge a book by its cover, Tabs started to draw up a mental list of what she might need to take with her this time. How would she get in? Perhaps she'd need to take a few tools again. She'd need a new black rucksack, yes, maybe velvet fabric. That would be nice and Christmassy. Maybe she would treat herself to a new set of spanners and screwdrivers? A small portable set. What were they called? Her father used to have one in his special drawer of dad-stuff in the kitchen. A 'Leatherman' was it? Tabitha sneakily opened up the Amazon shopping app on her phone which was resting on her lap discretely and started browsing for some new treats for her hobby. '*Happy Christmas to me*,' she sung to herself quietly as she filled her online basket with goodies.

The bell rang and Tabitha scooped up her teaching resources for her next lesson. She was supposed to be revising oxidative phosphorylation with her A-Level group as they had a mock exam straight after the holidays, but she had a feeling the few that did turn up would just want to talk about Ruby and what happened to her.

'*Thank you, your order has been placed*,' appeared on her phone screen. Have there ever been any other words so sweet? She stashed her phone in her bag and trundled off to class smiling.

'Tom?'

'Yes Miss'

'Ozora ?'

'Miss'

'Clare?'

'Miss'

'Gemma ?'

'Yes Miss'

'Solly... Solly..?'

'He's not here Miss. Him and Liam have been off all week,' one of the students piped up. 'Taken it pretty bad apparently. Liam was shagging her, you see. They'd been hanging out together at McDonalds together for ages. He was always buying her milkshakes.'

'Thanks for letting me know Dean. I had heard that they were an item.'

Tabitha finished off, then closed the register and gathered the students round the front of the class. She managed to summon enough emotional energy to carry the class through a brief revision session before chatting about the funeral arrangements and discussing what she should write in the Biology eulogy she had been asked to put together before dismissing the class a few minutes early and going home. The way she saw it, her mind was only able to focus on two things at the moment. The uncertain cause of Ruby's misfortunate, tragic death. Or her next planned outing. She chose to think about that latter. It kept the bad butterflies away.

CHAPTER ELEVEN -- THE RAVE

They'd left Bristol just after midnight after having listened carefully to the directions on the party line phone number that Sky had been sent earlier that evening. Casper was feeling proud that he'd managed to fix their sound system so he and Sky had bought in an eighth of cocaine to celebrate. As they left the bright city lights behind them, they became part of a noisy convoy of battered-up old hatchbacks and large, converted trucks and campervans; some decorated with graffiti and stickers, others uniquely self-built from wood and reclaimed parts.

It was a cold, crystal clear night and the stars were beautifully visible in the sky. It had been under an hour's drive from Bristol and rigs from all over the south-west had come together for the annual winter solstice rave. As soon as Casper, Sky, Emma and Soma had ditched their old Volvo estate down a nearby lane along with the vehicles of hundreds of other attendees, they set off into the night. The excited group followed a snake of others who had just arrived, using head torches or the light from their mobiles to guide them down the winding, country lanes.

They followed the pounding sounds and the strobe lights firing high up into the night sky up several muddy tracks and across two fields until they came to a driveway leading to what looked like a collection of abandoned air hangars, each brimming with partying revelers.

'Mate, this is immense. There's got to be at least five or six rigs here. How the fuck did they set this up? There's going to be complaints... hope it doesn't get shut down too early... quick, let's get amongst it whilst it still pumping,' Sky grinned from ear to ear and jumped onto Casper's back. 'Onwards, my mighty steed, for much fun is to be had.' Sky jabbed her chunky 16 hole army boots into Casper's knee caps and screamed with raucous laughter. They galloped off together into the warehouse in the depths of bumbly Paulton.

Draped black and white, razzle-dazzle, hypnotic banners and large inflatable virus-shaped dangly things hung from the ceiling. UV strip lights chucking out the most unnatural of purple glows spread over the hundreds of revellers as they danced or chatted or scuttled up and down the corridors of the old factory to get from one room to another. The noise was deafening and the rave-elders and more sensible amongst the crowd had foam earplugs in to try and offer some protection against the inevitable tinnitus that would come from years of this kind of sound abuse. Considering it was winter and not far off Christmas Day, the building was sweltering, with sweat dripping from the rafters and people everywhere were glugging on water or alcoholic drinks from cans and bottles. The floor was already a thick carpet of empty cans and finished packets of rolling tobacco, which would all be cleared away in several days time. The ravers were noisy but they were usually tidy. There must have been over three or four thousand people here at this illegal collective celebration of the winter solstice, repetitive beats and drugs. The noxious stench of diesel-powered generators, fags and ketamine being cooked up could be detected outside the warehouse, with some of the more slightly fraggled party goers huddled around a large fire that'd been started using some of the old furniture that had been ditched round the back of the warehouse.

The clientele was a motley combination of spoilt trust fund kiddies, drug dealers and opportunistic thieves, students, creative traveller types, DJ's, happy, hedonistic life-long rave devotees and a minority of people who generally just seemed completely lost in life. The impressive light shows and projected audiovisuals happening on the inside must have taken hours to set up and the sound systems in each room amounted to thousands and thousands of pounds worth of equipment. It was all put on for the pure love of music and entertainment and despite the overall quite eerie appearance of the event to any outsider, most of the youngsters coming tonight and having their first taste of the underground rave scene would certainly be hooked.

Emma and Soma, hand-in-hand were skipping from one rig to the next, giggling and taking it in turns to swig from a bottle of cherry brandy that Soma had pinched from her gran's house a few months ago. It had had been since sitting on her bookshelf, waiting for a special occasion.

'Aw. I can't believe you guys are all off to Thailand on Tuesday. I'm going to really miss you.'

'Yeah. It won't be the same without you there, Somes, but I've got to make the most of these long university holidays. My funding is going to run out soon then I'm going to have to get a real job. Become an adult and stuff – behave like a grown up.'

The girls hugged. Emma scrunched up Soma's fluffy bunch of ginger curls and gave her friend another extra long squeeze.

'I've got us all a little something to celebrate too,' said Emma with a sly grin. 'Let's go and find the others.'

'Right that's it for me on the booze,' Soma said, passing the half full glass bottle to Emma. 'I've got shit to do tomorrow. I've got to get the train up to Leicester for a family do so I'm going to drive back to Bristol at sunrise.'

'Ah, really? Well take some of this for while I'm away,' said Emma, pressing a small glass vial in a plastic sealable bag into Soma's hand.

'What is it?'

'It's Bleach. I got some off the dark net. I've been wanting to try it for, like, forever but if you want to drive back in a few hours, maybe save it for another time?'

'Ah cheers Emma. How exciting. An early Christmas gift. I haven't got you anything yet, I was going to bring something back after the break.'

'No worries, sweet cheeks. You don't need to get me anything. Just empty the bloody ashtrays out in the front room a bit more often.'

'Ha ha, nice one.'

The pair bounced around merrily together for the next hour or so before eventually bumping into Casper and Sky. They found their housemates huddled around one side of the fire with a few other familiar faces from Bristol. Casper was slowly pushing the leg from an old wooden chair onto the pit of flames whilst seemingly engulfed in a deep conversation with Sky. They both looked very animated as the warm, amber glow from the fire was reflected in their young, happy eyes. Rosy-cheeked and yarning away. Possibly from the immense amount of heat that was being kicked out, but more likely due to the local cider that the pair had been drinking all evening from the makeshift bar. Emma and Soma perched next to the others, initially squatting on tippy toes then both flopping back onto their bottoms, giggling and flinging arms around as each of them hugged the other. There was a spread of cold, dry straw on the floor and some large rectangular bales a little further back which had probably been dragged over from the nearby farm at some point to make the slightly muddy patches a little bit more comfortable. It turned out that Casper and Sky were making plans about their upcoming winter break to Thailand that they were making with Emma. Their flight was in 3 days and their rucksacks were already packed, passports prepared and tickets printed. They had an old copy of a Lonely Planet, probably too out of date to rely on for accommodation information, but full of inspiring photos of places that they'd like to visit. They'd been planning it for weeks now and had their itinerary down to near perfection. They were only staying out there for a couple of weeks but after flying into Bangkok, they'd planned to get as far north as they could in the time allowed. They were all hoping to reach the busy city of Chang Mai and then head on towards Pai, a small but beautiful rustic village on the outskirts of the jungle, for some cookery lessons, maybe a bit of jungle trekking and lots of Thai massage. They all wanted to cycle around old temples and soak in the scenery too. Friends of theirs had all been and done the island hoping and full moon parties that happened more down in the south of the country which they all fully intended to go back and experience when they'd all graduated and Soma could afford to come too. This short winter break was more of a relaxation, pampering and sight-seeing affair. Wholesomeness. Perhaps a bit of a de-tox too; a fortnight off the partying and alcohol would do them all the world of good before returning to their studies.

'So... how are we all doing this fine evening then?' chirped Emma, as she reached down into her belt pocket and pulled out several empty glass vials and small, plastic bags of lilac-grey powder.

'I thought we could all celebrate this beautiful wintery weekend with something new and exciting. I'm bringing you all a little Christmas cheer – who's in?'

'What's...'

'It's Bleach,' piped in Soma before Casper could finish his sentence. 'Emma got some off the net. Who's a clever geek then?'

'Clever wrong-un' more like,' retaliated Casper, winking and nudging her. 'I'd love to give this a go, I reckon tonight's the perfect vibes for it. Banging party going on in there. Maximum atmosphere all around. Yes... I'm in. For sure.'

'Sky? How about you, pickle?' Emma urged – not that Sky ever needed convincing to take drugs.

'Er, yar, obvs!' she replied, swashbuckling her drinking hand whilst pushing out a gorgeous grin. For some bizarre reason she had done her eye make-up to look like the clown from IT this evening, white and red, long black lines stretching from her bottom lashes to the middle of her cheeks. Sky always dressed for attention. She was so pretty she could get away with deliberately looking a complete disaster and still be hot.

'You'd better wipe that shit off your face first, Pennywise,' shrieked Emma. 'If I have a bad trip, I don't want to be seeing that bastard.'

They all laughed and watched as Emma started to pass the vials along to Sky and Casper.

'Somes – you can look after us all,' Emma said.

'With pleasure. Don't I always? Gis' a bump of coke Sky so I can stay awake and look after you bunch of feral twats then.'

Soma scraped her red hair back into a tight pony tail so that it wouldn't get in the way as Sky reached into her pocket. Sky tapped out a mound of white Bolivian-marching-powder on to the back of Soma's hand. She snorted it up her nostril then licked the rest off before rolling herself a cigarette. Sky tossed the wrap towards her buddy. She probably had a good few more grams about her person amongst god knows what else.

'Help yourself dude.'

'Cheers bud,' Soma replied. 'It's nice having you rich bitches as friends,' she joked grinning at her crew before blowing smoke into their faces.

Casper opened up his little plastic baggy and took out the glass vial with his left hand with a puzzled expression on his face. He flicked it gently with his right hand and watched the dark grey powder settle to the bottle of the tube.

'What do you do with it, Emz? Do you snort it? Why's it in this glass thing?'

'We need water,' she replied, pulling out a bottle from Casper's backpack. 'Can we use this, Casper? I can't believe how many cans of paint you lug around with you – your back must be fucked.'

'Yeah sure thing chicken wing. Help yourself. I'm totally all about having some Thai beauties walk all over my spine next week. Sort me out a treat.'

'You sexist twat. Hope they stamp on you and snap you like a Twiglet,' Emma retorted.

Emma delved back into her pocket and pulled out a plastic, purple syringe, the sort parents use for giving medicine to babies with.

'So I got this from the pharmacy. You need to take up about a half mil of water then mix it in with the powder until it's all dissolved. Then you drop it in the corner of your eye, or get someone else to do it for you. It takes a few minutes to work.'

'Woah. Weird. It's like DIY acid or something. How will you guys know when it's working? You twats are feckin' loons at the best of times,' Soma joked.

'How long does it last, oh Oracle?' Casper asked Emma. 'Do I need to lie down and will I piss myself when I'm on it? I've not brought any clean clothes.'

'Oh shut up you twat! Just do it. It only lasts about twenty minutes. It feels like a lot longer when you're on it though – bit like K – only this stuff is fucking A-mazing. MDMA-zing And it take you to heaven bay-bee,' Sky had obviously heard a lot about this drug and was filling in for Emma who had already drawn up water from the bottle and squirted it into her vial.

'Yeah. What she said. Trust me. You'll know when it's working. And Soma, check out our eyes in approximately three minutes... you'll know too.' Emma issued instructions whilst not even looking up at her mates. She'd been looking forward to this for ages.

'But didn't some guy die from it recently? Some old dude in prison? And some kids nearer Bristol?' asked Soma, showing slight concern for her friends, as she was starting to sober up and thinking a little more coherently than the drunken trio.

'Yeah I remember. He was old though and probably on smack too. Same guy that broke into Buckingham palace. There's been no proof about the other deaths I don't think. The media just blows things out of proportion. Tory government trying to clamp down on our fun. Other than that I've only heard awesome things about it. It's so new and I reckon it'll spread like wildfire now you can get hold of it so easily from the internet,' said Sky, nodding like an excitable puppy 'hey Ems?'

'Yeah, maybe. So what you guys been chatting about anyway? Looked like you were having a right old mothers' meeting. Super-intense discussion... putting the world to rights,' said Emma as she steered the conversation back to their Thailand discussion.

'Oi oi. Mothers' meeting indeed. Now who's being sexist?! I do have a willy don't you know.'

'Yeah and don't we all know it mate. Stop shagging all our mates while we're on the matter of cocks. It'll erode if you keep rubbing it and from what I've heard there's not a lot left to play with,' Emma winked then tipped her head back and dropped three or four drops into each of her eyes before blinking frantically like a strobe light for a few seconds. Sky and Casper followed suit, dripping the liquid into each other's eyes whilst they continued sharing their travel plans.

Soma cleaned the surface of her I-phone with her sleeve and gently tapped out another sprinkling of cocaine, rolled up a fiver, snorted it then stood up and laughed loudly to the night sky as she watched her friends all recline slowly, with the pallor of ghosts and the frailty of porcelain dolls. She was glad she hadn't partaken as she was pretty sure that this bleach would definitely not be compatible with driving, although she was also slightly envious of the expressions on her friends' faces. Each of them had turned as white as snow, eyes like chalky marbles. But they were smiling like the Cheshire cat in a comedy club and all appeared to be communicating with the atmosphere around them by some form of slow motion, jellyfish sign language. Soma over-zealously started to move around to each of her friends, putting their hoods up for them, zipping up their tops and generally tucking their clothes in, using any spare material like a blanket to try and keep them comfortable on their trip

Each of them appeared to be in their own little corner of the universe, laughing like a pack of far-flung hyenas to a joke that Soma didn't understand, but not a sound came out of their mouths. Soma wondered if the world in which they appeared to have been transported to had not only momentarily taken the colour from their complexion but also the noise from their throats.

Several minutes passed and Soma was somewhat captivated by watching the strange horizontal performance that her friends were unintentionally putting on for her but she was also starting to feel impatient – too much cocaine. The bass line was being churned out hard from the rave inside; she needed to stomp and had run out of tobacco. Soma left the fireside and decided to go on a short reccy whilst her friends finished whatever strange journey they were on. After blagging enough Golden Vagina and Rizla from some other kids sat around the fire, Soma went for a little dance in the main warehouse. After half an hour or so had passed, not only had she warmed up but could feel the agitation of the cocaine wearing off so she decided to go and check up on her mates. On her return to the fire she could see that the colour had returned to their faces once again and they were all sat, more clear-headed, chatting fervently, with elation in their words, cutting over each other, with the listening skills of disobedient toddlers as they all tried to share their personal experiences of the bleach. Their Halloween make up was smudged and dripping down their faces and they had beads of sweat on each of their brows like they'd run a marathon in the desert.

From what she could gather, they had all experienced something similar. It sounded beautiful, yet slightly haunting. The trio spoke of being surrounded by a scaffolding of dense forest and hearing the sounds of many creatures they'd never seen before along with the gentle soothing gush of fast running water as if a waterfall was nearby. They said the sensation of the air on their skin felt different and all three of them had felt sweaty with each inhalation packing a pure rush of humid, gold dust into their lungs. Sky said that as she explored and looked around she couldn't see her own body or her friends yet she knew that they were there with her too as she could sense their inaugural energy. Emma likened her field of view as moving with her as she slowly moved her head but slightly delayed as she tried to take on board all of the beautiful intrinsic detail in the nature around her. It was like when she tried to run out-of-date software on her computer or when a television aerial didn't work as it should, creating that trippy, pixellated effect. But as she relaxed into the experience further, her visual acuity sharpened and as she looked at her surroundings more slowly and with acceptance, the detail and beauty in what she was seeing had moved her to tears.

'I couldn't see any colour at all yet I could feel so much vibrancy. Everything glowed. I could see birds. So many beautiful birds. I could see the detail in their feathers if I looked closely like they were under a microscope' Sky said. 'It was so strange, as I've never really liked birds but there they were, everywhere, in this tranquil, overwhelming heaven. And huge insects too. It's like they were in four dimensions, like aliens or something. Like they were me and I was them yet they were separate from me but connected with some kind of invisible energy... Like glowing strings that you could feel and control but yet they also controlled me.' The group sat, huddled and chatted rampantly for hours.

'I could feel these gigantic mountains all around me just outside of my peripheral view. I could feel them slowly breathing in time with the universe, taking in minerals as they formed over millions of years and passing out elements as they slowly eroded. I couldn't see them though as there were too many trees around me. The trees were beautiful I kept trying to reach out and take some of the fruit from them but I couldn't.' Casper reached out in from of him and grasped the air with disappointment on his face like a novice playing a VR game.

'Okay... You guys are weird. Nothing you've said makes any sense. You've definitely lost the plot, come on, back up out of that rabbit hole and give me a hug, I'm getting cold,' said Soma. She was confused by their babble and also very envious at this point. It sounded amazing.

The friends took it in turns along with the other people sat around the blazing fire to collect more wood as the music continued to pound in the background. The warmth of the alcohol and drugs flowing in their veins kept them up all night until eventually, the light of the low slung winter sun could be seen creeping over the horizon. Soma had fallen asleep a few hours ago with her head in Casper's lap. The others had cooed over the fluffy mass of ginger curls and freckles gently snoring away. The light of the morning and the coldness of her damp and now sober feet woke her up.

She hugged her pals goodbye and wished them luck and all the fun in the world on their trip to Thailand as she huffed and puffed about having to catch the train back to visit her family for Christmas. As she walked back to the car alone as fast as she could, her legs felt freezing cold and heavy as sodden with morning dew. She felt pretty rough but it was worth it. It always was. She clasped the vial of bleach that Emma had given her to try at a later date through her rainbow woollen mittens excitedly. Her friends' descriptions had reminded her of a book she'd read about shamanism a while ago and she wondered perhaps whether they'd actually travelled through the *axis mundi* or passed through the point at which heaven and earth are connected with their third eye. What had they seen? She couldn't wait to find out at a more convenient and comfortable time. The words of her grandmother, a devout Christian, resonated in the back of her mind.

'The Devil is in the detail.'

Yet the detail sounded so exciting.

CHAPTER TWELVE -- MRS LOCKBRIDGE

Valerie-Ann Lockbridge had dealt with other people's shit for years. Abusive shit from family, lovers and literal shit from the residents in the care home she'd devoted herself too. She was a woman recently retired who'd realised that what life she had left needed to be lived. The doctor had given her months - a year at best. After researching the side effects of the invasive treatment she'd been offered which may only extend her life by a short time, Mrs. Lockbridge had opted to face her cancer head on – however foolish friends might think this was. Fortunately for her, she had no friends, by choice, so the opinion of others didn't really matter. She fully intended to make use of every second she had left rather than wasting away trapped and alone, connected to multiple cannulas and lines, confined to a bed and a sick bowl.

It'd been her decision to return to work after fighting off the big C first time round. She worked hard, sometimes several 14 hour shifts or nights in a row at the care home for the elderly. She enjoyed the chats she had with the residents and offered a real patience and kindness to the ones who were in the process of or had fully lost their marbles. The irony was that she herself would probably not be making it to such a ripe old age as her body was now so riddled with cancer. Her diagnosis came just weeks after her retirement send off at work and although a terrible shock, Mrs. Lockbridge knew deep in her bones that it had come back with a vengeance and was now, well, deep and in her bones.

Despite the lethargy, the relentless coughing attacks and the feeling of heaviness in her soul, Mrs. Lockbridge had been told that it had yet to reach her brain and whilst she still had some cognition left she had a few very important things she needed to do before she passed. She'd observed for most of her working life old timers drifting through the last twenty or so years of their time on earth and she'd she witnessed her residents troubled by arthritis, incontinence, mobility issues and the like, and had decided that old age wasn't a place that she was that bothered about visiting anyway.

Generally, Valerie-Ann kept herself to herself and gained all the social interaction she wanted or needed in life from talking with her residents and colleagues and if she ever needed to let off steam she knew that a quick rant to one of the patients in the dementia unit was all she needed. Her shared words would fall on deaf ears allowing her anger to sail away as dissipating waves into the ether, never to come back and bite her on the bottom as they had the habit of doing when one discussed ones feelings with other members of staff.

Since retiring, she'd had some thinking time. She'd put her will together at the advice of her doctor and had started to slowly donate any superfluous belongings. She had no relatives left to pass anything on to so she'd made several trips into town on the bus with bags of things she would no longer need. She had one more job to complete before she wasted away, before she finally gave up, before the visiting healthcare worker would force her into a care home like the one she had just retired from. Worse case scenario, she'd end up being escorted to a hospice to die in a strange place surrounded by people she did not want to be around. She wanted to die on her own terms after she'd done the tasks she had set herself. They weren't pleasant tasks and tonight would be the biggest challenge she'd faced yet.

The four walls of her remote, smallholding cottage had felt like they were pressing in, pulsing and squeezing like a tachycardic prison earlier in the day as she'd spent what felt like forever waiting for the sun to set, pacing the rug in her lounge, clasping her 12 bore in one hand and a framed black and white portrait photo of a young, solemn faced child in the other. She eventually wrapped the shotgun she'd occasionally used for rabbit hunting along with several brick red cartridges in a large, delicately patterned French scarf and then again in an old beach towel before placing it into her old school gym holdall. Her motorbike leathers were so warm but it was bitterly cold outside and she had a long journey ahead of her. She took one last swig of her strong, black Nescafe. This was followed by one last look at the address and list of handwritten directions she'd drafted days before on a piece of paper and committed it to memory before tossing the paper onto the wood burner, slamming the fire door shut and sliding the portrait inside the breast pocket of her leather jacket. She then left the oppression of her cottage and mounting her trusty stead. Mrs. Lockbridge took in a slow lung full of the icy night air which caused her to cough for several minutes until she collected a small clot of bright red blood into a hanker chief. Her exhaled breath hung like miniature diamonds in the cold winters' air. Blood diamonds. She donned her helmet and set off down the frosty track on her motorbike. Revenge was a dish best served cold.

CHAPTER THIRTEEN -- OLD MAN DON'S HOUSE

The sun had set on the eve of Christmas Eve. Not that anyone observing the horizon would've noticed the difference. Clouded, low-hung, grey sky became slightly darker, slightly cloudier and slightly lower hung sky. Time plodded on, day slipped into night as pyjamas, nostalgic festive movies and warm blankets could be heard beckoning with careless whispers from lunch time onwards. Tabitha had just put her overexcited son to bed. Perhaps it would have been easier to not tell preschoolers about Christmas until they were four or even five years old? It would certainly have saved her a lot of money and made December bedtimes a hell of a lot easier. As he snoozed deeply, she kissed him on the forehead and then peaked out of the curtains to double check that Don's house was sitting silently in the dark before setting out for the evening, leaving her husband at home in the warmth.

As she pulled up quietly a short walk from the night's project, number forty-one, she smiled at the twinkling Christmas lights framing many a window along the road. It was cosy and comforting to be in her bubble, her mind redolent with memories of Christmases past. The hypnotic act of counting the repetitive '*tap tap*' of raindrops striking her windscreen had almost made her forget that after parking and undoing her seat belt the next obvious step was to undo her door and exit the car. A loud bang suddenly woke Tabitha from her hazy daze. She sat up abruptly, alive in the moment. Seconds passed and several further short, sharp thuds ricocheted through the air, each instigating a cold rush of adrenaline in Tabitha's bloodstream. She froze - unsure whether to duck and cover or pull away. Tabitha's subconscious decision had been to keep her body perfectly upright and still; somewhere half way between the two possibly more sensible options. Frozen like a rabbit in the headlights. Seconds passed and the noises appeared to stop. Tabitha rolled her eyes to the left and right, head remaining central, as still as rigor mortis. Then again she moved her eyes left and right followed by a slow turn of her neck to scope behind her. The back road alley was dark and motionless other than the constant downward drizzle. Not a soul could be seen or heard. No animals, wind or vehicles could've caused the disruption. How strange she thought, heart racing.

Tabitha decided to sit tight for a little longer. Sit and wait. Sit, wait and watch. Just in case. Her legs felt tired and although she'd been looking forward to her mini-mission this evening, she took this noise as an excuse to remain put for a little longer. She stared at the cluster of houses, three out of three she'd have explored after this evening. It felt nice to achieve a personal best, a full house, one hundred and eighty. Mrs. Burrows was at Women's Institute and would be for hours. Knitting and baking away in one of their weekly 'lock-in sessions'. Her lights were all switched off bar the welcoming light in the hall which Tabitha had noticed that she kept on permanently. There was no loud music pumping out from the student house. Only one light appeared to be on in their front room, all the curtains and windows were closed, even their back door was firmly shut. She had noticed it seemed to remain open pretty much twenty four seven with various muddles of dreadlocked youths tumbling out to smoke rollies whenever anyone was at home so Tabitha presumed they were all out, possibly even home for the Christmas holidays.

Tabitha, wrapped up in her new, black, velvet coat and hat, started to nibble on the emergency Tracker bar she'd put in her glove box months ago in case of a break down (of the car or her toddler). The slightly stale crumbs absorbed any moisture left in her mouth and she instantly regretted her snack choice once again, but persevered for the odd hit of chocolate drop. She occasionally investigated her peripheral surroundings, anxiously passing fleeting glares to her left and right. To an onlooker, not that there were any, she looked like a plump squirrel that'd just woken from hibernation. Ten minutes had passed, her Tracker bar was long gone and she'd heard or seen nothing of any interest from the safety of her metal drey. The rain had eased so Tabitha pulled on the inner door handle and stepped out into the night, her floor length coat offering her the blanket of camouflage she had desired.

Tabs hitched up her coordinated velvet bum bag, felt the outline of her new metal toys through the softness of the fabric and smiled. She'd gone for a svelte female Batman ensemble, courtesy of Amazon and her rainy day savings and with each step she took towards the old house she was about to break into, she felt marvellous and all the woe of the past few weeks temporarily melted away.

'Curiouser and curiouser,' Tabitha muttered as her confidence turned to caution as she approached the old man's wooden back door. It was several inches ajar and by all accounts it looked as though someone had beaten her to it. The lock had taken a strike or two, broken completely and splintered wood hemmed the handle like an unkempt moustache. She ran her fingers over the damaged entrance carefully so as not to acquire a splinter and tried to evaluate what had happened.

Perhaps old Don had lost his key and drunkenly smashed his way in? Perhaps it had always been like this. Surely not, no-one would live so insecurely in a city. Perhaps someone else was robbing the place? Although what would have enticed anyone to this particular abode Tabitha was unclear of. The place didn't exactly hum of wealth, more stale beer and yesterday's kebab. Someone must have broken in.

Her concentration lapsed and her finger pricked on the damaged wood. The sharp pain caused her to draw her hand away rapidly. Zeus's lightning bolt surged through her chest; an adrenaline rush which she had learnt to love and somewhat crave. But this time it felt different. She felt out of control. This was HER Christmas gift to herself. HER break in. Who else was here? How dare they ruin her event. Should she proceed with this mission or should she abort it? God, she hated that word, abort. So final. So unnecessary. She was no quitter anyway. She didn't have a free slot for days now with Christmas fast approaching. This was her only chance for exploration. She brushed the strange combination of fear and jealousy aside and slowly pushed the door further ajar, wide enough so she could step inside. She grappled with the new head torch which swung freely around her neck, keeping her thumb firmly over the power switch in case of needing light.

The lights were off but Tabitha could just about trace the surface outline of the kitchen worktops which were occasionally interrupted by piles of poorly stacked dishes and empty beer cans. She edged forward into the unknown, bumping gently into a thigh high waste bin overflowing with smelly refuse. More beer cans were stacked around the outside of it and more again wedged into several carrier bags, overflowing like alcoholic vomit onto the floor surrounding the bin. It reminded her of a documentary she had watched about hoarders. People collecting stacks and stacks of useless belongings, afraid to throw it all out and say goodbye to the past attached to it all, but in this case, he seemed to mainly be hoarding empty beer cans or perhaps he'd just missed recycling day.

Hygiene rating award zero stars though Tabitha to herself as she tried to wipe off some bin juice from her new coat with the back of her hand, almost retching at the feeling of the cold, vile liquid penetrating through her gloves. From what she could make out, the place appeared barren; certainly free of excess other than trash. No festive decorations, no trinkets, no wall mounted family photos, just the basic necessities for maintaining a human life – a fairly bleak one at that. Some wall paper was peeling badly above the hob and in the corner of the kitchen she noticed polystyrene tiles, partially ripped off making a disgusting, outdated, dangerous feature appear even more atrocious.

From the next room, most possibly the hallway presuming the house followed the same basic layout as its neighbour's, came a short, scuffling sound, like a very heavy mouse punctuated with a short sharp squeal. A wince of pain perhaps? Tabitha froze, every ounce of blood in her five foot six, velvet-wrapped frame dropped instantly to her heels. She drew in a fast breath and paused, dead still. What the actual fuck was that. Someone is here. Or it could be an animal. Whatever it was, it sounded injured. Tabitha's maternal instincts would normally overpower any other feelings; she was always the first one to offer a crying child a tissue and an optional hug at school, but in this case she just froze. What if she got caught - what the heck would she say? She could pretend she was out distributing leaflets for her husband's door company. But she didn't have any bloody leaflets on her. She could pretend she'd heard the noise from outside and had come in to see if anyone needed help.

But why on earth would she have crept up the back path in silence laden with small tools dressed like the Milk Tray Man? Shit.

What had she been playing at? The vacuity and irresponsibility of her behaviour suddenly dawned on her. There would be severe consequences if she got caught stumbling around in strangers' houses. She would lose her job, maybe even end up in prison. Who would care for her son? Thoughts were streaming through her mind now and snowballing like an avalanche of negativity dashed with sharp, spiky rocks of fear.

She turned ready to zoom out of the back door as fast as she could. Left foot in front of right, left in front of right. The motion of her feet was about all she could focus on, each felt like a dead weight, laden with the guilt of what she was doing and what she had already done. The smell of stale beer and ashtrays seemed to be infiltrating her pores as sweat started to pore out of them. Her heart pounded faster and faster as her eyes jumped from the filthy worktops to the source of the noise and back again.

Then it creaked.

The door between the kitchen and the hallway opened wide. As wide as the pit of pure panic and despair Tabitha had just dropped into.

It spoke.

'You. You. YOU. I SEE YOU don't you dare go,' hissed the loudest whisper she had ever heard, ripping through the blackness of the night from the bottom of the stair case.

It was a lady's voice, rough and warbled. A rasped sound, female yet elderly; vignetted around the edges due to the passing of time and possibly a lot of nicotine.

'I'm hurt, don't leave me. I can't move.' The tone sounded begrudged yet desperate.

This was it. Fight or flight. She had taught this so many times to her Biology classes, now it was her first hand experience.

Logically, Tabs should have bolted, but something was stopping her from leaving and it wasn't just the stickiness of the beer-encrusted lino floor. This woman was hurt. This woman had seen her. She had already been caught red handed. This woman was in pain and she was asking for help. Surely she wouldn't grass her up to the police if she stopped and helped her? If she behaved like the 'Good Samaritan' that didn't just walk on by, she wouldn't get into trouble, would she? She would help her as best she could, maybe call for an ambulance anonymously and then leave. It had worked when she had discovered the boys taking their strange drug in the lane. She'd called anonymously and helped them without getting involved, they were safe. No more deaths from Bleach had been reported in the news following the situation – she had gotten away with it. She could scarper now, make a quick 999 phone call and then go home and shower for an hour or so to cleanse her mind and body of the guilt and general filth of Don's house. Then she would dive underneath her duvet, hide under the bed covers and curl up tightly with Oscar until the events of the treacherous evening disappeared.

Tabs turned her head around like a barn owl, her body still not entirely convinced this was the best idea, still facing the exit.

'Who are you? W-w-w-what's wrong?' She stuttered.

'Who am I?! Who in the world am I? Ah that's the great puzzle.' Came the flippant reply.

Tabitha decided to switch on her head torch at this point and aimed it directly towards the slumped pile of old lady on the floor. A sharp beam of white light struck the recumbent woman in the face like a wet slap.

A wrinkled, cross and tired visage that was lit up like the moon glared back at Tabitha as she pulled up her free arm to try and block out the torch light instinctively. She was lying on her left side, feet still touching the bottom of the staircase. She was huddled around a large holdall onto which she clenched even more tightly as the light shone towards her, like a cobra addressing its newly claimed pray but with more an expression of sheer panic on her face than hunger. She screwed up her face, tightly closing both eyes to protect them from the light then withdrew her hand from probing around in the air like a dalek's proboscis and used it to reach for something. She rapidly shuffled something heavy, long and clunky back into the bag in a furious spate of movement, grimacing with pain at every move. She yanked the zipper closed and then, still grasping around the sack with her full body length, again steadied herself with her hands.

Now looking at Tabitha directly who had since kindly redirected her beam of light to the floor in between the pair of them, she opened her mouth to speak. Tabitha was unsure what she'd just hidden, but seeing as she was trespassing she had no moral high ground on which to start asking inquisitive questions to this potential burglar. The tone of the lady's voice switched from flippant to angry, almost bellicose in nanoseconds.

'You stupid girl just help me up can't you see I'm hurt?' The lady pointed to her left leg which Tabitha could see was clad in skin tight, dark leather. Not quite the attire she'd expected such a voice to be wearing. Tabitha edged cautiously closer to the woman and inspected the area with her head torch.

'W-w-what do you want me to do?' Tabitha quaked in her plimsolls, no time for pleasantries. There was no blood visible, but as Tabitha gently touched the lady's ankle, attempting to somehow roll up the cuff of her leather trousers, the lady recoiled in pain and a row of expletives rougher and faster than anything she'd heard from some of her most foul mouthed of students poured out, tarnishing the air. Tabitha drew her hand back instantly, fearing more for her own safety than for inflicting any more accidental pain.

'I've buggered my ankle. Came down the stairs whilst doing some cleaning for the old man. You'll need to get me to my friend's house immediately. I can't stay here. I don't do hospitals or doctors. I've got a phobia. A bad one.'

Cleaning? In the dark? At this time of night? She must have been way past retirement age – and who cleans in leathers? Every part of what she'd heard rang alarm bells but Tabitha just wanted to help this lady quickly and get the hell out of old Donald's cesspit. There was no doubt in her mind that whatever reason this lady was here for, it was just as, if not more questionable than her own.

Tabitha shone her head torch accidentally around the hall way and stair case in a state of mild panic, somehow looking outwards to her otherwise desolate physical surroundings for advice on how to help and on what to do. She saw a dripping, vermillion stream of fresh blood trickling down from the top of the stair case. Tabs padded on the floor around the legs and head of the old lady frantically trying to work out where the blood was coming from. 'There's no blood around you. Where's it coming from?' Tabs asked.

'I'm not bleeding. There's no blood, it's just a nasty sprain' she barked. The only blood is going to be yours unless you help me out of here schadenfreude.'

'Erm... sure... um.... are you sure I can't call an ambulance? I've really got to be on my way now.'

'No. Absolutely not.' The elderly lady's face was bright red with rage and infuriation now.

'Sure. OK I understand,' she replied, glancing back to the top of the stairs and then straight back down to the bundle of wrinkled peach and black skin, human and cow, simultaneously trying to hold back some tears of distress that had started to collect in her eye ducts. Not understanding at all but too scared to probe further, Tabitha decided to do as she was told. She didn't need this lady having a heart attack on her on top of her other injuries.

She strapped her head torch tight to her forehead to give herself both arms free to help and in doing so, the beam shone down on the old woman's holdall which she was grasping the handle of so tightly with her right hand. She made out three letters which were demarcated on the outside of the bag, possibly scribed in pink nail varnish.

V....A....L.

Val.

The bag was labelled Val.

It was an old bag. A pair of old bags thought Tabitha to herself, which amused her enough to temporarily remove her mind from the dire situation she had gotten into. Her grandmother used to do the same with all of her clothing and bags either with nail polish or with rather messy embroidery. Occasionally she'd tie a piece of yellow or pink ribbon around something to claim it as her own.

'Val,' Tabitha murmured to herself, seeing how the word sat in the air.

The lady looked up at her face, realising she had been caught out in responding to her own name. 'Hmm? How do you... ah. Balderdash. Yes. Val, I'm Val.'

'Hi Val, I'm Tabitha,' replied Tabitha. Whether this was too honest or too foolish, Tabitha was beyond caring. They appeared to be two women both in a situation that neither of them wanted to be in and hopefully in a matter of minutes, they would never have to see or hear from each other again.

Finding it strange yet choosing to ignore the fact that the old lady had not asked her what she was doing at Don's house either, Tabitha bent down and with all her body strength helped the old lady up. She was surprisingly light and can't have been more than five foot one or two in height and perhaps six stone at best. The leathers had made her appear to be larger than she truly was.

'Darn my blasted decaying body. How dare it let me down like this,' the old lady cussed and muttered as she arranged her left arm around Tabitha's neck, almost digging into the skin with her spindly, sharp fingers. 'Get me out of here.'

The lady stood and realised straight away that she wasn't going to be able to walk anywhere on her own. Her injured leg could take no weight whatsoever. She was still clasping onto her holdall tightly with one hand and around Tabitha's neck with the other.

She appeared panicked yet Tabitha could see from tiny movement in her eyes as she stared at the floor and looked out towards the back door that the lady was thinking intensely, calculating some master plan.

'How did you get here? Did you drive?'

'I... um... er... yes I did,' replied Tabitha who'd always been a terrible liar.

'Get me in your car. Now. I need to go to... to go... to... to go to my... my friend's house. You'll take me there now,' the lady said.

'Yes. Yes sure,' replied Tabitha. Tabitha was just keen to get out of the house and away from the imminent danger of being discovered by Don returning home from the pub.

Tabitha ran to the back door and closed it gently. She pulled it firmly into place and tried to hide any immediate evidence that the door had been broken open by sweeping the fragments of splintered wood from the floor into a dark corner.

'My car's closer to the front door, which appears to be a Yale lock. It's not double locked I see. We can go out the front and get to it much quicker. I don't think I can help you walk all the way around if we go out the back.'

'Oh. Sure. Whatever, dear - let's just get out of here. Get me to my friends.'

Tabitha sat Val down on the second to bottom step of the stairs and carefully opened the front door, looking immediately outside for signs of anyone, Don in particular, returning home early. She stretched her body as far as she could whilst holding onto the door frame but couldn't see any further onto the street as she feared she would lose hold and lock herself out. It seemed quiet enough though; the occasional car drove past but she couldn't see that far due to the large bush growing either side of the short path from the front door. The two ladies struggled out onto the path and then left through the low gate, allowing the front door to gently close behind them. They hobbled onto the pavement and then they both froze - not just because it was near Baltic on this mid December evening but because there, outside of the student house next door to Don's stood three youths. On the curb stood a boy and two girls, late teens or early twenties, dressed in hiking boots and carrying 50 litre rucksacks stuffed to their upper limits with several weeks worth of clothing, books and equipment. Three students who were about to catch a taxi to the airport to get on a flight to Thailand for Christmas.

Tabitha drew a deep breath and held in a squeal as Val elbowed her in the ribs before muttering 'act normal you fool' in her ear as they limped past the trio. They managed to briefly exchange muted looks signalling season's greetings and Tabitha even managed to force a quick smile as once again adrenaline seemed to be the only thing keeping her legs moving forwards and preventing her body from collapsing into a pile of despair.

Casper, Sky and Emma all looked at each other surreptitiously once the pair of women had hobbled passed and started to giggle.

'Looks like old Don's been having sex parties again, dirty old trouser snake,' joked Casper. They all guffawed and continued to wait for the Uber to the trains station that they'd booked.

Tabitha and Val struggled onwards, their surroundings lit only by the light pollution of the city, their exhaled air forming transparent beads suspended in front of their cold faces, but eventually they reached the Corsa around the corner. Tabitha plopped Val into the passenger seat, where the lady screamed into the folded elbow corner of her leather jacket sleeve in agony as she dropped like a sack of potatoes into the chair. Val still refused to let go of her bag which sat on her lap, taking up almost as much space as the lady herself and cussed sporadically until Tabitha started the engine to pull away.

'Farrier's Lane, Farm Road. It's in Gloucester. Get me there swiftly so I can let my friend treat my leg,' she barked, obviously feeling more confident now she was out of the house.

Tabitha plugged the location into her Sat Nav and sighed slowly and quietly as the display provided her with step by step directions to get onto the M32 - the only motorway that seemed to have a calming effect on her. Perhaps Val would doze off like her son used to on this stretch of road giving Tabs some much needed headspace to process what on earth had just happened.

The first ten minutes of the journey was spent in silence although the silence, in Tabitha's mind anyway, at first felt louder than the loudest alarm could possibly sound but as they drove past the inflatable, lit snowman signalling the sale of Christmas trees and past junction three, they eventually left the M32 and headed onto the M4, Tabitha felt like she had subconsciously managed to re-collect maybe half of the marbles she'd just lost and watched roll away from her control over the last hour or so.

Tabitha began to relax slightly as distance fell between the women and Don's house and eventually she plucked up the courage to start a conversation.

'So, Val. Or should I call you Valerie?'

'Pah! Valerie indeed. My name is Valhalla. But... you can call me Val,' she replied, cutting in to whatever more pertinent question Tabitha was about to pose.

'Wow. Ok. Valhalla. Yes of course. Valhalla and the Valkyries. The slain Norse warriors chosen to fight again in Ragnorok. Something to do with powerful women. I remember learning about that at sch...'

'Yes yes. Yes, I'm a strong woman....and no. No I am not a lesbian. Although all men are pigs – trust me I should know.'

Tabitha nodded in agreement. A little confused as to how the conversation had moved towards justification of the elderly ladies' sexuality, but in agreement nonetheless. Her husband had once been her Ragnor Lothbrok, her Nordic Viking heartthrob, but times had changed, wedlock and birth had occurred. Although he wasn't a pig as such, definitely not one of those cute miniature house pigs anyway, that would possibly be an improvement, she found very little pleasure in what was left of her relationship with her husband and realised that she wasn't in any rush at all to return home that evening to watch him sat in front of the TV, drinking the same beer he drank every night, his dirty plates probably on the floor by his feet where they'd remain until she cleared them away in the morning. Her mind drifted to the empty void that was her home life after Oscar had gone to sleep- it was the same whether her partner was home or not. She would largely be ignored, listen to the radio, clear up the mess from the day that had drawn to an end and then spend several hours working at her dimly lit office desk under the stairs before retreating to bed. Her mind had drifted to an empty place again...

'Oh lady. I've been through some times.'

Tabs realised that Val was in fact still talking to her and it would probably be wise to pay attention to whatever this strange lady had to say.

'Not that it's any of your business,' snubbed Val, once she could see she'd got Tabitha's attention and lit up a cigarette.

'Oh please I'd rather you didn't smoke in here, I have a son and...'

Tabs turned around to point at the car seat fitted in the back of her trusty Corsa, to hint at the fact her son really doesn't want to be sat in stale smoke on his next journey to nursery but before she had a chance to justify her request, Val had started to cough, lobbing her barely touched, lit cigarette out of the window. This wasn't a normal cough, this was some kind of torrential Kundalini-cough that seemed to come from the visceral depths of her frail structure, that shook her whole body like foundations destabilised by a high scoring Rictor scale quake.

She drew out a mottled handkerchief, also embroidered with the letters VAL, from a pocket inside her leather jacket that seemed to keep giving like Mary Poppins' carpeted bag of dreams and tried to stifle her cough by submerging her grey face into it and facing away from Tabitha. As the attack eased, Val drew the old rag away from her mouth and nose and quickly stuffed it back into her coat pocket, hoping that Tabitha had not seen the crimson blood that she had brought up.

'Pah. Don't taste like they used to anyway, not since the Tory's got in and whacked the tax up.' Val winked and smiled at Tabitha and Tabitha smiled back in a moment of subliminal connection.

The slight emotional wave of warmth was however quickly controlled and dismissed by Val. She was a frosty woman, but Tabitha could see that beneath her exterior, just like herself was a lonely soul craving for interaction with someone who would listen. Listen and not judge.

'Let's put the radio on shall we?' Val suggested as she dabbled with the on/off volume control of the inbuilt Vauxhall stereo and eventually stumbled onto a classical channel.

They left the motorway and drove from major to minor roads. The minor roads became more twisted and poorly lit and Tabitha had to revert to full beam lights for the last ten minutes or so of the journey. Tabitha had begun to feel a little sleepy so she wound down her window. It was black outside and the still, clear air of the wintery Gloucestershire countryside was helping to keep her focused on the challenging roads. She could see Val was uncomfortable and had lent forward slightly, possibly due to a mixture of pain and anxiety, and was tapping her spindly fingers on the top of the glove box. Nearly an hour had passed and the conversation had been stilted. Val clearly needed to say something but wasn't sure how to start a conversation. Tabitha tried to break the ice as she could see Val was becoming frustrated.

'Gosh I'm tired. What a journey. Glad there wasn't a big tractor coming in the opposite direction. You couldn't fit an anorexic whippet in between me and that hedge.' She paused and glanced sideways, hoping for some kind of response. Nothing. She continued to chat in a feeble attempt to offer an olive branch to this strange lady sat next to her.

'Any chance I could come in for a coffee before the journey back? That is, if your friend doesn't mind?' Tabitha frowned and returned her eyes to the road ahead. In her head, she reflected on the selection of failed attempts at starting a conversation she had just made, wondering if she'd sounded like she was trying to make wise cracks or if what she'd said came across more like the gibberings of a buffoon.

After a short pause, she looked over at Val, opting for direct eye contact and a forced smile to try and hide her own confusion which probably made her look even more insane, she noticed Val appeared somewhat distressed and Tabitha presumed straight away that she'd said the wrong thing

'Absolutely not. No. No. She doesn't have coffee. She won't have it. Tea either. Nothing of the sort. You'll have to stop at the services on your way home. You will.'

'Um sure ok,' Tabs responded. Strong and stubborn she is. Such a ball of fire she is - the voice of Yoda had crept into Tabitha's head. She really needed to get home and get to bed. Tiredness was tipping her over the edge of rational thought. Her Sat Nav instructed her that they were just three minutes from their destination. Thank goodness.

Val unexpectedly launched into a monologue, without making a nanosecond of eye contact with Tabitha, all the while staring into the dark out of the passenger window.

'You have a car, ergo I presume you have a garage.' Val said, not leaving time for a response. 'My motorbike is on the road outside of number 52 or 54. It is valuable. I do not trust it to be left outside this evening. It will get vandalised or taken. You will need to get it for me this evening when you return and keep it safe until I can collect it from you. What's your address? I will come as soon as I'm able to walk and get it back from you. Shouldn't be long, I think it's only a nasty sprain. My body has been through much worse and recovered.' She reached inside of her leather jacket pocket and pulled out a single key on a long ribbon and placed it into Tabitha's coin pot.

'But I'm so tired Val, can't it wait until the morning? Do you really have no one else that can help nearby?'

'No. You must do it. You weren't meant to be in that house this evening. You don't live there, You were creeping around in the dark so I think you should jolly well count your chickens and do as I say.'

This was starting to sound a lot like blackmail and Tabitha was becoming riled at the way this woman seemed to be able to flout and exert power over her. Yet in her heart, she knew she had no choice but to do as she was told. She didn't want to get into trouble with the law. She had her son to think of.

Tabitha replied, telling Val where she lived in her most disgruntled of voices. Cross with herself for revealing such private information but also feeling trapped between a wall and a hard place.

'But why were you there?' Tabitha finally broke. 'I don't believe you were cleaning there. The house looked filthy for a start so you can't have been doing a very good job and why were all the lights off?'

'You're correct, I wasn't cleaning. But it is categorically none of your business.' Replied Val laconically, still looking out of the passenger window. A long, silent minute passed. Tabitha could see Val was thinking again, her eyes darting from the bag she was still clutching tightly on her lap, to out of the window to Tabitha's face and back.

'You have a son you say? You have a lot more to lose than I if you were caught in a place you shouldn't be. Let's leave it at that shall we? Now drop me off here, return to Bristol and safely store my bike. I will be in touch in the next few days when I am more mobile. Then go home and be with your son.'

Tabitha was flabbergasted. But Val was right. She did have more to lose and certainly wasn't going to risk being exposed if she could avoid it.

She mulled over her limited options for the last two minutes of the journey until they eventually arrived at their destination. A security light switched on as Tabitha's car approached the drive way.

'Please don't go up the drive, you'll get stuck in the mud. You'll have to help me walk the last few metres,' Val instructed. Tabs sighed and looking up at the stone brick farmhouse with its lead framed windows and a rickety roof. It was quite a quaint looking building, she imagined it would look quite idyllic on a summer's day with a few geraniums blooming from the window boxes and wild flowers scattered about the front lawn. It was about 10pm and if anyone was home it looked like they had gone to bed as all the lights were off.

Tabitha looked up at Val with acrimonious contention and then folded her arms. She raised one finger in the air as if she were about to tell off a year seven for throwing wet tissue at a window but Val stopped her in her tracks and merely muttered, 'your son, Miss. Tabitha. Your son is at home waiting for you. I strongly suggest you think wisely.'

Tabitha sighed loudly, turned off the engine and got out of the car. She opened Val's door and tried to take the large holdall from her grasp in an attempt to carry it separately to the front door. Her reasoning being it may reduce the coming struggle of guiding Val up the path. Val outright refused to release it, gripping on with a pained expression, so Tabitha rather roughly hoisted the elderly madam up and out of her seat and awkwardly shuffled her to the front porch like a drunken three legged race, feet swathed in thick, fresh country mud by the time they arrived at the door.

'You may go now,' Val curtly instructed as they arrived at the single slate step at the foot of the porch, where she now steadied herself independently and placed the bag on the floor. Her body weight was entirely balanced on her good ankle.

'Will you be OK? Is your friend home?'

'It is none of your business. I'll be fine. Now off you go. Do not forget to make my motorbike safe. I'll be over in under a week. I've survived much worse.'

Val knocked three times abruptly on the front door and stared straight ahead, deliberately avoiding further eye contact in an effort to shut down any further exchanges.

Tabitha took this is her queue to leave. She had another long drive ahead of her and really wanted just to be snuggled up next to the steady rise and fall of breath from her sweet Oscar.

Being the prepared ex- Brownie guide that she was, Tabitha opened her car boot and pulled out an empty shopping bag which contained a clean pair of shoes that she kept in the car for such situations, well for slightly less odd situation, and lent on the back of her car to change. She watched Val from afar. Val had turned to see if she was still there and then knocked again at the front door, waiting impatiently.

Tabitha closed the boot of her Corsa quietly and sat in the driving seat. She paused and considered very briefly whether leaving this elderly and injured woman alone outside in the middle of the cold night was the right thing to do, feeling a slight bubble of guilt in her belly and then she looked at the time on her phone. It was getting really late. She had to go home or Jack would ask questions. Possibly - if he'd even noticed that she'd not returned from Women's Institute yet.

'Well. Umm. Merry Christmas?' Tabitha offered out of her wound down window. The well-wish came out as more of a question than a greeting as she turned the key in her ignition. She got no reply, which she half expected and a deafening silence hung in the air like a garrotted corpse swinging from a tree. What an indignant, stubborn old woman. Tabitha disliked her strongly but also felt a strange connection. They say the characteristics you often dislike about others are actually the parts of yourself which you have yet grown to recognise, accept and love.

As she pulled away slowly, she continued down the drive until it joined to a slightly wider, slightly less muddy country path and flicked on her indicator switch. Prime example of a conditioned response – there wasn't a single soul other than her, Val and Val's friend for miles yet she still felt the need to let her presence be known to other road users. The conditioned brain does strange things.

Val looked back and saw Tabitha pulling off so she withdrew another small set of keys from inside the biker jacket pocket. She turned the lock and pushed the front door open. Ah, she was glad to be home.

Mirror. Signal. Manoeuvre. Just prior to flicking up her indicator switch, Tabitha had also taken an automatic glance in her rear view mirror to see Val withdrawing her front door key and opening her own front door.

'It's her house,' Tabitha sounded out to no one, gasping and confused as she pulled away. What a strange, lonely lady Val was. Tabitha could feel tears once again rising, this time unsure whether they were tears of sorrow or relief. She let them flow. Sometimes it was important to express your emotions, even if you aren't really sure what they are or where they have come from. If your body is telling you that you need to release tears, then so be it. Jack didn't understand this. Tabitha had often come out to her car to cry after they had rowed or if she had had a particularly hard day at work or with Oscar. If she cried in her car alone, if Jack hadn't seen her and told her to turn off the waterworks, then it hadn't really happened and she had not faltered or weakened. She shed a final tear, the release of the emotion now complete, and she found a smile as she realised that she would be home soon with her son and she could relax - until she looked down at the motorbike key in her coin pot and started to think instead about the logistics of how she was going to lug a two tonne heap of metal down the road at midnight in order to store it discretely in her garage.

CHAPTER FOURTEEN -- THAILAND SEEMS FAMILIAR

To say it was hot was an understatement. It felt like each of their beads of sweat had beads of sweat and the smell of old perspiration was deeply ingrained within the crazily patterned minibus upholstery. The squashed travellers swayed from side to side as they ventured up and up the winding, narrow tracks that passed as roads as they moved further and further away from the hustle and bustle, flashing neon lights, ping-pong bars and dual carriageway concrete lines of Chiang Mai centre.

The bus took a sharp turning off from the track and then slowed as the tour guide stood up in the centre aisle firing out directions in several different languages instructing the visitors to keep themselves belted up until the vehicle came to a complete standstill. Casper, Sky and Emma undid their belts as instructed and stretched out their backs and legs, as they rose from their seats to collect their bags. They each tipped the driver a few baht as they clambered out of the bus. It was still hotter than a British summer as they exited the vehicle but at least there was some air flow outside as an occasional waft of breeze hit their pink cheeks. They were chatting loudly to each other but their conversation came to an abrupt stop as all three of them stood side by side.

'Are you thinking what I'm thinking, girls?' Casper said slowly and quietly at the foot of the tourist bus as each of them stepped off into the dusty clearing.

They'd taken a trip to the very north of Thailand as part of their holiday to a beautiful village called Pai where they were going to learn how to cook fragrant Thai food and experience gong baths deep in the jungle. The journey to Pai had consisted mainly of the three of them ribbing each other, sharing music on their phones and practicing (with minimal success) Thai phrases from their guide book on locals. It had been a seven hour monotonous trip, broken up only with toilet and cold drink breaks and the opportunity to buy locally crafted jewellery made from recycled fishing nets and ring pulls. For the first time in their travels, the three of them stood in pure silence after Casper uttered this question. They were all thinking the same thing.

The tour guide and the other tourists all marched on ahead yet the three of them remained in the same place, gobsmacked. Eventually, Emma cautiously took several steps forward to look further afield. They were surrounded by beautiful forest which started just metres away from the car park clearing. Tropical birds were within clear earshot and if one cranked one's neck skyward, a few could even be seen with their beautiful primary and jewel coloured plumages in the branches above.

Emma closed her eyes to allow her other senses to confirm what she'd been thinking and turned around slowly, breathing in the surrounding tranquillity, her heart thumping as she got the confirmation she sought. It was the same place. The same exquisite place they'd visited in their trip at the solstice party together.

None of them had been here before and despite their unconventional attitudes and approach to life, they still remained doubtful to the point of being cynical over such strange concepts as magical synchronicity. Casper would always be the first to mock somebody for trying to realign his chakra or offering to amend his soul with reiki at a free party, joking that the hardest part about using healing crystals is dying when they don't fucking work. Yet here they all were, in a place they'd thought they'd jointly imagined, synergistically created whilst high at a party only a few days ago.

'We... we... we've all been here, right? But we haven't? Have we?' Emma said, mind-blown yet trying to make sense of it all.

'It's exactly the same. Smells the same, looks the same... It even sounds the same. Up there. Up over there if you follow that path there's a brook. Look – it's exactly the same.'

They both followed Emma, as she stomped over to a gently babbling stream which became divided by three large rocks and trickled past, surrounded by luscious flowers and greenery. The colours were so bright they spoke to their senses directly, luring them in closer. The wondrous nature of the Thai jungle, out-glorified only by the amazing possibility that they had seen it all before in some joint, mystical vision. The soporific yet strangely energising noise of the moving water interspersed sporadically by tweets, honks and burrs from the exotic wildlife echoed the visual experience they had all felt whilst eyes a-washed with bleach.

Sky, usually the loudest of the bunch sat down on a protruding rock and eventually spoke. She seemed shaken and was clearly overwhelmed with exhilarating feelings of joy.

'We were talking about Thailand before we took the drugs weren't we? It's taken us to where what we were thinking about, what we were discussing before we did it. We came here in our minds and now we're here in our bodies. And it's beautiful. It's so striking here. I don't know how this has happened. We must have seen it in a brochure or on television before we came? I just don't get it. I'm... I'm not making sense am I? We need to follow the tour guide. Let's ask some questions.'

'I hear you. I feel the same. It's incredible. I want to sketch it – it's beyond beauty. It couldn't just be a coincidence could it? I want to capture it on paper. Do you guys mind if I chill here for a bit?' Casper stuffed his camera back into its case and dropped down onto the rocky outcrop besides Sky yanking his pad from his rucksack before using it as a cushion. Sky and Emma nodded in agreement and he watched them walk towards the rest of the tourist group, as he unzipped his tatty leopard print pencil case. Emma and Sky walked in silence, holding hands, tuning in subconsciously and walking rhythmically to the entomological beat of the forest like a charming white noise radio station, beads of sweat forming and dropping from their brows. Sky fastened a red and white polka dot neckerchief around her hairline to capture her perspiration. They stared at each other and smiled, as the elation outweighed the fear of this strange situation. It was a situation that to most people would seem unfathomable, unspeakable, nonsensical even, but to these three who had taken a variety of hallucinogens in their short lives it seemed to make sense. It was like their experience at the solstice party had now come full circle, they felt blown away, but complete. It was definitely the most intense situation they had experienced to date though, and one which they would talk about for years most likely. Their smiles stretched from ear to ear as their hearts raced in the heat.

The pair tried to explain their strange situation to the tour guide using some form of bizarre, spontaneous sign language and using broken, poorly pronounced phrases from their Thai guide books that probably spilt out offence more than helping to get them any answers. The group chatted and paused, in a constant cycle of astonishment and disbelief for hours that day as they ambled around the Asian forest which they'd all somehow visited before on their psychonautic adventure. The conversation veered from a tangible feeling of hormonally-steered teenage excitement to cynicism at their own analysis and conjecture of the trip.

Something strange had happened and they were all excited to see if it could happen again when they returned home. They'd already planned their next session with the bleach and as the day trip to the jungle drew to a close, they were excitedly discussing what they were going to try and create with their words and their minds next time. They'd have to get Soma involved too this time.

As the burning sun sank beyond a horizon inundated with rich greenery, the weary, sun-kissed travellers boarded their bus. As they sat in their seats for the journey back to the local town, they all kicked off their hiking boots and looked out of the window. They'd given up trying to probe for help, unable to make sense of what was happening to them or to see if anyone else there had ever experienced anything like it. The familiar scene disappeared as the bus departed and the last of the sun's light faded behind them. Had they somehow predicted their future surroundings by using the drug?

Perhaps they'd somehow been so high they had teleported their own spirits? Perhaps they'd messed with the linear nature of time? Perhaps they'd just seen it all before in a brochure? This felt unlikely considering they had no recollection of researching the area on the net or in travel pamphlets. The only explanation seemed to be that taking the drug had somehow allowed them to visit the place they'd been thinking about just prior to dropping the bleach into their pupils. How or why this had happened, they hadn't a clue, but it had been beautiful and bonded the trio more closely than ever imaginable. It had been an experience they would share with all of their friends and their grandchildren one day possibly.

At least they hadn't bumped into the Dalai Lamar whilst hopping around on the astral plains of their dreamscape world thus avoiding a good old telling off from the wise monk.

CHAPTER FIFTEEN -- HAVE YOU HEARD THE NEWS?

Yule tide gooch. The strange perineal period between Christmas and New Year had passed slowly for Tabitha, the highlight being watching her boy's face as he opened his gifts and licking the brandy butter spoon on Christmas day. The lowlights had included a crap selection of Christmas movies on the television and having to feign interest in a long conversation with her husband and in-laws about the qualities of sliding versus bi-fold glass doors and the surging rise in popularity of the folding patio door otherwise known as the 'infinity window wall'. It wasn't all wasted time though, as she had however learnt about the largest ever door in the world. Apparently the Vehicle Assembly Building in Cape Kennedy has doors around four hundred and fifty-six foot tall which allows them to accommodate thirty-eight story high space rockets and each door takes a full forty-five minutes to open or close – which could provide useful if it ever came up on The Chase or Pointless or Opportunity Knocks.

The last Christmas cake crumb had been hoovered up, the in-laws had finally gone home and Tabitha had finished taking down the decorations. It was New Year's Day and therefore festivities were officially over in her home, none of this stretching it out until mid January nonsense. She'd done a great job of finishing off the last of the chocolate-based Christmas comestibles last night whilst struggling to stay awake until ten o'clock (let alone midnight) to see in the New Year. She was feeling lackadaisical, aware of a gentle hangover braying in the background although she wasn't sure if it was the half bottle of red or the sugar overload that was causing the headache. Biscuits were only to be of the non-chocolate variety from this point onward – a resolution she could stick to as technically, custard creams were still a permissible snack.

Jack was upstairs hiding from his parental duties (or 'working on his laptop') and Oscar was seeing how many plastic dinosaurs he could fit inside of his nappy. Poor old stegosaurus had gone in the back. Tabitha watched from the comfort of her sofa, slightly bemused at her son's actions and too snug to help remove the *terrible lizard*. Back to normal life at last. Christmas was lovely but the build up and preparation always felt like a bit of a marathon and she was always glad when it was over.

She extended her right arm, button-stick in hand and aimed the infrared beam at the television. The news popped on and out of the unnecessarily massive thirty two inch screen into her front room.

Still trying to maintain some kind of holiday tranquillity, Tabitha would normally have turned it straight over to a quiz show or nature program. The cadence of the reporter's voice could have been offering up good or bad news, he used the same expression and inflection for either, but something caught Tabitha's eye about the female portrait photo being displayed on the screen in HD technicolour. Her bubble of Christmas isolation had popped. She re-awoke from the slumberous fug of Christmas indulgence.

'*Soma Bond, 20, of Wigston, Leicestershire, yesterday evening sadly died in the Leicester Royal Infirmary at 11.27pm despite the best efforts of all staff involved. Her death is currently being treated as drug related, however, investigations have being launched by the coroner and forensic pathology department into the exact cause of death. A post mortem investigation will hopefully yield further details.*

Her parents were by her side as she passed, after tragically suffering excruciating symptoms for several hours. Soma, a student at Bristol University studying Theatre, was at a house party in her home town celebrating the end of the year with other revellers. It is a tragic loss to all who knew her. It's believed she had been experimenting with new street drug 'Bleach', also referred to as 'Diamond White' or 'Dropout' by users. It is believed to be a novel synthetic chemical, source currently unknown, that has caused twelve deaths around the south of the United Kingdom, a further three in Wales and one in Scotland. As yet no reports of supply or usage outside of the UK have been documented.

The characteristic white-eyed appearance of bleach users has been recounted by security staff in nightclubs and public houses all over England over the Christmas Period. It is believed that many drugs were available at the house party and the police are currently taking statements to try and source the supplier.

Her parents are asking to be left alone to mourn in private, but questions will undoubtedly be coming their way as Police investigate this new street drug death. The consultant who Soma was under as she was brought into A&E early on New Year's Eve was unavailable for comment but onlookers and medical staff have reported seeing a young girl brought in on a stretcher appearing to display symptoms similar to extreme intoxication and needing to be restrained by medical staff due to extreme muscle spasms.

'Her body was white as anything. Her eyelids were peeled right back, like massive ping pong balls. Her back was arched. She looked like something out of the Exorcist,' one onlooker informed us.

The cause is currently presumed to be overdose from or allergic reaction to a chemical although the police are awaiting toxicology reports for confirmation. Police wish to issue a warning to people, especially at this time of year of celebration to be aware of this drug and to report any sightings of it to the police immediately.

The Home Secretary is placing this new psychoactive under new temporary classification as a Class A drug for the next twelve months whilst research is done by the advisory council for the misuse of drugs into sourcing its point of manufacture and supply network.

The rapid increase in popularity and illegal administration of legal highs in the UK in recent years led to the passing of the Psychoactive Substances Act in 2016, which specifies that anyone who is found guilty of supplying or producing as yet unclassified psychoactive substances will receive an unlimited fine and additionally up to seven years in prison.'

Tabitha recognised the girl straight away from a photo she'd seen at the student house she'd visited weeks ago when she disabled their sound system. She had such beautiful green eyes. Tabitha remembered thinking how stunning she was with her rare features; a head of leonine, russet curls and a smattering of freckles. They'd used the same photo in the news. How terribly tragic. Ruby and Soma. When will young people stop experimenting with drugs she thought to herself, pulling the dinosaurs out of her son's rather saturated nappy before sloping off into the kitchen to take her Sertaline.

'Jack... Jack... ' she called from the bottom of the stairs, plonking her empty tumbler on the radiator cover whilst fumbling for her trainers.

'I'm going for a run. New Year's resolution. Can you come and play with your son? He's got into a predicament with a pterodactyl and could use some help.'

Tabitha had decided that she was actually going to use her trainers as the God of New Balance had intended. She was going to try running again. It was a clear enough day and the excess mince pies and chocolates that she'd caringly tidied away last night were queuing up around her waist like a rubber swim ring. As she heard her husband reluctantly slam shut his laptop lid and holler back 'fine' with the grudged disinclination of a teenager, she pulled the front door behind her, locking it for safety. She didn't think her son would be adventurous enough to leave the house but she also wasn't one hundred per cent confident in her partner's ability to notice if he did. She pushed her front door key along and around the silver circle of her key ring until it was safely attached next to the garage key which she'd taken from the key hook in the kitchen and held onto tightly as an attempt to keep her husband from going out there. Neither of them really went out there anyway in the winter.

The garage was more of a storage space for the clutter they didn't want in the house but weren't quite ready to dispose of yet. Fifty percent old clothes, shoes, toys and 'craft projects' (to the untrained eye, merely taped-together toilet rolls) Oscar had brought back from nursery, thirty percent tools that in all honesty neither of them knew how to use confidently, a lawnmower, a bicycle that Jack had bought to get to work on several years ago in a fleeting moment of environmental concern that passed faster than a fart in a wind tunnel and lastly, a motorbike, an eff-off massive, motorised bike.

She had so far been successful, but seeing the key in her hand triggered the butterflies of anxiety in her stomach to somersault and flap as it reminded her vividly once more of the night she found Val.

Launching into some kind of half-baked leg stretch she had seen carried out with much more finesse in the movies by people who could presumably touch their toes without dislodging a vertebral disc, she embarked on a gentle walk with the intention of building up to a gentle jog. Her sneakered-feet led her down the road and cut through to the road behind, stretching her arms up and out to the heavens, feeling some of the pent up, festive stress flow out freely into the chilly air around her. She was going to walk and think. Think and walk. A think... And a... Walk her mind said with each plod she took.

She had Val's address.

Val had hers.

Should she wait for Val to contact her?

Was Val okay?

Elderly people can go downhill very quickly with leg injuries. She had read a while ago in something a student had written about mortality rates that one in five people over the age of sixty-five who break a hip die within the year due to complications. Imagine that. Working your whole life in a job that you probably find innocuous at best to then have a few sherries, take a tumble and conk it before ever getting the chance to blow your grandchildren's prospective inheritance in Las Vegas slot machines.

She would contact Val. Later that afternoon. if she could get away for a couple of hours she could drive out there and maybe offer the cantankerous biddy a lift back to her garage if she was able to ride, if not, she could take some fruit over and offer to help out with any chores. Maybe they could watch some television together, or get a takeaway.

Tabitha paused, taking in a deep breath as she was aware her thoughts and her feet had wondered off the beaten track. She wasn't even sure where she was going and the voice of reason in her head was now suggesting she should plan a mate-date with someone with whom she had nothing in common and met in suspiciously muddy circumstances. It was probably not one of her best ideas.

Head held high, she took in her surroundings. Tabitha scanned the grey, heavily housed road and the similar yet geographically higher road behind it and noticed that a tumultuous knot of people were congregated near the trio of homes she had recently visited on her evening missions. A huge cluster of people were milling around the back garden of the student property.

Her heart started to pound like a startled doe. What on earth were they all doing there? A pair of policemen and a suited professional were walking away from the thong down a side lane towards a parked up police car. The cluster of five or six people bumbling around the back garden of the student house appeared to be holding cameras and Tabitha also spotted the black snout of a sound boom being waved around like an excitable Russian wolfhound fresh on the scent.

Once again Tabitha's stomach felt a writhing intensity as her intestines twisted and squeezed, her feet unsure whether to return her home as fast as possible to mull over what she'd seen or whether she should inconspicuously continue her afternoon exercise and pry further.

She remained indecisively frozen, paused in a position not unfamiliar to a surfer, one foot pointed forwards towards the animated assemblage and the other foot pointed back towards from whence she had come. The startling flash of a silent siren pulled past her and whizzed towards the gathering which snapped her out of her hesitatory stance. A blue, fluorescent yellow and white Mercedes Sprinter van emblazoned with 'Forensic Investigation Squad' on the side panel pulled up behind the parked police car and out stepped two further uniformed officers, and from the back of the van, two more in white boiler suits carrying with them a role of blue and white Police tape and a fistful of metal sticks. The latter pair headed towards old Don's back door and began to hammer in the metal crook posts to which they then began to fasten a long stretch of crime scene tape.

In Don's back yard, Tabitha noticed a petite, pony-tailed lady with an expensive looking camera strung around her neck. Her heavy head hung in her hands. She was crying and an awkward looking policeman with a notepad was sat next to her trying to offer comfort without losing his soaked-to-the-bone constabulary arrogance. The crime scene tape now encapsulated the two investigating officers in their white, disposable suits, the seated, awkward policeman and the distressed journalist.

The cluster of standing press photographers was now migrating away from the student property and moving en masse towards the newly established crime scene two doors down like an inebriated V-formation of migratory birds, with the member at the back of the pack constantly flapping and striving to move towards the front. The occasional flash light firing off could be seen, as a silent bullet to the competing news-rag's face. The three students Tabitha had seen on that hellish evening she had found Val on closed their own front door behind them and followed the bustle with slightly terrified expressions on their faces towards Don's back yard.

Curiouser and curiouser Tabitha thought; the eruption of moths in her belly drawing her oddly, against all reasoning, towards the flashing bulbs of the press. Breaking into a gentle jog, she climbed the steps a stone's throw from the crowd and tried to maintain some pace, breaking into a canter. She figured posing as a New Year's Day runner would appear as significantly less suspicious than a walking, nosey neighbour loaded perhaps with undertones of guilt.

As she came to the top of what felt like a mountain but was probably only thirty or forty weathered steps, she saw a policeman outside of the newly secured crime space shooing the press away with his hands after firmly addressing them to leave the area. Investigations were underway. The press started to disseminate slowly, buzzing around like worker bees at the entrance of a hive, high on nectar, torn between obeying 'The Law' and getting their front page spread. Tabitha pushed forward with her run as she could feel the caboodle of cameras shimmying towards her.

Suddenly a six foot something rod of navy blue topped with a silver-badged custodian helmet stood before her.

'Excuse me madam. Would you mind if I asked you a few questions?'

Stalling somewhat and also unable to speak, Tabitha grimaced and nodded. She had pushed her body to its aerobic limits scaling the steps and her cheeks were crimson red as she folded at the waist, hands on thighs panting for what felt like considerably longer than normal for a non-smoking, middle-aged woman within the upper limit of her recommended BMI – just. She glanced at her Fitbit watch which she had received from Jack despite not asking for one. He said it was in the sale. She had accrued a total of twelve calories, not even half a coconut éclair. Her pained expression dropped to a frown as she hinged her upper body back up to vertical slowly, eventually regaining control of her breathing to respond.

'Um, certainly officer. I'm just a local neighbour. Just out for my regular jog. What's going on?'

A face to palm moment occurred as she realised she looked and sounded like the village idiot. Tabitha's eyes glanced rapidly between the two houses and the policeman's stern face. He couldn't have been older than thirty yet sported a thick, black moustache Tom Selleck would've been jealous of - yet bald as a polished peanut up top she noted as he lifted his hat to scratch his head. Why do men overcompensate with facial hair she pondered as she pushed her dangly front bits of fringe out of her eyes and felt across her upper lip with her index finger to see if she needed to wax again. Suddenly conscious that it may have looked like she was sniffing her fingers or mocking his choice of facial decoration, she whipped her finger away sharply.

'Well madam, I'm afraid were not unable to say too much at this stage. If you've seen the news this morning, you'll have heard that a young student who resided at the house over there sadly passed away last night. We were visiting to interview her housemates as we start our investigations to try and piece together the events leading up to her death. At the moment it's presumed that it was a drug overdose of sorts. They were very upset. Last thing they needed was the press knocking on their door. Just got back from Asia and understandably jet lagged. Once the cause of death is established officially we may pull them into the station for further questioning, possibly return with a warrant. Too early to say at the moment.' The officer pointed to the house in which Tabitha had spent over an hour just a few weeks ago. Tabitha's thoughts drifted to the smell of patchouli and the sight of the array of drugs she'd discovered there.

'One of the hacks went door-knocking and discovered that the entrance to next door-but-one had been left ajar, blood marks down the stair case. The first officer on scene has since located a body there. Suspicious circumstances. We don't think the two deaths are related. An elderly man. Looks initially like a bullet wound. Of course, we need his identity to be clarified by next of kin. Although to be honest, I think Path will be basing it on his dental records. Not a lot left to identify. Don't be alarmed Miss, Mizz, Mrs erm.'

'Mrs. Fox,' Tab replied, all colour having drained from her cheeks as the police officer sensed mild panic in her response.

'Mrs. Fox, don't be alarmed, our officers will get to the bottom of it. There will be police presence for the rest of the afternoon and we will send patrol cars out this evening. It's our duty of care. Did you know the owner Mrs. Fox? Or the any of the kids next door? Do you have any information you could give us to support our investigations?'

'Erm no... No... I mean, I might have recognised their faces, you know - down at the shops or whatnot but no, I've never spoken to either of them. Any of them... any of the kids that live in that house or the old man... Nothing in common really I suppose.'

Suddenly, the gravitas of the situation metaphorically thumped Tabitha in the guts. The reality of what may have actually happened on that dark night with Val dawned on her and the five minutes of exercise combined with the sudden shit sluice of guilt landed in the pit of her stomach all at once. She felt like she was spiralling down a tunnel, new beads of sweat were collating into rivers on her forehead, were her feet even touching the ground still?

Oh no.

Her heart jumped up to her throat then sunk rapidly to her heels. Sick, she was going to be sick.

'Sorry officer,' she gulped, 'I've got to go, left my hair straighteners on.' She realised she was stroking her upper lip again and gripping her sour belly with the other hand.

And off she ran, faster than she'd ever run before, fast enough to burn off a whole green triangle. She pegged it to the nearest hedge out of sight to throw up the equivalent of the rest of the box of Quality Street.

'If anything comes to mind...,' hollered the policeman as she shot off, 'don't hesitate to contact us at the station or on 101 Mrs. Fox...' He turned around and marched with a weighty swagger back towards the blue-grey cloud of law enforcement.

Tabitha ran all the way home, albeit mainly downhill. It was the furthest she'd covered at that speed since the egg and spoon race in year six. She fumbled for the garage key as she approached the rear entrance to her home. She couldn't let Jack and Oscar see her like this but she wanted to hide away from the world. Hide away from everything and pretend none of this was happening. Kids were dropping like flies from some scary drug. She didn't want her son growing up in a world where he might experiment at a party and die in such a horrendous way. And she was practically an accomplice in cold-blooded, first degree murder.

The key turned in the lock and she slid the large garage door up slowly and over her head as quietly and inconspicuously as she could before entering the garage and closing it again slowly behind her. There were no windows in the garage. She stood in near darkness, tracing the outline of all the bulky objects with her eyes, trying to focus on getting control over her breathing again.

The bike, the bloody motor bike - it was still there. Of course it was still there. It was covered by a large, green blanket used previously for summer den building in the garden. Back when everything was sweet and simple, now the green blanket lay draped over this metallic beast, cocooning key evidence.

It all made sense now. That bag. That dreadful, tatty, old bag had been enveloping some kind of gun. She'd shot him. Val had killed Don. Those bangs in the quiet of night as she'd been sat in her Corsa - she heard them again and again in her mind as she flopped down against the cold garage wall, curling inwards. The noise repeated like a scratched record that she couldn't turn off despite placing her sweaty hands forcefully over her ears and closing her eyes as tightly as she could bear.

Head in hands, too panicked and dehydrated to shed tears, full Lycra camel toe, too distracted to pluck it out. What on earth was she going to do?

CHAPTER SIXTEEN -- IN THE LAB

'Thirty-two people dead. Thirty-two people. How on earth has this happened? It's a bloody good job the majority of the British public are mouth-breathing buffoons otherwise they'd have made the same connection that we have by now. This has *got* to be chemical weaponry. There are too many similarities. Have the Russians beaten us to it? Is this a terrorist attack or an accident? It's just too similar to be a coincidence. A couple of crooks died from it in the Summer in Wormwood Scrubs – I'm not surprised a full post mortem wasn't carried out though so it's mainly speculation – waste of tax payers money I expect HMPS would've said. The Scrubs is the penal dustbin. No one turns a blind eye inside that shithole. Valueless life, that of a violent career criminal. One of the poor buggers was a homeless man apparently. Probably better off inside than he was out. 'Til he O.D.'d on the stuff that is.'

The Professor spoke with an air of unchallenged authority and with such furious passion that the blue veins in his forehead popped out against his un-sunned complexion. The corners of his mouth were encrusted with white remnants of saliva and spittle flew through the air with each stubborn sentence he bellowed.

There were four of them huddled in the well-concealed, subterranean government genetics lab, and all three of his audience were doing their best to avoid eye contact for fear of becoming the verbal target of his invective tirade.

Unbeknown to Jon, the lab technician who had been working for the research team in the recesses of the ministry of defence's scientific department somewhere on the plains of Wiltshire, there was a high staff turnover in this particular department. This was partly due to the Professor's insatiable temper and partly due to previous technicians resigning when asked to administer lethal concoctions to the caged mammals that were being used. Professor Birch, who was older and slightly more affable than Wilder had worked there for much longer than the others and Dr. Cook was also fairly new and didn't want to face Wilder's wrath or risk being his next victim so they both kept shtum. Jon could sense the temperature rising in the room and all three of them avoided his glare.

'Now it's kids though. Kids dying left, right and centre. With the same godammit white eyes. Bleached eyes. Like our trials. The same dead, white eyes.' He grabbed a newspaper and waved it in the air angrily. 'A '*torturous death*' the Mail is describing it as. '*Zero-Zero, Bleach, Dropout*' the Telegraph is calling it. Christ, the youngest was only seventeen – a school girl from Bristol –front page of one, two, three papers.' Professor Wilder sifted through the collection of the morning's press in front of him as he addressed his team.

'We've got samples coming in for evaluation later on today. I've asked the Chemical Processing lab on Level 3 to assess them and let us know what we might be dealing with, see if they can get a match on anything out there and try and sort this out. If it's coming from Russia or China, we've got big problems. We need to be two steps ahead of them, not cleaning up their fall out.'

'But isn't what we're doing wrong?' Not usually a man of conscience, Jon spoke for the first time whilst fiddling with his Ministry of Defence lanyard draped around his neck, shifting his body weight from left to right as he awaited a response. A tremendous wave of guilt had flooded over him when he'd heard about the first death in the news back in the summer, before the press had even linked the consequential six or seven deaths that had occurred over the heat wave to a new drug on the streets. A sudden rise in deaths over the Christmas period had meant HVN-1 had hit the headlines hard that morning.

Jon had been 'hand selected' by Professor Wilder from the local university after he'd failed his first year Biochemistry exams. Professor Wilder occasionally lectured there. He simply hadn't bothered to turn up to a couple of his end of year finals after partying a little too hard the night before. It wasn't the first time he'd failed in his education after being expelled from his sixth form for a foolishly botched burglary attempt. A delinquent yet annoyingly bright child, he'd also been arrested as a thirteen year old juvenile for shooting and injuring local cats with a ball bearing pellet gun. After being expelled from sixth form for trying to break into the science department, he'd eventually finished his A-levels, scraping a handful of C and B grades under the supervision of the youth offending team during a short spell in prison.

The professor shot Jon a glare that made him want to shrink into the porcelain-smooth, deep Belfast sink.

'Jon. Thank you for your concern,' the professor responded sarcastically, pushing his half moon spectacles back onto his aquiline nose. 'We don't have time to run through the works of Galton, Mendel, Dawkins and the complete history of ethics this morning, perhaps if you want to chat about this at greater length you should come and discuss it with me another time... WHEN WE DONT HAVE A NATIONAL EMERGENCY ON OUR HANDS.'

He slammed down the collection of newspapers onto the waist-high laboratory desk in front of him, sending a box of Gilson pipette tips flying across the highly polished floor which scattered like tens of tiny see-through cockroaches then he placed his head in his hands in total despair.

His cheeks rouged with embarrassment, Jon bent down and started to collect the dropped lab-ware, picking up each tip and placing it in his spacious Howie lab coat pocket. Jon was usually the one dolling the verbal abuse out amongst his peer group; he was unsure how to handle it when he was the recipient of it. An intelligent young man with illicit rogue ambition, he'd been in and out of trouble most of his twenty-one years, but for the first time in his life he'd been given a chance by Wilder to earn a ridiculous salary for simply measuring liquids, feeding and cleaning out the research rodents and the odd bit of washing up in the depths of the government research laboratory.

'If I m-m-m-ay, Jon, Ivy, Professor W- W- Wilder? M – M – M - Myself and Professor Wilder have been working on our n... n... neo-genics programme under the permission of HRH for over three decades now. I should have retired last year but I felt that we were so close to making a breakthrough with our HVN-1 trials that I stayed on, committed to see it through. We've managed to successfully biosynthesize a knockout gene-linked dissociative that the lab mice are keen to self administer which over time brings about a statistically significant proportion reduction in albinos versus pigmented. Only the mice lacking pigment, with the red eyes, are dying. Yet they're all still gulping it down, lapping it up,' the portly scientist declared with animation. 'The drug is only killing the animals with the gene we selected. Genetically specific euthanasia.'

Professor Birch lit up like a candelabra as he started to pour out his research details once again to a trapped audience. He continued.

'Prior to that, the D-D-Drosophila trials were also statistically supportive; we managed to take out the white-eyed fruit flies, every single one of them, leaving the vermilions unaffected by the same drug. A 'euthanogen.' A selective chemical with lethal power that is usurped by its magnificent hallucinogenic property. It could be... It will be the next big thing in the improvement of livestock. Young cattle and pigs carrying recessive and therefore hidden forms of certain useless, disadvantageous genes, characteristics that they may carry hidden and pass on to their offspring that could cost the farmer significant financial loss could be terminated without having to be screened for defects.

Eventually HVN-1 could be used as a tool in counter-terrorism. Just knowing we had it, stocked up ready to supply on the streets of whichever politically screwed dictatorship next poses a threat to us would keep them all in check – without the worry of hurting the genetically superior. A tailored bio-weapon. So much more specific than a nuclear warhead.'

Jon looks at the clock on the wall. He normally went for a cup of tea and a breath of fresh air at this time in the morning before cleaning out the furries. He had lost track at 'neogenics' but tried to feign interest and didn't want to appear ignorant or rude as he could see the usually quieter of the two professors was about to launch into another high-brow science lecture.

'K - k - ketamine seems to be inadvertently taking the weak out of the underclass at the moment. Difficult to believe it was manufactured with the intention to be a replacement for PCP as an anaesthetic as PCP was deemed 'too addictive.' Look how the government are exploiting its formerly illicit importation now. What about the occasional batch of one hundred percent pure heroin that the government allows to filter through the system in order to take out a dose of useless junkies sporadically – yes – it's cleaning up the streets, helping a reduction in petty crime but it's so vague, so unspecific. That Bob Geldof's pretty daughter overdoses on the junk, just like her mum and there's a huge hoo-haa about it.'

'Peaches – she was called Peaches.'

'Y - y - yes. I'm sure she was, thanks Ivy. By the end of the Spring I'm hoping we have enough data to start attempting to link the dissociative to a different gene... Scale things up a little.'

'Really?' Interrupted Ivy again with an unsettlingly keen look on her face.

'Y- yes. Of course. With a gene-tailored psychoactive, we could take out any particular genetic subsector we, or the MoD rather, need to – by voluntary, self administration. In our lab we've managed to knock out the un-pigmented rodents by designing our drug to only be lethal to the rodents lacking the gene needed for a particular skin and fur pigmentation molecule. The brown hamsters are fine, the albinos, weakened to the point of death. All of them high as a kite, oblivious and happy to keep on self-administering. What a power to have. With a few more years work, after we've isolated genes unique to each particular race... We could take out all the Chinese if we needed to....'

Wilder flashed Birch a threatening look and cleared his throat at several decibels louder than necessary. 'We're in the line of defence not attack of course Professor Birch may I HASTEN to remind you.'

'Yes, yes... Of course Professor Wilder. Of course. I'm merely making my point about the potential of this research as a counter weapon. M – m - many events and investigations have come and passed that... mmmm... in the eyes of a layperson may seem unethical, not quite right or even downright corruptive.'

Dr Birch stuttered, his left eye twitching more than it usually did, amplified by the tension they were all feeling no doubt.

'The a – a - anthrax spillage of '68 on the south coast for example - although technically *B... b... bacillus globigii* – may well have been responsible for several birth defects over the following few years but without carrying out the germ warfare tests, we would've left ourselves exposed to future international threats. Bird flu, ricin, yellow fever, dengue fever, small pox – the bloody Yanks and Ruskies have weaponized all of these delights. It's a game of ensuring we are in the ship of one-up-man first I'm afraid.'

'If you don't mind,' Dr Cook politely interrupted, 'SARS – a perfect example of modern day defence. I believe the Americans seeded it in China deliberately. They lost so much trade as a result of it. It wasn't virulent enough – didn't spread fast enough either.'

'Yes – g - g - g - good example Dr. Cook. SARS didn't take off as well as whoever seeded it believed it would and then the Americans started to claim it was caused by a man in the Guangdong province eating a pangolin.'

Professor Wilder nodded in agreement but drew the discussion to a close with the power of his commanding body language alone. Wilder was a serious man, a few years off retirement and had worked alongside Professor Birch and a handful of other brain-achingly intelligent scientists for the best part of his working life. He was in charge of, and overseer of, all scientific research on Level sub1b. The labyrinthine maze of scientific offices and labs were all based below ground level and access was only by one of three separate ID-activated lifts. He'd needed a laboratory technician to take care of the rodents being used for the phase two trials of the top secret neo-genics programme and had chosen Jon after developing a soft spot whilst lecturing him as part of his undergraduate degree. He'd felt that despite his troubled history he was a bright enough boy capable of carrying out the mundane lab work necessary for the trials and had also lost his father in service to the Army, as had Wilder, Iraq and Vietnam respectively. Most importantly, Jon, like Wilder, was easily manipulated by money. He'd arranged for his early release from prison in exchange for a well paid job with himself and Birch.

The fourth member of the emergency meeting that Wilder had called that morning was Dr Cook, a recently divorced, post doctorate research scientist who, despite having risen that morning, and every morning at 6am to prepare lunch for and pack off to holiday club her three children, was always the first to arrive at work and the last to leave. Her work-life balance was atrocious and her disposition was bitter but she was a committed, efficient if slightly right-wing scientist. She was fully aware that even in this day and age a woman had to work thrice as hard to achieve half the credit. Even in 2020, only around twenty percent of UK academic professors were female. She was especially enjoying the fact that as of last month she was to be addressed as Dr Cook rather than Mrs. Cook and thus occasionally avoiding a certain amount of patronisation she'd received in the past in the still sexist world of science. Despite being slightly resentful having to be at work on

New Year's Day, she'd been sat down attentively taking minutes on her laptop but the question Jon had raised on morality had prompted her to look up from her screen.

Wilder corrected his posture and readdressed the team. 'Our research is paramount. Can I remind you all that protection of MoD information is crucial to the safety of our country.' He then turned away, left the lab and entered his adjacent office. He was furious and pulled his door as hard as he could. The fire door closed painfully slowly behind him as Professor Birch, Jon and Dr Cook all sifted through the pile of headlines he'd left on the desk.

'Unfortunately the likes of the Nazis and fictional media like Gattaca have given eugenics a bad name,' Dr. Cook said grimacing. 'It's a terrible shame all of these people have died but if they will take drugs...' She raised an insinuating eyebrow and paused. 'My money's on the Russians. It's either them testing the waters, seeing if we've come up with an antidote yet or Trump has made a terrible mistake – stupid man that he is. What we're doing though, what we're working towards here in the UK is no worse than pre-implantation genetic screening, giving a woman the right to chose abortion if her child isn't going to look the way she wants it to. Designer babies. Or it's no worse than diagnosing potentially life-limiting conditions prior to conception or birth to allow abortion. Or medics treating terminal conditions such as cystic fibrosis with gene therapy to allow sufferers to live beyond their prognosis. Although gene therapists seem to be more focused on extending the life of those suffering. Something I will never understand. Or the Chinese, restricting couples to just one child. We're just more of an...'end-point' project.'

She paused for breath, clearing her throat and smoothed out some creases in her polyester slacks before continuing her spurious out pour.

'I'm constantly amazed that humans are so preoccupied with the selective breeding of cows, horses and even dogs more than they feign any interest in trying to improve their own species. We allow people to mate willy-nilly with catastrophic results. My three are as pure as snow. I terminated a fourth. Down's Syndrome. If we don't get there first, another lab will. Looks like they already may have. Having the technology and the scientific capability is one thing. It's what you then chose to do with it that makes it right or wrong.'

Jon understood part of what his superiors were saying, although a lot had gone over his pock-marked, stubbly face.

'Yeah, whatever, I'm not that bothered, I just like the money you know. Just rented a flat near the centre. Don't want to lose my job.'

'Do you like reading, Jon?'

'Yeah sure. Not much else to do here at lunch time seeing as we're not allowed our mobile phones on site or on the net.' Jon read Viz and the odd manga magazine as a teenager, but truth be told he couldn't remember the last book he'd picked up. People rarely say no when asked if they like to read though for fear of looking ignorant.

'Here, go to the library and see if you can borrow this title. It's a beautiful read. Pure fiction, but sums things up better than I ever could. It's pretty old, 17th century I think. Don't let the language put you off. It paints a glorious picture of how better society could be. You know - if things were tidied up around the edges a little.'

Dr Cook rummaged in her bag with her petite hands for her notepad and biro, scrawling down the title of an old book she'd read moons ago. 'City of the Son by Campanella.' She tore it off carefully and passed the note to him before scuttling off down the corridor into a different laboratory where she'd probably spend the rest of the day analysing blood samples from the rodents without having to interact with another human if she was lucky.

Jon twiddled his thumbs and stared at the floor. In all honesty he cared not for what the team were 'working towards'- his interest was purely selfish. He was however feeling nervous and slightly guilty, but not because he'd caused friction in the lab that morning with his questioning over the professors' project, but because some time back he had read the mainly incomprehensible bumf hand-written on the side of the tub of powder that Professor Wilder had given him. A little bit of knowledge had proven to be at first a gainful, powerful thing, but had, in a series of misfortunate yet financially quite rewarding events, ultimately turned out to be a complete and utter disaster.

Wilder had been given phase two clearance to begin experimenting on animals with his novel research chemical. A collation of a potential dissociative, a quasi-crystalline matrix of DMT and PCP with a synthetic section of messenger RNA coding for a particular gene linked to it. The gene coded for a protein which caused the production of a pigment in the small mammals they'd worked with so far. The theory was that by using gene targeted therapy, a particular drug that could cause harm or benefit could be activated only in individuals carrying the specific gene.

Jon had always found it hilarious that humans share sixty percent of their DNA with a banana. Around ninety-six percent of human genetic material is identical to that of a chimpanzee and he'd always ribbed his granddad Pete with his low hanging hairy knuckles, hunched back and ridged brow that he shared perhaps slightly more so. The rodents in the *in vivo* lab had about eighty-five per cent of the same coding genes as the average Joe Bloggs on the street. It was actually quite mind blowing to think that every single human being on planet earth has DNA that is ninety-nine percent identical to the next person, despite an array of amazing differences in skin, hair and eye colour, body shape and so on. All of the differences we see between us and another soul come down to just one percent of the DNA being slightly different to theirs.

Professor Wilder and Professor Birch's ultimate mission had been to create a bio-chemical that would be willingly taken by a population deemed non-useful by the government to the future proliferation of the human race that would effectively cull a proportion of them. It was of course, never to be used, but merely held as a counter-terrorism threat of Trident proportion. There were many reasons for this highly secure research to be carried out. Professor Wilder and Birch had put a detailed funding request case forward to HRH many years ago, blinding her better judgement with science somewhat and had since continued to plod on, un-moderated, in rather an unethical manner in the safety of their underground haven. When you are the Oracle, head of your game, top in your field, the Chief Egghead, the one with the most knowledge, the Governess of the Chase – who is there to challenge you?

The government would likely never unleash such an atrocious form of chemical warfare on the world but knowledge was power and understanding the process was crucial in controlling its production and utilisation elsewhere. The implications of their work would be immense, and, according to Wilder and Birch, it was a line of work being undertaken in other governmental laboratories across the world, with North Korea, the KGB and the Chinese all making headway.

Back in the summer when Jon had been recruited to work at Porton Down, alongside daily cleaning out of the animal cages, topping up of various consumables and reagents, Professor Wilder had instructed him to mix a miniscule 10mg of the HVN-1 powder with the measliest of 0.5ml distilled water and to put just one small drop no bigger than a human tear into each of the hamsters strange liquid food each morning. The rodents were given the choice of pure food, or food that had been tampered with by the addition of the HVN and could dispense nutrition by pressing a small button. The small mammals chose the adulterated rations every time. The cages were split down either side of the livestock lab, with currently ten golden hamsters, one per cage on one wall and ten hamsters of an albino variety distributed along the other side. Over the months, Jon repeated this daily process and enjoyed how excited the little rodents always were to see him and gulp down the delicious grub-fluid he was providing them with. He also began to notice that the albino hamsters started to become most unwell, eventually over a course of weeks, all dying, where as the golden hamsters with their beady eyes, pink stubby tails and auburn top coats seemed to thrive, even gaining significant weight and scored highly on carefully constructed intelligence tests and maze challenges. The dead rodents were disposed of and replaced as the tests continued in the name of data collection. They fed, they were tested and probed, the chestnut hamsters thrived, and the albinos died. Yet they all went white in the eye.

Although he'd felt a pinch of guilt when the fluffy beings started to keel over, snowy-eyed, wasted abdomens, no more than skin vacuum packed onto frail bone, he continued his role as he had never earned such good money. He was feeling guilty for an entirely different reason. A reason he truly hoped he would not be caught over.

You see, whilst bored in the laboratory one day, Jon had read the words 'DOPAMINE/SEROTONIN EXCITOR' on the side of the powder tub (amongst a load of other incomprehensible, scrawled chemical information) that Dr. Wilder had provided him with at the start of his new job and having some basic knowledge of biology and chemistry and a much greater knowledge of street drugs, supply and demand, he decided to help himself to a generous few scoopfuls for a few home experiments of his own. He had himself tried the substance on his Grandad's yappy old Patterdale terrier who simply could not get enough of the stuff. He'd observed the dog's shiny black, keen eyes turn a glassy ice white, contrasting amazingly with its fine brindle coat and for a good quarter of an hour he watched the dog smiling. The dog was flopping around on the floor laughing his little grey socks off.

He'd tried the powder himself, a miniscule crumb under his tongue after a drunken night at the pub and he'd loved it. And he'd loved the new friends and girls it brought along too. It was like nothing else he'd ever taken. He'd felt like he'd jumped right into the middle of Grand Theft Auto with infinite lives. Although it tasted foul. He shared it with his mates. They tried diluting it in water and drinking it, rubbing it in their gums -so bitter - and eventually dropping it in their eyes. His mates loved it. So then he sold some to his mates, and then he sold some to mates of mates; and his mates sold it to their mates. The tub he'd filled from the lab had stretched and stretched like a bottomless pit of fun. The powder percolated far afield via friends and friends of friends and with due course it spread to the streets. It flooded the streets as a squirt of bubble bath would flood a bathtub with effervescent, soapy suds and when Jon's well ran dry, he took more from the lab. As the huge stockpot depleted unnoticeably, Jon's bank balance rose substantially and then eventually, so did the death toll.

CHAPTER SEVENTEEN -- UNEXPECTED REUNION

Tabitha slowly drew up the pillar box red garage door, redundant to the fact that no matter how long she sat there thinking, she would need to return to her house and take care of her son at some point. Oscar must've been with his dad for at least two hours now. God knows what state the house was going to be in. She always needed to have a quick tidy up around midday whenever they were all at home to prevent the evening tidy up from cutting into her precious other free time which was reserved for cutting her toenails and marking. On returning via the back door, Tabitha noticed that the house was strangely spotless, spare a handful of dinosaurs on the floor of the kitchen scattered around a potty which was filled with a relatively fresh turd. Oscar's shoes and coat were gone from the hallway and Tabitha spotted a note scribbled on the back of an old birthday card which lay prominently on the table.

'Nipped into work for a bit. Oscar at Izzy's. Curry for tea please.'

For Christ's sake, Izzy would be charging him at least triple time for working on a bank holiday. Couldn't he at least bare to spend a couple of hours with his own child? What a way to start the year. Her husband was indeed a workaholic - married to his work. Tabitha was convinced that he'd probably spent a greater amount of time in his life clearing out guttering than he had actually on his hands and knees playing horses or finger painting with his son. She grumpily threw open the freezer door and plucked out a Tupperware box filled to the brim with chicken curry and dumped it on a clean tea towel next to the note. She had enough on her plate, metaphorically speaking, and she certainly didn't have time to start cooking up something fresh for his dinner plate too. Slightly eased by the fact the pair of them were out for at least the next couple of hours, she wrote a reply on the bottom of the note.

'Defrost 8 minutes full power. Gone to gym. Back late please bathe O and put to bed.'

She hated passing her son over like a relay baton but time was important and she had a potential crisis to deal with. She could not... would not be getting into trouble over this. She'd after all merely snuck in to check the old boy was okay after hearing some noises from outside. Surely that didn't make her an accomplice, did it? She wasn't in any part responsible for what had happened to him. Yet she'd seen the blood dripping down the stairs and she'd seen that Val's leg was not lacerated and deep in her heart she'd realised that something more sinister had occurred that night, yet she did nothing about it. The guilt had fuelled the volatile butterflies that frequented her stomach which were now on overdrive. She wasn't sure if she was going to be sick again as the emotions rose inside of her so she rushed to the kitchen sink as a precaution.

Warm spit flooded her mouth, but no sick. She focused on her breathing and eventually made it to a wooden stool tucked underneath her kitchen island. She glanced down at the other stool in the room that Oscar had kindly left her, the smell of which suddenly hit her olfactory system. She jumped up, hunched her stressed body over the sink and vomited out some more shock from her system.

Scraping off the formerly dangling strands of brown hair that were now slightly vomit soaked and stuck to her cheek, Tabitha stood up and looked out at the garage at the end of her garden. She had decided that she needed to speak to Val as soon as she could. She needed that motorbike off of her property ASAP. Then she needed to think up an alibi for that December evening. But what about the students? They'd seen her leave. They'd seen her practically carrying Val out in a hurry. Had they seen anything else? Her heart started pounding again, and she wretched once more, empty of all solids and liquids yet full to the brim of anxiety, she turned her cold tap on and for some reason started to run her wrists under the cool stream of water.

Ding Dong.

The front door.

'Dammit,' she spat, out loud to a plastic triceratops. Tabitha twisted off the tap, dried her hands on a nearby tea towel then squatted down and hid behind the oak-topped island, staring at the washing machine all the while, waiting for whoever it was to go.

Was it the police? The knocking repeated.

She needed to think this all through before she spoke to anyone. Maybe she should just hand herself in? But what about Oscar, she might go to jail. Who would bring him up? Jack wouldn't last a second, Oscar would end up in care... All the worst thoughts a mother can have came streaming through her displaced, fractious mind. She pummelled at her stomach with one hand and bit the dry skin framing her thumb nail from the other.

Nearly a minute passed. The unwanted visitor knocked again, this time louder, Tabitha stayed still. Then a third time. Her bell rang, accompanied with a firm rat-a-tat-a-tat-a-tat-tat. They weren't going anywhere. Tabitha was just considering whether to sneak out through the back door and go once again to hide in the darkness of the garage when a familiar voice which sent judders down her spine came through the letterbox, raspy and booming, like a judge court-martialling a war criminal.

'Tabitha. Tabitha? I know you're in there Tabitha. I've been watching you, waiting out here for a quiet moment – waiting for a chance to knock.'

The grit grey, rubber-bung stub of a walking stick came poking through Tabitha's horizontal letter box aggressively. She knew in an instant. It was Val.

She must have heard the news thought Tabitha, unfurling her squished body from the wooden floor and walking hesitantly towards the door.

'Come in, come in.' Tabitha opened the door and hurried the elderly woman into her kitchen, railroading her gently into a corner where a small, plump arm chair sat, guiding her down into it softly. Then she went around the kitchen, lounge and hallway and pulled all of the venetian blinds down, closing them tightly. God knows who else was watching.

'Your leg's better then?' Tabitha offered, trying to act as normal as she could, 'tea?'

'Yes, yes. Still giving me a bit of jip at night but I'm on so many analgesics for my c...'

She trailed off.

'Your what, sorry? I didn't catch you,' Tabitha responded, bundling tea bags into the teapot with one hand whilst frantically filling an overflowing kettle with water with the other, nail beds raw from chewing and nerves clouding her senses.

'Nothing. I'm fine. Let's move on. I've no time for small talk.'

'Yes. I'm sorry, glad you're feeling better.'

Tabs moved over to Val, bringing the wooden stool with her and sitting on it in the corner of the room.

'I'll be taking my bike back today. I suppose you've heard the news.'

'Which news?' Tabitha asked with dismay. Surely there couldn't be any more bad news.

'The old git. They've found him. Of course. Surprised it was so soon. I doubt the bastard had any friends visiting him.'

'Don? Yes Don. W... w... what happened?' She asked with trepidation, already knowing viscerally the answer to her own question.

'I shot him. Blew his bloody brains out.' Val placed her hands on her hips, arching her lower back slightly, puffing out her chest like an eccentric robin almost with pride at what she had said and done.

The audacity of her response shocked Tabitha. Surely only a cold-blooded murder would speak like this? A psychopath. Not a frail, old lady. But that's exactly what she was, a cold-blooded killer.

Tabitha began to actually shake, now definitely regretting letting this mad lady in. She was probably going to off her too – get rid of any witnesses, or maybe she was just a total psycho, enjoyed killing. What if she'd already hurt Oscar and Jack?

'Calm down. Calm down, you're shaking like a wet dog after a bath. I'm not going to hurt you if that's what you're thinking, dear.' Val reclined back into the chair and her facial expression softened somewhat. 'I came to explain. I came to explain what happened – it's only fair – if there's a chance you're going to go down with me, it's only fair you know what happened. What he was like. Then we've got the youths to deal with. They saw us leave. We'll need to speak with them. Have words.'

'What are you going to say to them?' Tabs murmured, unsure if any sound actually came out. She felt like a school girl who'd been summoned to see the headmistress for smoking in the toilets. How did this old bag of bones exert this force over her? In her own home?

'Well, I'll explain my situation, explain whatever they need to hear, appeal to their better natures....and if that fails, I'll whip out my knife.' Val drew her hand inside of her zipped, leather breast pocket and started to fumble around for her flick knife.

'No! No... No... I don't need to see it. Please keep it in there ... There is no need for that please. Let's not add insult to injury.'

'Injury? Pah! I bloody blasted his face off. Total scumbag. I wish I'd done it sooner. My whole life I've wasted, living every day in fear that he'd find me and beat me ten shade of blue. I made sure I put him in the grave before he ever got the chance. I wouldn't actually hurt the poor babies. I'm not crazy. Just a 'vengeful lady with a murky history'.' Val made the inverted commas sign with her spindly fingers either side of her inappropriate grin.

Tabitha felt choked up hearing Val declare with the confidence of a strutting peacock that she wasn't crazy.

'I just need to make sure the buggers don't say anything to the police. I don't want to spend my last few months locked up in a cell, pissing in a pot. I'm sure you don't either.'

'Last few months?' Tabitha squeaked

'Ah, yes. I suppose you need to hear this.' Her solemn face looked to her feet. 'Now is as good a time as any other.' She rolled her eyes as if bored with her own terminal diagnosis. 'Well you see. I'm ill. Stage four metastatic lung carcinoma. I'm ridden with the stuff. Like a fruity cheese that nobody wants. Probably more tumour than not in this pile of junk.'

Then, as if on cue, she started to cough. She pulled a hanky from her pocket and caught all manner of disgusting, blood tinged phlegm in it. After several minutes, the breathless, coughing fit passed and Tabitha noticed for the first time how pale the old lady was, her skin almost translucent, clinging to her cheek bones and backs of her unsteady hands as if for dear life. What a way to go. Tabitha felt a strong twinge of pity for the poor lady. She'd lost her own mother to cancer and knew just how horrible the last stages were. Heavy medication, hallucinations, a hospital bed often set up in the lounge for weeks or months until eventually a protracted death in a hospice. The stench of a body rotting whilst still pumping blood, changing of dressings, frequent visits by hospital staff day and night to medicate a pained, vociferous individual back into a hazy stupor. She'd seen her mother go through this and wouldn't wish it on her own worst enemy or even on a calculated murderer.

'Oh. God. I'm so sorry to hear that. Is there nothing the doctors can do? Well, you look remarkably well. Here, let me pass you some water.'

Tabitha suddenly strangely more at ease chatting with Val, her vulnerability now apparent. 'Why did you do it if you don't mind me asking?'

'A brave question young lady. A brave question. He destroyed me. Stole my youth. Stole my dreams. The bastard beat me daily, cut and burnt me. Tied me up whilst I healed so no one could see the damage he'd done or the bruises he'd left.' Val unzipped her jacket and exposed part of her chest to Tabitha. Tens of small circular marks where skin looked like molten peach wax showed the scarring of cigarette burns. The silver-grey slice marks on her collar bone, evidence of razor cuts. She fastened her coat in silence then continued her story. 'Raped me regularly. Then my son came along. That changed things for a while. He left us to it, started staying away for long periods of time. I didn't ask what he was doing. Didn't care. Just glad to have a roof over my head and enough money to feed myself and my boy.' Val sighed and sipped on her water.

'Then it started again. The beatings. The violence. Oh, the names he called me, the things he said. Almost worse than the punches and the throttling. When Stephen could walk, he started on him too. He would put his Lambert and Butlers out on the soles of his feet so no one could see the scars. That poor boy. My poor baby. He was taken from me. Pulled through the care system like a doll. I tried to keep in touch, I sent birthday cards every year, presents when I could afford it, I've no idea if they got to him. I wasn't allowed near him. Things were different back then. Poor boy.'

Tabitha filled up both of their glasses with water and took Val's hands in hers as she sat down again and continued to listen.

'He died recently, my Steve. Overdosed on drugs. Alone. In prison. He'd been on the streets. I'd tried to approach him years ago. I wanted to build a bridge; make amends but he blamed me of course. It's awful how memories distort. I never laid a finger on him. Loved him with all my heart and soul. No child should be dragged up like that. No child should die like that before their parents.'

'No. It's awful; what you've both been through.'

'When I saw him on the news, I knew it was him straight away even though I've not seen him for time. His beautiful red curls were shaved off short. He had freckles just like his granddad.'

A tear appeared in the corner of Val's eye, Tabitha's too. As Tabs dabbed at her own face, she offered a fresh tissue to Val.

'Oh no dear. No dear. I'm not crying with sadness. I'm crying with joy. He's gone. No longer will I have to worry that he has tracked me down or that he is doing what he did to me to anyone else. He's gone. The world will be a better place without him I assure you. No-one will miss him. You see dear - that's why I did it. He killed my son. What he did to me and Steve, it made him turn to drugs; it killed Steve. So I've killed him - balanced the tables. And god, dear, it felt good. What have I got to lose?'

Val drew in a deep breath through her nose and sat up straight, slapping her hands down on her thighs, drawing her chin towards her chest whilst holding back a cough.

'Well dear. I take it I have your support Tabitha? Seeing as you're, well, technically my wing lady in all of this?'

'I... I've always found honesty to be the best policy.'

'And what exactly were you doing at the bastard's house anyway? You were bloody lucky he didn't catch you, whatever you were up to. In a way, I think I may have saved your life. Oh Tabitha, Tabitha, Tabitha. We're not reporting this. We are covering up our tracks and we are disappearing back into the ether from which we once came. I'd rather hoped you wouldn't make me say this but if you even think of grassing me in I will implicate you. You will end up in trouble with the law. How would your son feel, mother locked up through his formative years?' Her confidence was waning. She didn't know if Tabitha would bite.

Tabitha could see that despite this outrageously forthright attempt at blackmail, Val was a desperate lady, grasping at straws.

'Well. What are we going to do then? How are we going to prevent his neighbours from telling the police what they've seen... if they haven't already. By the time the forensic team have finished with Don's body they'll be able to work out that he's been lying there for a few weeks. Damn it. If I hadn't fallen with the push back from the rifle I'd have been able to properly deal with his disgusting body. They'll speak with the neighbours and ask them if they heard anything suspicious. We have no choice. We have to get to them before the police do.'

'You're blackmailing me Val. That's really not on. I'm a professional. I've got a child. I want to help you I really do... it sounds horrendous what he did to you and your son. God, if Jack ever laid a finger on me I'd be out of here like a rocket.'

'Yes, well things were different back then. Feminism was a dirty word. Many young wives were assaulted by their husbands, both sexually and physically and laughed at if they tried to report it. I was trapped financially, emotionally, societally and in the worse cases, physically. Many a night I spent locked in the bedroom. He'd pass plates of dry toast through occasionally if he wasn't too drunk.'

Tabatha sighed, 'Oh Val. I really am so sorry. I'm here and we will sort this out. Let me think.'

Tabitha cleared away the empty glasses and put some biscuits onto a plate and passed them over to Val. She began to pace the kitchen, picking up various strewn toys as she did and placed them in a basket whilst Val nibbled like a mouse.

'Sorry dear. Not much of an appetite these days,' said Val, placing the majority of the biscuit back on the plate.

Tabitha picked up her phone and started scrawling and tapping, searching her photos folder for something she'd saved from weeks ago. Several minutes passed. 'Yes! Got it. Right... I do have an idea if we can't persuade them to keep shtum.' She showed Val the photos and explained.

'Sweet Jesus what the actual fuck?' Casper said as he exhaled a thick cloud of vape smoke into the front room of the student household. The other two were slumped down either side of him on the bedraggled sofa, the Indian elephant themed purple and orange throw clinging desperately onto its back.

They'd just returned from peeping next door to see what had finally distracted the swarm of journalists away from their own door, their heads all spinning. It'd been an exhausting morning to be interrogated first by the police, who seemed overly keen to make it clear it was just a friendly chat but that they would probably be back with a warrant at some point, and then by the press who weren't as friendly and so bloody persistent with their questioning. The trio had only just arrived back from Thailand the day before and despite being still somewhat jet-lagged were also in a state of shock to return to such devastating news.

'What happens now then? Should we go and see her family? I can't believe she's gone. All her stuff... her stuff is still here. We've got a big tub of soya ice cream in the freezer that we both chipped in for. I can't eat it all. She can't be gone.'

Sky got up and went to retrieve a roll of toilet paper from their downstairs bathroom. She wasn't crying yet and felt strangely hollow inside but she could feel a wave of horrendous emotion snaking up through her body. She wilted back in her spot next to the other two and plonked the roll on the coffee table. They hadn't even unpacked their rucksacks yet which she could still see stacked ungraciously at the other end of the lounge.

'What about her clothes? What about our rent? When will the funeral be? Are the doctors going to have to hack her body up to find out what happened? Oh god. poor Soma.'

And then the damn opened, and as Sky started to cry so did Emma and so did Casper. They remained clustered on the sofa for over an hour, crying and blowing their noses, braking only for Casper to get and pour a family sized packet of quinoa and spinach crisps into a bowl. The crisps remained relatively untouched, partly as they were too distressed to eat and partly because although they were fair-trade and organic, they tasted disgusting. They continued to console each other on the sofa with deep hugs and heartfelt conversations and shared memories as the low-slung winter sun moved across the sky. The excitement outside slowly petered away as all of the press moved on to their next story. The police vehicles and officers that had accrued slowly pulled away one by one until just a solitary patrolling officer remained outside, guarding the crime scene whilst one more remained inside collecting the remaining evidence needed.

At just before four, just as it had started to darken outside, Emma leant forwards, using all of her core strength to draw her tiny self out from the depths of the sofa's miserable mouth and stood up. She brushed off the crisp crumbs and stood as if to address the other two, hand on hips.

'It's my fault. It's my fault. I gave it to her.' She fell to her knees and wept harder than she'd ever wept in her life. Sky rubbed her back, gently teased her hair out of her face and then knelt down on the worn carpet next to her.

'It's not your fault Emsi. It's not. It's really not. We all know the risks every time we take something, yet we continue to choose to do it. The chance of something like this happening is so small. It's a tragedy it really is, but it's not your fault. It could've been anyone of us giving her something. When we take something we usually don't know where it comes from or how it's made or what's in it. It's Russian roulette every time. We all know that. But she chose to take it, Emma. You didn't force her. She would've taken it with us at FarmTek before Christmas if she didn't have to go see her family. She said she was jealous and wanted to try it. If she hadn't got it from you, she would've found it somewhere else.'

'I'll never forgive myself for this. God I'm going to have to face her parents at the funeral. I can't go. But I can't not go. What if the police come back? They said they were awaiting further information on the exact cause of death. They're obviously going to get a warrant. What if it's confirmed that it was the bleach? What if they come back and search the house, arrest me. I need to get rid of it now. All of it. Or should I just turn myself in? I can't go to prison... for murder. I can't do that. I can't do that. I just can't'

Just as Emma managed to peel herself off from the floor with every intention of marching up the stairs and emptying each and every one of her tiny packets of drugs down the toilet, there was a loud rap-rap at the front door.

'Oh god, it's the police. They've come back for me... Shit. What do I do ? Casper, Sky, help me.'

'Calm down, Em, it's not the police.' Casper had risen from the sofa and had started to walk towards the net-curtained bay window at the front of the house cagily, moving the draped lace to one side slightly. He managed to make out the outline of two familiar figures who were crouched in a huddle at the front door, squashed up strangely against the thick hedge as if hiding from the outside world.

'They can't just come back and search. They'd need a warrant and they'd need a reason. It would take them longer than a couple of hours. Don't panic. They have no way of connecting you with what's happened to Soma other than speculation. I'm pretty sure they can't just come crashing in here. They also said they understood we were all in shock and I could see the lady PC... PC Fuck-Biscuit or whatever she was called was concerned about our welfare more than anything. She gave the press a right talking too. I'm pretty sure they want to protect us if anything. Bloody good job that old git died next door. Took the heat off us.'

Casper tried to make light of the situation but he could see from the looks on both of the girls' faces and the tugging feeling in his own pericardium that this was definitely not the time for jokes.

'He didn't just die, Casper, he was shot. Right next door to us. Shot,' said Sky directly.

'Well it definitely wasn't me – I was in Thailand,' said Casper unsure what point Sky was trying to make. 'Come on girls, let's not fall out over this. Now more than anytime we really need to stick together.'

'Who's at the door then?' asked Emma, unsure whether she wanted to know the answer.

'It looks like the old woman and that lady who lives down the road. The pair that were here the night we left for Thailand – remember? They looked well odd creeping out of Don's house that evening. They look pretty odd now to be honest. They're both crouched in our bush. Shall I let them in?'

Another loud rat-a-tat ensued, this time harder and faster.

'It sounds like they're not going to go away.'

'Let us in. We know you're in there. Let us in right now.' Val hissed through the letter box in a forcefully decided voice.

Emma turned towards the stairs 'I'm just going to lock my room. Wait until I have before you answer it.'

'Hang on Emma, come here. It can wait.' Sky pulled her friend back into the sofa and hugged her tightly, then yanked off several meters of toilet tissue and split it between them. Even on New Year's Day after a 26 hour split stop flight, Sky's face had been bejewelled with blue mascara, glitter and gems which had since streamed and dripped down her cheeks mixing with her tears. She asked Emma to help wipe her face clean, more to distract her friend from despair than vanity this particular time though. The girls both huddled up under a soft blanket and as Sky reached again for the repulsive hippy crisps, hoping perhaps that the flavour had miraculously improved since her last dip, she gripped Emma's thigh firmly with her hand, placing her other arm around the weeping girls torso comfortingly.

'You're okay, Em. You're okay. We'll sort this out - don't worry. We're here for you and we'll get to the bottom of this dilemma. Let's not do anything hasty. Let's talk this out.'

Emma felt mildly reassured. She had hundreds if not thousands of pounds worth of drugs upstairs .In her bedroom, stashed in a tin under her desk was a stash greater than Dr. Gonzo's suitcase, all in little bags, hundreds of little bags and cling-film-wrapped portions of powders, tablets, liquids, dried mushrooms, DMT and strange bits of what looked like tree bark she'd scored from some old dude at the Black Swan on a very drunken night out which she didn't even know the name of or how to use it. Drugs were just so easy to get hold of with the dark net and living in a busy, creative city like Bristol. Not so easy to dispose of though. She agreed she needed to talk it through.

The knock at the door resonated through the hallway like a pinball machine. 'Let us in,' Val shrieked in a whisper in a way only she could.
'OK. OK. Calm down. I'm coming.' Casper unlocked the door and slowly opened it half way, blocking the women from being able to see inside with his body.
'It IS those two ladies we saw coming out of Don's the night we left for Thailand,' he called back to the girls in the lounge. 'They're in our bush.'
'What on earth do they want?' Sky asked Emma with a puzzled expression on her face. 'I hope they're not just here to have a nose. Tell them to bugger off, politely if you can, Caz.'
'Yes?' Casper said through the door.
'Let us in.' Val stood up and brushed off a smattering of shrubbery from her biker leathers with one hand whilst grasping her stick firmly with the other. She leant on Tabitha unannounced causing her to buckle slightly under the unexpected load as Val used the end of her stick in an attempt to push the door fully open.
'What do you want? You can't just come in.' Casper replied curtly
'Trust me,' Val said, her abrupt annunciation causing her already wrinkly smokers-pout to wrinkle furthermore. Her eyes fired out a 'don't mess me' with look that reduced six foot two Casper to a bucket of scared kittens. As they entered, Tabitha offered her condolences to the trio over the loss of their friend, telling them that a girl she taught had also died after using the same drug.

'But that isn't what we came to see you about,' Val interrupted, throwing an icy glance to her partner in crime. 'Tabitha. Keep on topic, dear.'

Casper huffed and rolled his eyes, 'Jeeez... Pick your timing ladies. Now really isn't a great time.' He gestured at the girls on the sofa, screwed up piles of glittery, snotty tissues scattered around them like jilted-at-the-alter bridal confetti.

'Well,' Val said 'I'm afraid there is no time like the present. What we need to say can't wait.' She slowly eased herself into a high back chair with Tabitha's help and Tabitha perched on the arm rest next to her resembling a ventriloquist's puppet.

The pair of odd allies divulged what they'd shared with each other earlier. The three students now with additional woe on their heavily burdened shoulders were shocked to hear the horrific stories Val unfolded. Casper and Sky seemed convinced that with everything going on, with Soma dying maybe the ladies had a good idea in asking them to keep hush hush about seeing them creeping out of the old man's filthy house at night. Val had told them all now that she'd killed him. She'd admitted to first degree murder to Tabitha and now to three other total strangers seemingly with little remorse. Tabitha was in it up to her eyeballs now. Her body was exhausted from the constant ebb and flow of anxiety and panic she'd experienced over the last few hours.

Emma, however, still felt vehemently unconvinced by the request to conceal evidence from the police relating to Don's death. Obviously still worrying about her own ordeal and what her next move should be with respect to supplying Soma with the drugs that killed her just the night before, she really didn't want to open another can of worms.

It was almost too much for her to take. Why should she cover up for the pair of old bags? If they said that they hadn't seen or heard anything that night and got caught out, it would definitely enhance the suspicion of the police further. Why would they cover for people they'd never met properly before? Yes, what Don had done to Val and her son was atrocious but she was an old woman, at the end of her life. Emma had so much left to do. She couldn't go to prison.

'No. No!' Emma exclaimed. 'I can't lie anymore. Casper, Sky, we've got enough on our hands. Well, I've got enough blood on my hands anyway.'

Realising that she'd let slip perhaps more than she had intended to in front of the two newcomers to the household, Emma slumped back into her chair crying, head resting in the palms of her hands. Her nails, like Tabitha's, had been chewed to stumps in the last twenty four hours alone.

'I just can't take anymore of this. I'm sorry Val, Tabitha, but I just can't lie for you. I've got so much to think about.'

'What have you done?' Asked Tabitha suggestively, detecting a resounded waft of guilt from Emma. 'It's the drugs isn't it?' Tabitha spoke out loud what she had meant to internalise.

'What drugs?' Emma said. 'How do you know about the drugs?'

'The drugs. The drugs that killed your flatmate... Sarah, Samantha... dammit what was her name? Soma?! You gave her the drugs.'

'What on earth? You can't just come into our home making false accusations like that you crazy woman. Look at us. We've just found out we've lost one of our best friends.' Casper yelled as he stood in the centre of the room, hawking his long arms into the air like a heavily antlered deer, attempting to defend his harem.

'Falsely accused? Are you sure about that?' Tabitha had put two and two together and come up with the solution to The Times' cryptic crossword.

She grappled for her phone from her bum bag, which she'd taken to wearing on and off 'house investigation' duty due to its excellent combination of style, comfort and functionality.

'Look,' she tapped on her screen. 'Look. Here... your drugs. I've seen your drugs. You have loads of them. God knows what they all are. You must be the Pablo Escobar of St. Werburghs. And we've got evidence of it all. Look...'

Tabitha showed the students photo after photo of pastel coloured powders and tablets, the box that Emma kept the impressive collection in and even a selfie of Tabitha holding up a bag of green coloured tablets and grinning like a loon.

'What the actual fuck?' Emma stood up then sat down again, her breathing becoming irregular, panic kicking in. Sky rubbed her back, offering soothing words and reminding her friend to breathe.

'How on earth did you get photos of inside of our house? Inside of her bedroom?' Casper spoke, red with rage. 'You've been in here haven't you? What the fuck were you doing?' Tabitha quickly locked her phone and returned it to the safety of her zippered pouch.

Sky stood up and lassoed Casper with her arms, reigning him in, guiding him down to the sofa to avoid things getting any further out of control.

'Yes. I've been in your house. It... it was when you were out. I thought I saw a burglar and I noticed the door was open so I came in after them. Turns out you'd just left your ridiculous glitter ball on.' She was really thinking on her feet now as she pointed to the corner mounted party light.

'What a loud of utter shite,' Casper retaliated from the sofa, gesticulating like an octopus, shaking his arms at the ladies, clearly still very hot under the collar.

Tabitha paused to collect her thoughts. They were all in this now.

Sky had given Emma a paper bag in which to breathe and after a few seconds of silence that felt a like eternity for all five of them, the colour had slowly started to return to her cheeks as she inhaled and exhaled her way slowly out of a panic attack. They were indeed all in it together now. Each as guilty as the next. There were no winners.

A Mexican standoff. Deadlock. Stalemate. Each of the players were pointing a finger at the other.

CHAPTER EIGHTEEN -- NOT THE FINAL TRIP

Tabitha and Val were half way up the path leading away from the student house. The clear, crescent moon was presented in the sky like a single white eyelash on a blue velvet cushion. The amber-grey clouds on the horizon where the sun had just set meant it must have been tea time. Tabitha could hear her stomach grumbling. She'd thrown up most of her lunch. Luckily she had an emergency Twix in her bum bag which she opened it up and then offered a stick to Val.

'No thanks dear. Not much of an appetite with this cancer malarkey I'm afraid. Anything chocolaty makes me cough.'

'Ah, okay. I can fix you a salad if you like? At mine? I'm glad that's over with. Let's just hope they stick to their word.' Tabitha said, feeling a strange sense of accomplishment and satisfaction with the threat of blackmail she'd laid thick and fast on the table.

'Meh. It went OK. Didn't need to get out the old blade.' Val smiled with a glint of humour in her eyes. Little did Tabitha know that Val didn't really care if she was arrested or not. She was coming to the end of her life, months at best and she'd done what she'd set out to achieve. She'd merely wanted to ensure that Tabitha had not been brought down with her and it just so happened that Tabitha's act of good will towards her may have also have helped keep the wolf from her door for a little longer too.

The pair of them, linked in arms, strolled slowly onwards with slightly less weight on their shoulders, and Tabitha with slightly more Twix in her tummy. Tabitha smiled softly at the beauty of the young night sky and wondered what to put in their salad.

Val stopped suddenly, almost dropping her walking stick. Her mind was a machine that was constantly working, slowly ticking away, mulling over several problems at once. She'd set out to right wrongs before she passed and she had just had a light bulb moment. Clear direction as to where her final days might take her next.

'Bleach you said, huh?'

'Sorry, what?' replied Tabitha..

'Bleach. The girl you taught. She died from bleach. And the student girl. Bleach.'

'Erm... Yes... It's terrible. I hope they catch the suppliers. Such a tragic waste...'

'Cut the crud, dear,' Val snappily interrupted with a look of elation, as if she'd placed the final piece of puzzle in a one thousand piecer.

'Bleach. They all died from bleach. That girl. Emma. The mousy one. She had a case load of it you say?'

'Erm, she had some. I think. She had loads of drugs. I have no idea what most of them were. It's not really my forte.' Tabitha reached for her phone, shoved the last of the chocolate bar into her chops and pawed through the images to show Val the images she'd taken once again.'

'We're going back. Back into their home. Back now please. Turn me around.'

Val instructed Tabitha to slowly rotate her on the knobbly path so that she would return to face the front door they'd just invaded and left from. Leaning on Tabitha, Val elongated her walking stick as if it was the tongue of a thirsty giraffe and tapped it hard on the door.

Inside, Casper had just turned around to go and comfort the girls once more and suggest that they went for a walk to clear their heads when he jumped with the noise.

'For fuck's sake,' he muttered under his breath, realising it was just the pair of swindling women he'd thought he'd seen the back of. He opened the door with caution. 'What do you want?'

'We are coming back in,' Val declared, once more forcing the door open with her cane, leaning on the boy to help her over the threshold.

'Hang on. Hang on. We need to invite you in.' Casper angrily spouted

'I think you'll find that's vampires, dear,' Val replied, making headway at snail's pace to the upright chair in the front room. 'I want to help you. Grant a dying lady a final wish will you now?'

Tabitha hadn't the foggiest what was going on, but followed Val and once more perched on the arm rest next to her new friend.

'These youths. The school girl.'

'Ruby.'

'Yes, Ruby, Ruby and Soma. They took bleach didn't they?'

'Yes. Yes they did. We've also taken it before. Me, Em and Sky. To be honest with you, it was amazing. Didn't hurt us at all. It's so fucked up. Why did Soma have to take it? Wish we'd been around. Maybe things might have turned out differently if she'd had her mates closer.'

'I can see you are all hurting terribly my children. I want to help. My son you see, my son Steve. He was older than you. He would have been forty-four yesterday. Terrible time to have a birthday is New Year's Eve. Not that it mattered for me as I haven't seen him since he was eleven. He took the stuff too - when he was inside. He died from it. Horrible death. Ruined his fair complexion, washed his freckles away so the press say. His beautiful hair, his eyes, even the purple veins under his skin faded to white. I want to find out where this awful stuff comes from. I want to take it off the streets. Off the streets before it does more harm. Will you help me? You will help me. You. You... Emma?'

Val pointed at Emma, who was looking drained on the sofa but also eager to find out just how the old lady could help her. She would take any help she could get to help her scrape her way out of a prison sentence.

'Yes?' she quietly answered.

'You have some, don't you? Where did it come from? Who did you buy it from? I'm going to find them. Find where it came from. Destroy it.'

Emma sunk back into the sofa with disappointment. 'I can't help you I'm afraid. I have no idea where it came from. I bought it on the dark net.' Realising the old lady's face looked like how she'd felt hearing her tour guide just last week speaking to her in rapid fire Thai, she clarified. 'The internet. I bought it over the internet anonymously. I don't even know which country it came from although it arrived the next day so it can't have been far. I'm sorry. I truly don't know any more than that.'

'Ah well. It was worth a try,' Val sighed. Her body sank with disappointment.

Val placed her frail fingers firmly down on the chair arms and as Tabitha stood to help ease her onto her equally frail feet, Casper spoke.

'I've got an idea. Hang on Val, rest your bones. Let me put a cuppa on. I think I've got an idea that might help us right a few wrongs. I'm not sure any of you are going to like it though. But hear me out will you?' And off he strolled, through to the kitchen to find some chamomile teabags from amongst the odd collection of mismatched jars clustered on the shelf, pondering at the irony of all the healthy organic food that the four of them had insisted on eating, only to then go and poison their bodies with varying concoctions of illicit substances every weekend.

Casper returned to the lounge, where the silence of hopeful expectation hung heavy.

'So... hear me through.'

'Ok. This better be quick. I need to start flushing my stash.'

'Sure. Hold on, Em. Just hear me through...We want to know where this stuff comes from. Who makes it. Then we can somehow stop it from getting onto the streets somehow? What do we know about it already? It's fucking amazing yet potentially deadly at the same time. It's a powder not a plant. It's all over the south of England – not heard it being used abroad...yet. At Czech Tek back in the summer those Czech dudes had never heard of it when I was chatting with them – remember Sky? When I was trying to find some?'

'Yeah. Yeah, vaguely. I think so.'

'It's a new drug. How is it made? Where is it made? A novel research chemical the press are saying. So it's coming from a lab. Somewhere. My guess is somewhere in the UK, or its coming in from China – like all that ket that flooded the streets a few years back that stank of rose water.'

'Alright, Walter White,' chipped in Sky, 'where's this going. None of us are scientists. Not sure how this is helping.'

'Um, well I am actually,' said Tabitha. 'I'm a science teacher, used to work in a lab, but now I work with kids. I teach science – for what it's worth.'

'Um, well thanks, but I don't know if it will help. Hear me out.'

Casper was getting annoyed by the interruptions at this stage. He was fumbling around the lounge as he spoke, pulling on the two sets of blinds and curtains to make sure nobody outside had a chance of peeping in. All the press had long gone and the forensic team had collected all that they needed from next door, but h was feeling edgy and couldn't stand still.

'Um. Tell me where it comes from. Then I can stop it from getting onto the streets,' Val said. 'There's no need for you to get yourselves in this any deeper than you already are.'

'Erm... okay... So, here's what we should do. The bleach. Emma still has a few vials of it left don't you, Em?'

'Yes. I've got enough for two, maybe three trips but not for much longer. It's all going down the drain as soon as this ridiculous conversation is over.'

'No... No. Hold onto it for now. In fact... go and get it.'
'What?'

'What?' Screeched Sky, 'Seriously Casper, two people have died, we're all suspects and you want to get high?'

'No, no... No, of course not. Well, yes. Yes actually.'
'Wha...'
'Hear me out....'

All of the women were sat with arms folded in various states of confusion and dismay. 'Hear me out. The bleach. The bleach right, we've all done it, right, girls? It's been fine. Amazing in fact. Definitely not the experience Soma had. It took us to Thailand after we'd been talking about Thailand. It took us all to the same place. The place we'd been talking about. Thinking about. God knows how. Seriously, only god must know how. It was mind blowing. But we were all there, and then we witnessed it with our own eyes on holiday.'

'Hmmmmmm,' let out Emma, engaged yet afraid of where Casper's plan was leading. 'What if we thought about where this stuff comes from. Where does it come from? What country, what region, what laboratory? Where does it come from? What about if we thought all that and then took some. We would get taken to...or see, where it came from?'

Casper clasped his hands together to signal that he'd finished what he'd wished to say and by saying it aloud he realised how totally nuts it was but also how totally genius if they could pull it off.

'The. Last. Time. This will be the last time we do this.' Casper tried to reassure Emma and Sky who were now looking very nervous as the immensity of what they were about to do after losing a dear friend to it dawned on them. It had to be the last time, they all needed to clean their acts up for Soma's sake, plus this was the last Emma had of the bleach.

God knows how Casper had managed to talk them round. Val and Tabitha sat on tenterhooks, totally oblivious to what they were about to witness.

'We'll be fine. Don't worry. Try not to over-think. We need to focus on the Bleach Lab. Where is it made?'

'Sure. Okay Casper. I'm putting my faith in you. I hope this works out. Val, Tabitha if any of us get ill, here's my mobile. Call an ambulance from it and run, get out of here.' Sky passed her phone to them over the coffee table.

'Run?' Laughed Val. 'I'll do my best dear,' she chuckled, tapping her injured leg.

'When we know where it is Val, you can do what you like. Do your best. I'm going to draw what I see when I come round, like I did in Thailand. I could feel the angles, the curves, the smells and sounds and colours. After I get past the fractals, the kaleidoscope tunnel, once that other reality starts to appear I'm going to search. Search for anything useful. Then I'm going to try and draw what I see – when I come round... if I come round...' Fear started to encroach in his voice yet he pushed it to one side like a defiant toddler. 'Then we take it from there.'

'Draw it?'

'Yeah, he's good. Don't worry. You should see some of his pieces. We'll show you later, he's an amazing artist.'

'Okie-dokie,' said Val, giving them the nod of authority.

The trio each mixed the powder with a tiny bit of water using a plastic needleless syringe and started dropping the lilac fluid into each other's eyes, trying to recreate the first time they did it before Christmas in happier times, sat around the fire outside of the rave.

How the circumstances had changed, how the mood of the friendship crew, now minus one had changed, yet they upheld the same order, the same routine and the same ritual that they'd carried out before and all hoped for and wished for a positive experience.

Casper tilted his head back, blinking like a flickering star. 'Think about the Bleach and the lab. Focus with all your energy. Where did it come from?'

'Okay,' the girls nod in agreement. 'Where did it come from?' they unintentionally chanted together and started to focus on the origin of the chemical being dropped into each of their eye. Gambling with their very essence.

'I'm doing this for you, Soma,' Emma said, all sense of reasoning gone. She was so drained emotionally yet still riding high on a massive wave of guilt that was clouding her judgement. Casper's idea seemed to make sense. If they could somehow find out where it came from and help the police to shut it down they'd save lives. If she got caught, then perhaps she deserved to. After all if it wasn't for her, Soma would still be alive. What's the worst that could happen? Well, she could die she thought but unlikely as she'd done it before and been fine. No greater risk than any of the other research chemicals she'd dabbled with. 2C-i, 2C-b, bath salts, N-bombe. The list was endless. She squirted the last drop into Sky's left eye and they placed the purple syringes onto the table in unison, clenching fists and blinking.

Drip...

Drip...

Drip...

Drop out.

Within seconds, the three of them were rolling back further into the sofa, arms and legs everywhere, writhing around like medusa's hair before becoming placid, entranced, catatonic; three supine students, snow-eyed and still like hypnotised sharks, vulnerable, absent once more in a state of tonic immobility.

Val gripped Tabitha's knee a little too hard with one hand and subconsciously rubbed the threadbare, dark green fabric on the arm of the chair quite hard with the other, causing a bald patch to enlarge as the two of them held their breath in shock whilst sitting on the hard backed corner chair. They stared at the strange performance the three students were putting on, almost convinced that they were acting until their eyes changed. Ghostly.

All three of them were clumped loosely into a listless, entangled pile. Bug eyed. Displaced. Some place else. Their faces were practically glowing, illuminated by the effects of the bleach in the darkness of the musty student digs. And then pale, ashen, white as snow.

'Sh... sh... should we call for help,?' Tabitha stood, tense, and faced Val, fumbling for her phone. She was starting to regret the fresh Pandora's box of trouble the group may've just opened. She'd felt like this before, once as a child at secondary school, in a peripatetic music studio, sat in the dark after school before hockey practice playing with an old Ouija board her friend in the year above had brought in. Pure terror.

'They don't look well. I've never seen anything like it. I don't know what to do. Is this normal? Isn't this what happened to Ruby and Soma? Their eyes went white too. Then their hair, their skin. Everything.'

Val took a deep, sharp in-breath, stifled a cough and arched her back, taking on the prim posture of a girl trying to graduate from finishing school. 'They're still breathing. They look... well... kind of happy. Deliriously so,' Val stated, not really answering Tabitha's flurry of questions.

'We.... I should use their phone? Right?' Tabitha had picked up Sky's phone and was frantically trying to work out how to make a call. 'Ah blasted new I-phone. Why can't everyone just use the same phone as me! I've no idea how to use this. For fuck's sake.' She tossed the phone on the table. 'I can't use mine .They'll want to know why I'm here. I'll be traceable. This is a mess. We should never have come back.'

Tabitha was becoming more and more flustered and was considering just upping and running. She wanted to pretend she'd never returned to the student house, pretend as if she had nothing to do with any of it. But she couldn't leave. She was knee deep in proverbial muck. Trapped in every aspect of her life. She couldn't leave them. With one death already on her conscience, no one else was going to die today. She marched out into the hallway with her own phone trying to get some kind of signal. 'Gargh! St. Werburghs is a technological black hole.'

'Tabitha... dear...Tabitha... please calm down,' said Val, 'they're coming round. They're coming back to us I think. It's going to be okay. Their eyes - the colours are coming back. They're coming around.'

Several minutes had passed, which felt like a lifetime to Tabitha and Val and had felt like something totally immeasurable by the three students who were now all sat up straight, speechless, each with a look of pure euphoria on their youthful yet tired face. Slightly elevated heart rates, brown, green and blue irises present and correct.

Tabitha hurried back into the room and crouched in front of the three astral travellers, who appeared to have returned safely from wherever they had been on their cerebral journey.

'The colours... all the colours,' Casper softly spoke, 'so much detail... I can't describe it with words.'

'But so simultaneously monochrome. I was seeing... hearing... no, feeling in shades of off and on, present and not present, in and out, up and down. There was no black. No white. I can't describe it. I'm going to get my pad.' Casper slowly rose, rubbing his eyes like a 4am start. He plodded up the dusty stairs and again up to the attic room to retrieve his sketch pad and pens.

'The animals. The poor animals.' Sky was speaking now. 'Those poor animals. Some of them were dead, lying in the bottom of their cages. There was a wall of adorable chestnut coloured hamsters, or gerbils, I'm not sure. And a tower of albino ones. Tens upon tens of tiny, basic cages with nothing but a thin layer of saw dust and a small furry rodent in each– some alive, some dead. I could taste the death in the air. How could anyone do that to such harmless creatures? How could they just be treated like that?' She looked at Emma who was the last of the three to come around, perhaps having taken a slightly bigger dose.

'There was wire, bundles of the stuff. Tonnes of thick, angry looking barbed wire. I just passed through it though. Or was I part of it? I went into a huge building, must have been six or seven stories high. Such an ugly building.

'Yes. I was there too. It was a huge, rectangular, brick building in the middle of a vast stretch of flat, barren land. I reckon it was some kind of industrial site or protected area. I remember a sign over the fence: '*Danger, Hazardous area*'. There were more big signs on the towering gate: '*MOD property. Keep out Ministry of Defence Property*'.'

The group paused, an invisible veil of silence shrouded the room as they all contemplated what had been done and said.

'That can't be right,' chipped in Val, breaking the silence. 'The Ministry of Defence? Well, stranger thing happen at sea I suppose.'

'I had twenty-twenty vision of a laboratory. One of many I think. It was strange as it was dark yet I could see and feel everything. The walls resonated. It was like I was part of it yet aware of all of it at once. It made me feel angry and sad. It was nothing like our last trip,' Emma spoke. 'I could see a highly polished desk, not like the tatty, vandalised desks we had in the labs at school, this one was, like, made of marble or something smart. It was covered with Macbook Pros, printed documents, racks with test tubes in, some weird injector things with plastic hats on the end.'

'Pipettes?' offered Tabitha, feeling pleased that the fact she was a science teacher had been useful after all.

'Yes, I think so. I didn't really like science at school. I spent all my time on the computer, sorry.'

'No offence taken,' Tabitha replied and smiled gently.

'There were no windows. I couldn't see outside. No windows at all, like we were underground.'

Casper returned with his sketch pad and frantically scribbled on and shaded in his A3 page. Tabitha was fascinated as she listened astutely to what the three of them reported back but also by Casper's amazing talent. He drew an unfriendly looking building, definitely not a home or a shop; it was the same building the girls had talked about. A cube-shaped government building. No expense wasted on aesthetics. It had large, glass doors and windows all with blinds pulled down. A building built for efficiency and discretion definitely not for tourist appeal. And it had tall gates in front of heavily barbed barriers and an additional fence ran around the perimeter of the large space in which the building and a few other out-houses were occupied.

He whipped the page over and tore it off placing it on top of the junk on the coffee table and started on a second. This time, it was an image from inside the building. Inside a particular laboratory, a sign saying '*BGH Lab*' clearly hung above its electronically sealed, secure door along with a large, clear '*Keep Out- Security Level D*' sign alongside it.

His pencil continued to dance over the page. Immaculate detail, as clear cut as a photo. Tall glass-faced fume hoods mounted with industrial extractor fans at the top, floor to ceiling translucent-door ovens or storage cupboards of some kind, several containing row upon row of bottles and flasks with unpronounceable chemical names on them. Strange pieces of unidentifiable bulky machinery sat on the desks in the corners.

Signs were everywhere. Tabitha studied the universal lab safety symbols that Casper had drawn so she could explain what they meant to the rest of them, although symbols depicting skull and cross bones, flaming, shattering circles, thick black crosses clearly weren't welcoming images. 'Toxic, Irritant, Dangerous to the Environment,' Tabitha translated.

Casper continued wildly, tearing the second drawing off and discarding it onto the floor. He drew like a man possessed as the other two girls nodded in agreement with everything he penned down.

His third picture was of a display wall, with near on fifty small portrait photos, like a family tree of all of the scientists who worked in the underground zone. One sub zero level entitled '*Bio-Gen Hazards Lab – restricted access*' branched off. Casper circled it furiously with a marker pen and then proceeded to add detail to the faces that he could remember clearly - the faces of nine members of staff who worked in the lab that their trip had taken them to under which, were their names.

'Oh my god,' Sky squawked, 'this is unbelievable. You're unbelievable.' she patted Casper on the back, the three of them beaming at each other with excitement.

'There. Through there.' She pointed to another door that led out from the lab Casper had drawn.

'I went down there. There's animals in there too. Hamsters or rats. I'm not sure, the Bleach wore off. I was one of them. I felt their pain. I physically felt their pain. They were being tested on with something. They were all ill. We need to stop this. Whatever is going on – it's wrong'.

'Do you really think this is where the Bleach is coming from?' Emma spoke cynically. 'Do you really think the government released it on the streets? Why would they do that?'

'I have no idea. I really don't think they would do something like that would they?' Replied Tabitha, seeming unsure about what was being revealed. It all sounded so surreal. So surreal and so unlikely. She was expecting, hoping almost for Jeremy Beadle to appear from the grave around the corner, waving a camcorder about with his tiny hand shouting '*you've been framed*'.

'Who knows. They've done worse in the past. I tell you all in truth, I've worked in care homes for most of my life, watched the nurses and doctors dishing out medications for the elderly. The amount of times mistakes have been made - many accidentally, but occasionally deliberately. I've seen it with my own eyes. All governments... all management systems lie through their politically rotten teeth. Our government, developed country or not, certainly isn't the morally, honourable establishment the public think it is.' Val paused to take a sip of her water. Her chest was starting to burn. She needed to take her next dose of pain relief.

'I heard at work before I retired that over twenty thousand deaths a year are caused by medication 'mistakes' within the NHS alone and this is all above ground stuff. God knows what goes on in those research labs.

'Hang on. Hang on. I've an idea,' Emma said and she pulled the image Casper had drawn of the outside of the daunting building from the ever increasing pile of sketches he was producing. She picked her phone up from down the side of the sofa. It was full of holiday snaps she'd yet had the time or inclination to browse through. She switched it on and tried to steady her hand as much as she could to take a photo of his drawing.

'What are you doing, Em? You can keep the original if you like, I'll even sign it for you,' Casper joked.

She ignored the joke, fully focused on what she was doing. 'Reverse Google search. I'm reversing the search. I've got the image, now I'm using it to find out where this place is or what it is.'

She opened the Google app on her phone, tapped Updates and turned Google Lens on, then pointed the camera lens once again at Casper's artwork. In under a second, an array of various similar, soulless looking heavily defended buildings popped up on her phone screen, all five of them were peering at it in expectation.

Various gated communities in Brazil, Argentina and South Africa appeared which she scan read and swiped past. A prison with a watch tower and similar barbed wire fences, a section of Trumps border wall and Porton Down Science Park all followed on the small screen.

'Stop,' Casper shouted. 'That's it. I'm sure that one is it. That one there - tap it... Porton Down Science Park.' He sounded out his words slowly as if speaking for the first time.

'Yes that's it,' Sky echoed, 'where is that?'

'Looks like it's a government science park somewhere in Wiltshire...' Emma read aloud from the search engine description. 'In Wiltshire... Ministry of Defence... Science and Tech Lab. We've found it guys. We've found it.'

Casper high fived his friends. 'We found it. Now what?' The three on the sofa looked up at Val and Tabitha. Tabitha looked at Val.

'Oh, my giddy heart,' Val said jovially as she rose from her seat slowly, mock fist on chest. Tabitha could see she needed help getting up and aided her accordingly. 'My heart and my chest,' she said, smiling yet looking pale and slightly breathless. She excused herself to the hallway and lent on the stair case whilst she coughed and coughed and coughed.

As Emma fist punched the air, overcome with, albeit temporary, happiness at the success of her final time of experimenting with drugs her eye caught her favourite photo of the four of them together, stood outside of a massive speaker stack with 'Dissident' and 'Dirt Sound System' banners hanging down from it a year previously. They all had sun-kissed shoulders, youthful, cheeky smiles, somewhere in a field in Somerset. Soma was slightly pink, Casper had his shirt off as standard. The reality of what had happened to her closest friend sucker-punched her in the gut, propelling her back into a state of despair. She still had problems she needed to sort out. Serious problems, righting the wrong they'd done by somehow shutting down a government lab seemed impossible and still wouldn't bring Soma back. She could feel the tears well up inside her again, but she fought them back, stood up and brushed herself down.

'Well, parties over guys. I've got stuff I need to sort out. Sky, please help me flush all this shit down the loo and maybe we can melt all the baggies or something? I need to totally clear my hard drive too, maybe even sling it somehow.'

'Sure. Yeah. Sure Emma. I kind of lost myself for a bit there. Yes. We need to do that. If we're keeping tight on all of this, if we are all making a pact together to protect ourselves then yes, sure I'll help. No-one speaks to the police. No-one.'

Val caught Emma's eye and she signalled at Tabitha to pass her the photo of the students in happier times that she'd observed Emma looking at with reticence on the mantel piece. Tabitha looked at the students. 'Do you mind?' she asked as she grasped it carefully, folding in the velvet covered stand that was supporting it.

'No, not at all,' Emma said. 'That's Soma, second from left.'

'Yes. Yes I know. I saw her on the news. Beautiful girl. We really are truly sorry.' Val spoke on behalf of herself and Tabitha, Tabitha nodded in agreement.

Val continued to stare at the photo as comforting conversations took place around her, but her mind appeared to be elsewhere, and a single tear fell down her cheek.

'She was beautiful. Lovely looking girl. What a shame. She has, had sorry, the same red curls as my Steve. This frightful drug took him too.'

Tabitha, all-encompassed in the shared moment of grief suddenly spoke, somewhere in the depths of her mind, some rusty neurones had connected together. She'd seen a connection.

'What did you just say Val? Steve had red hair?'

'Yes, beautiful colour. People used to stop me in the street and say how special it was when he was a baby.'

'Ruby. Ruby, from my biology class. She had the same red curls. The same scattering of freckles and piercing green eyes. Let me see the photo again Val, please.' She took the photo from Val, stared at it intensely for less than a second, confirming straight away what she'd thought and immediately passed it to Emma, Casper and Sky.

'Look. Green eyes, red hair.'

'Yes, my Steve too. Lovely green eyes. Beautiful red hair. Until I think he started to go bold in his thirties, like his Granddad.'

Emma, on the same wave as Tabitha, had already reached for her I-pad and was searching for images of the other victims of the Bleach. One, two, three and four. She pulled up images and showed them to the others. Five, Six...

'They're all white, fair skinned, freckles... They've all got red hair.' All thirty-something of the victims who'd lost their life in the same painful, tragic way all had one thing in common.

'Genetics. They have similar genes,' Tabitha declared. 'This street drug, this bleach or whatever it is. It's working like a selective weapon. Dear god. It's like something the Nazi's would have introduced back in the days of eugenics.'

Tabitha's phone started to ring, her partner's face flashing up on the screen. 'Damn. It's Jack, I've got to answer this,' she said, and walked out into the hallway.

'Yes, I'm coming home now, just taking some trousers back to Next. Won't be long. You have the curry, I'll grab something here. Okay. Okay. Yes. Okay. Bye.' She hung up and took a pair of brown, starchy bananas from the students' fruit bowl on their coffee table, buried under stacks of sketches. 'Mind if I...?'

'No, be our guest. They've been there for weeks,' Sky replied and smiled. 'Sounds like you're needed at home?'

'Yes. Talk about bad timing. Val. What are you doing... your bike?'

'I'm staying here a while. It's cold out there.' Val was still coughing slightly but had made her-self as comfortable as she could, and had taken a handful of various coloured tablets from inside of her biker jacket pocket, knocking them back with gusto in between coughs, a stash almost on par with Emma's. After her coughing fit had finally subsided, Emma tucked her up under a crocheted granny square blanket and went to the kitchen to fix her a snack, whilst mulling over what Tabitha had said.

'Well, I've managed to keep Jack out of the garage up until now. I'm sure another day won't hurt.'

The students looked at each other confused.

'Let's all meet back here after breakfast, nine-ish, I should be able to sneak over then. It's still the school holidays.'

She gathered up the detailed sketches that Casper had made and rolled them into a tube, securing either end with a hair band from around her wrist.

'Don't mind if I look after these do you? I'm going to have a good hard think about what we could do next. What we should do next.'

'Sure, help yourself. I can make more if we need them. Anyway, we all saw it with our own eyes, or our third eye or whatever,' Casper mumbled, tiredness kicking in.

'We need to think about what we do with all this information to protect ourselves and to try and stop more people from dying.

Jack's back at work and I can leave Oscar, my son with the child minder. I'll see you all in the morning. Try and get some sleep.'

Tabitha was not good in immediate emergencies, she tended to freeze and dribble, like a stunned cow prior to slaughter. But organising... Organising was her forté. She needed to come up with a plan of some kind to take the project forward. She needed to organise the information they'd gathered so far. She'd need two pieces of A3 paper, sellotaped together down the longest side. She could use her new pack of pastel post-its she'd saved for a special occasion such as Ofsted or an Inset day and her 0.4mm nib calligraphy pen.

Casper and Sky nodded. Tabitha left. Emma returned with a hummus sandwich and half an avocado for Val, but she was snoring gently in the tall-backed chair. Emma left the sandwich on the table for when she awoke and scurried up to her room with Casper and Sky to start the mass disposal of any evidence.

CHAPTER NINETEEN -- THE FINAL TRIP

Tabitha eventually managed to drop off some time after midnight. Had she cracked it? She certainly seemed to have made some progress, although she was still unsure as to what the next step was going to be for her and her bizarre new group of friends. Could she call them friends? She loved her son more than life itself, but it felt nice to spend time with other adults. It felt like she'd had more conversation with Val and the students yesterday than she'd had from her husband for the whole of 2019. Radio 4 had provided her with more company at home than he had. They'd listened to her. This encouragement had egged her on; spurred her further towards completing her poster chart of what to do next. She'd even opened the fresh packet of Staedtler Triples roller pens to add a dash of colour to the plan.

Once she'd returned home that evening, she leafed through the drawings Casper had made and made a pertinent discovery. After studying each one in detail over and over again and focusing on the names he'd managed to bring back from his astral journey, she'd carried out internet searches on each of the staff highlighted as working in the lab they thought the drug was coming from. Tens of research papers carrying the names of the Professors and Doctor Cook popped up, none of them appeared to be accessible to the public. She managed to read the odd snippet of an abstract from a couple of papers, but even with her scientific background she really couldn't make head nor tail of what they were about. Something to do with genetics, in particular the genes responsible for pigmentation in skin and hair in small mammals and a medicine that had side effects so enjoyable that it encouraged patients to take it again and again. All probably preliminary research building up to the production of this Bleach that had done so much damage outside of the research laboratory in just a few months.

Then she'd started to study the fourth lab worker, a young lad called Jon Manley. A common surname, but the name Manley had rung a bell with Tabitha and as she'd inspected his face more closely after putting Oscar to bed, she'd realised that she'd met this young man before.

Jon Manley had briefly attended Farefield High - the school at which Tabitha worked. She hadn't taught him but his reputation preceded him. When Manley and his friend had broken into the laboratories a few summers ago, Tabitha was called in to clean up the mess they'd made. He was immediately expelled for this and was no longer allowed anywhere near the school, he may even have ended up in prison for it due to an accumulation of sins. He'd tried to get back in a few years later, claiming he was there to pick up his little brother Solomon.

Solly Manley was now in the sixth form and had somehow avoided expulsion like his older brother. He was also a bright boy but also easily led astray yet Tabitha had a soft spot for his cheeky personality but would always have to keep an eye on him whenever anything valuable was being used in class. The boys had lost their father in Iraq or at war somewhere when they were both small and their mother ended up becoming an alcoholic. Both boys ended up living with their grandparents at some point but the elderly couple struggled with the boys' behaviour and both of them had ended up in and out of the care system for periods of their life before their mother eventually got clean.

The penny had now dropped. Ruby's death, Liam, Solly and Bryce, and definitely Jon. It was all linked. They were all linked. Jon must have supplied something to the boys which Ruby ended up taking. If Jon had supplied it to his little brother or his brothers' friends, he was probably the source of the lethal chemical leaking from the research labs. It's why the boys had been absent for so long – yes – they were most definitely grieving for Ruby but they were also guilty of supplying the bleach to her.

What a stroke of inauspicious luck. She'd completed the puzzle, made the connection, cracked the enigma code. She'd solved the missing link. But what to do with this information?

Eventually curling up next to her snoozing son, Tabitha stroked his blonde curls and tried to soothe herself without waking him. Thoughts and ideas were running through her mind but she'd gone past the point of being productive and knew that she needed to try and get at least some sleep before sharing her discovery with the group in the morning.

Jon had been a bright but naughty boy at school, but surely he wasn't capable of murder? Was he being used by the government? Why were the scientists doing this? Was murdering all of those red-headed people what they'd intended to do? Were they on the brink of an epic disaster? Who was next? She hadn't studied history at school but this drug they'd put out on the streets of England was right up there with something Hitler would've done. They needed stopping. Her sleep was fitful and short that night but when she did dream, she dreamt in vivid colour. And in her dreams, her answers came.

Tabitha returned to the student house after dropping off Oscar. She waited cautiously across the road for people to pass so that she could knock on their door unnoticed by others. Sky let her in.

'Come in, come in. We were just thinking about taking this meeting outside of the house in case the police show up with more questions. Or in case the press start creeping around again,' Sky said, guiding Tabs through to the lounge where Val, still sat in the high backed chair seemed to have had some kind of glitter make over. The old lady was laughing as she put down the hand held mirror in which she'd been admiring her new look and looked up to Tabitha. 'It's your turn next.'

'Not a chance. I'm allergic.'

'What, to fun? That's obvious,' Val replied with a twinkle in her eye that Tabitha had not seen yesterday.

'Listen. Agreed. We need to get out of here, but we can't be seen together. I've got something to share with you all that might really help.' Tabitha pulled out a carefully folded piece of paper from her bum bag, the others gathered around in anticipation.

'Let me stop you there,' interrupted Val, 'you're right. We can't be seen together and there is a good chance the police will be back at some point. Where's my bike, Tabitha?'

'My garage. Where it has been since we first met. Where else would it be?'

'I want to see my bike. Let's meet in the garage. We'll go over separately of course. We can chat safely in there.'

'Erm....'

Tabitha couldn't think quickly enough for a good reason for this not to happen and all five of them made their way over discretely to her outhouse down the road.

Tabitha arrived first, unlocking the large, vertically moving garage door, dusting off and opening out some rather retro blue and yellow canvas garden furniture pieces for the others to perch on. She took the leisure-lounger, leaving little space for much movement around the garage. It was cosy but functional.

'Well, this is strange,' Casper said, trying to break the ice.

'What, stranger than taking a psychoactive disassociate after losing your friend to it just the day before and using it to travel to a hidden government laboratory where all manner of evil is occurring?' Sky replied.

'Hmm. Good point,' Casper retorted and sat down on the fold-up chair.

'Right, now were all gathered here, I want to share with you what I found out last night.' Tabitha once more opened up her carefully folded poster, fastening it to the wall with some blue-tak pieces she'd also brought, and then pulled out her laser pen from school which was stashed in her bum bag too before handing out a protein bar to each of the others.

Feeling relieved that her overloaded bag was now back to normal size and that they were all successfully gathered in secret to plot onwards, she proceeded to share with them what she'd found out about Jon Manley and how she felt that he must've been responsible for supplying the drug to Ruby and friends. Jon Manley was the connection. The leak.

'Woah. That kind of makes sense,' said Casper.

'Yeah. Wow. Good work Tabitha,' Emma added, Sky nodding in support.

Tabitha felt good. And bad. She felt good and bad. Good as she had the support of those around her who had hung on her every word and good as she had finally got to use her pastel Post-its and also good because she'd finally found a protein bar that didn't taste like dust and bad, well, because people had died, people were dying and more people were going to die if they didn't stop the lab.

'I'll handle this,' said Val, who'd been quiet since arriving at the garage. 'I'll handle this. I said I would and I must. I want to. This is my final wish. Leave it with me.'

'Handle it how? We can't let you deal with this. We all need to help. We all want to help. For Ruby, for Soma, for your son and for you Val. We're your friends,' Tabitha said and placed her arm around Val's shoulder giving her a gentle squeeze.

'Let me think.'

'Sure. You need time to think. We all do. Take it all onboard and think about what to do next.' Tabitha stood up and went around collecting the empty protein bar wrappers and made a make-shift bin from a red bucket shaped like a castle lined with an old carrier bag.

Several minutes passed. The students wanted to hear more about Ruby and the young boys that Tabitha had taught. Were they really bad kids or just misled youths experimenting with drink and drugs like many teenagers, like themselves even?

Val sat perfectly still, the cogs of her brain whirring at full speed. She hadn't touched the protein bar. Tabs popped it back in her bum bag for later.

'Help me up, Tabitha,' she commanded. Tabs helped her up and passed over her stick. Val looked at the poster Tabitha had tacked up to the breeze block wall, studying it with full focus. Tabitha couldn't help but feel a wave of pride that her work was being admired and utilised.

'We'll need some items,' Val said, choosing to remain stood as she dished out her instructions. Her leg seemed to be improving somewhat even if the cancer was weakening her noticeably more so each day. 'I'll need some hi-vis jackets and a large box. I'm going into the laboratory. I need to see it with my own eyes. If it is what we think it is. I will take it down.'

'How? How are you going to get into a high security building? You'd have more chance of raising the dead,' Casper said, 'and what exactly are you going to do when you get in there? You'll end up in prison.'

'I have nothing to lose.'

'I'm not letting you do this alone, Val.' Tabitha picked up a blanket shaking it free from any garage-dwelling spiders before placing it over Val's shoulders.

Val really didn't want company. She was generally a solo-mission-woman. She'd started this journey alone and wanted to finish it alone. Her cough was getting worse and worse and she hadn't managed to hold any food down for a few days now. She truly had nothing to lose and didn't want anyone else getting into trouble. But she was also still a little wobbly on her feet and the plan she'd engineered was most probably a two person job.

'Ahhh... Okay. If you insist. On one condition.'

'Sure. What?'

'If we get caught, you tell them I blackmailed you into helping me. You tell them exactly how and where we met – the truth – you tell them it's all my fault. Why were you in Don's house anyway?'

'Um, I followed a cat in?'

'Poppycock. Absolute string of twaddle.'

Tabitha still wasn't sure of the exact answer. Why had she taken to breaking and entering into her neighbours' homes? It seemed to temporarily fill a void of loneliness, gave her something to do, something just for herself. It certainly got the adrenaline flowing like she imagined skydiving or gambling on the horses might, but it never lasted.

Luckily, Tabitha didn't have to explain her actions any further to Val as Emma, Sky and Casper all spoke together, talking over one another with enthusiasm. They wanted to help too but Tabitha and Val firmly dismissed this. They had their lives ahead of them and Emma in particular may still have been in serious trouble for supplying drugs to Soma. It was agreed that t was best if they kept their heads down and supported the two older women from the safety of their home.

Tabitha agreed to Val's orders and Val issued a list of items she needed in order to get into the lab.

A spare helmet for Tabitha. Check. Casper could borrow one from his friend.

Two hi- vis jackets. Check. Tabitha could grab some from the prep room at work that they used for school outings. She nipped off to do so, picking up some sandwiches and drinks for the motley crew en route. Fuel and hydration were vital for such a project.

A large, plain cardboard box and tape. Check. Tabitha's garage was full of boxes and she had stocked up on parcel tape prior to Woolworth's going under, just in case.

A large container. Check. The students thought this last request was odd but they washed up a nearly empty organic peanut butter tub from their kitchen and brought it back to the garage.

Some kind of camera. Check. Emma offered her I-pad up and showed Tabitha carefully how to unlock it and take photos.

When the team reunited an hour or so later, all tucking hungrily into their meal deals, Casper asked what exactly Val's intentions with all the stuff they had collected together was.

'Well my dears, I'm going in. We're going to use a little bit of persuasive language and the like but I'm going in. Tabitha too, if you really must.' She turned and looked at Tabitha, who was chomping on her triple cheese. The protein bar hadn't touched the sides.

'What's the jar for? And the box?'

'Well dears, that's how we're going to get him out. A delivery for young Jon. Some fresh lab chemicals. He'll come out for them. Then he's going to take us back in with him. He won't like it, but he will. We're going to use him to take us in.'

'Like the Trojan horse?' chipped in Sky, happy that at last her Classics degree had come in some kind of use.

'Yes dear, like a Trojan horse.'

Tabs had arranged for Jack to collect Oscar that afternoon as she had a 'Women's Institute AGM' to attend and needed to do a last minute shop as she'd forgotten she needed to bring a plate of food along. How easy it had become to lie to her partner. She could have told him she was attending the Royal Wedding and he probably would've just grunted and nodded without even looking up. She texted him the pick-up time for Oscar and instructions to treat themselves to fish and chips for tea - otherwise he'd call her, asking how to operate the oven or complaining that there were no ready meals left in the fridge.

Val and Tabitha had waited until mid afternoon to set off together, Tabitha riding pillion on the motorbike. It hadn't taken them that long to collate all the strange ingredients needed for their adventure but Val had needed a short post-sandwich nap to gather all of her energy together. She awoke slightly more alert and with slightly more colour in her cheeks. After she'd necked a handful of pills and coughed a lot, she proceeded to wrap the empty jar of nut butter inside of the cardboard box.

Tabitha was puzzled as to exactly what the old lady's plans were but chose to follow the instructions given and not to ask any questions, she just did as she was told. For some reason unbeknown, she trusted Val and was rather enjoying losing herself in the drama.

Tabs pulled the motorbike out of the garage and donned her helmet as per Val's instructions before hopping on the back with Val at the helm. Another first. She'd never been on a motor bike before – it was exhilarating and the engine hadn't even started yet. The strange package was secured on the back of the bike. Tabitha was petrified yet there was no way she was pulling out now. She wrapped her arms around Val's frail waist, somehow holding onto Val's walking stick as well and held on for dear life. The two of them they tore down the motorway then the back roads towards the outskirts of the MoD land with their neon-yellow jackets flapping rhythmically behind them. It took them just under two hours to get there with a pit stop for coffee and a wee at the service station.

Val guided the bike down the poorly lit lane, surrounded by vast, empty fields until they came to a barbed fence and gate with plenty of signposts advising them against approaching any further. Val parked up her bike and they both hopped off. Tabitha felt wobbly; it felt strange for her thighs to be touching each other again and she was fully aware that she was going to be sore in the morning. She passed Val her stick and watched her retrieve the package from the storage box. Val passed it to Tabitha and hobbled over to the gate, where she pressed a button linked to a speaker and microphone. Suddenly aware of the multitude of cameras pointing down towards the pair of them, Tabitha realised it was now definitely too late to turn and run but was also having serious doubts about what on earth Val had planned. How on earth was a jar of peanut butter – in fact, an EMPTY jar of peanut butter - going to get them in?

'Hello?' Val directed her raspy voice into the intercom speaker

'Hello. This is government property. You are requested to leave immediately,' came the formalised response.

'We have a delivery.'

'All deliveries to Gate D.'

'Ok – thanks.'

Val and Tabs hopped back onto the bike and travelled slowly around the outskirts of the perimeter looking for Gate D. Eventually they found it – it looked exactly the same as their first port of call – Groundhog Day - but was slightly closer to the eerie looking building. Val pressed the buzzer once again and the same voice answered.

'Chemical delivery for Jon Manley, BGH Lab' Val confidently spouted, impatiently scratching away at the dirt by her feet with her walking stick.

'Hold one minute please whilst I contact the lab.'

The pair of them stood there. Unaware where this would take them – Tabs could now see uncertainty in Val's eyes too- what had they let themselves in for?

'You have no plan. No plan at all do you?' Tabs angrily mouthed

'Be quiet, dear, the cameras are everywhere. Stay calm. We have hi-vis jackets on – how could they possibly not let us in.'

'Hello. Mr. Manley says he is not expecting any deliveries this morning. Which company are you from?'

'Tell him it's the chemicals he has ordered from Solly's Scientific Supplies. They're on ice and need to get into the liquid Nitrogen ASAP please.' Val waved her stick at the box that Tabitha was holding.

'Solly's?' Tabs mouthed again. Tabitha couldn't work out if this was genius or seriously flawed. Val had pretended they were from a chemical company named after Jon's little brother, Solomon Manley. Surely that would get his attention.

'One moment please. Mr. Manley is coming down now.'

Several minutes passed by, the pair of them trying their best to look natural, Val leaning on the seat of her bike, stick in hand.

'You brought your phone didn't you?'

'Yes and the I-pad. It's all here.' Tabitha held the I-pad out to Val who slipped it inside of her biker jacket.

As she looked up, Val could see a slim, tall chap walking down the path with quite some pace sporting a mystified and slightly worried look on his face as he drew nearer and nearer to the gates.

'We have a delivery for you Mr. Manley' said Val, convincingly, waving her stick at the taped box.

'I think you're mistaken. We haven't ordered anything from 'Solly's Scientific Services' Never heard of them in fact. Who are you? How do you know my brother's name?'

'We know what you've been up to Jon. There's blood on your hands. We know about the drugs you've sold to your brother and his friends and lord knows who else. You have a high death count to your name, young sir. I think you have some explaining to do.'

Jon went white as a sheet, almost as white as if he'd just taken a hit of bleach himself. His heart felt like it'd missed a beat, blood pooled in his ankles. Who were these two strange women? He vaguely recognised the younger one although he couldn't place from where.

'I... I... don't know what you are talking about.'

'I very much think you do,' replied Val. Jon was literally shaking. 'Soma Lake, Ruby Wicker, Stephen Lockbridge. Do any of those names ring a bell? There are more...'

Jon remained silent.

'These are three of the many people whose lives have been lost due to you and your productions or whatever is going on in here. I demand that you let us in and take us to your laboratory or I will report you to the police immediately.'

Purely fuelled by fear, Jon led the two women down the dusty track back towards the building. Tabitha guided Val over the bumpy turf all the way to the tall glass door which led into the building's ground floor. Jon reluctantly used his ID card to open the main doors at Gate D and the group walked past the staffed reception. Jon nodded at the security guard manning the front of house after hours who nodded back at him.

'Alright Jon?'

'Yeah, just taking some deliveries through. Then I'm done for the day,' he replied hurriedly and signed them all in with a squiggle. The building was largely empty, the motion detecting lights came on automatically as the group moved along the corridors fairly slowly, two out of the three very apprehensively and the third hindered only by hobbling.

The strung-out young man guided the ladies down through a zig-zag of corridors before stopping at a lift.

'I can't take you any further. It's confidential. Top secret. I'll lose my job. I'll end up in serious trouble.'

'Losing your job is the least of your worries, dear. I think the information we have on you is going to get you into a hell of a lot more trouble than that, don't you?'

Jon called the lift using a red, square button. Then he typed in a six digit code. Tabitha quickly scribbled it down in her emergency note pad which she slid back into the front section of her bum bag before the lift doors closed behind them all and the lift began to descend.

'What do you want with me? What are you going to do? Please, let me go. I'm so sorry.' He was crying now, aware of the gravity of the situation. He was often on the wrong side of the law, but he'd never set out to kill people. He was now also very aware that he recognised Tabitha from one of his old schools so he knew that they weren't bluffing. They really did know Solly. They must have worked out what Jon had been doing; all for a bit of extra cash on the side and kudos.

'There's no one down here. There's no one else to get. Everyone's gone home. I was just washing up and getting ready to leave myself. What are you looking for?'

'Just open the lab, boy.' Val waved her stick threateningly.

Jon hesitated then threw his ID pass at Val before kicking Val's stick out from under her hand.

'Here – take it you old witch,' he panicked.

She didn't fall though, but managed to steady herself with the wall and slowly bent down to retrieve both her stick and the ID pass. He pushed Tabitha into the wall as he ran past her too, not hard enough to hurt her badly but winded her enough to give him just enough time to make off, back down the hallway, back to the lift and up out of the building.

Tabitha picked herself up and asked Val if she was okay. Val was already hobbling towards the double doors. The doors with the BGH Lab sign over the top of them. The doors that could be opened with the same six digit code that worked the lift and the ID card the boy had discarded through fear of being implicated in whatever the women were about to do.

'Yes dear, I'm fine.' Val said. She hadn't even taken the time out to look at Tabitha, she was already inside of the laboratory.

'How the heck did we get in? What on Earth just happened?' Tabs spluttered as she brushed imaginary debris from her velour bum bag.

'It's the hi-vis, dear – no one ever questions anyone in hi-vis.'

Tabitha looked back down the hallway and panicked that she'd never find her way back out alone, unsure if she wanted to follow Val into the Lion's Den. They were definitely in big trouble now if they got caught.

The lights flickered on in the lab as Val hobbled through, stick, left foot, right foot, stick, left foot, right foot, eyes scanning the shelves of bottles, jars and chemicals all around her. The ridiculous equipment on top and underneath the highly polished work surfaces must have cost more than a small third world country's debt. It was just as Casper had drawn it. Not one for showing emotion generally, seeing it as a sign of weakness, even Val had a look of pure amazement on her face. Tabitha quickly caught up with her crazy friend and linked her arm through Val's to steady them both. Tabitha's legs were shaking too now. She pulled out the protein bar she had stashed in her bag from earlier that Val had rejected and nibbled on it before placing it back in the zippered compartment. She couldn't eat now. The butterflies were having a rock concert in her stomach. Any food going in would most certainly be coming out sooner rather than later from one end or the other.

Val pushed open another door, a heavy fire door at the back of the lab and walked into an office type room to see a desk top computer switched off at the wall, a pile of yesterdays newspapers messily folded with an empty mug on top of them and a stack of documents in a font too small for Val to read even with her glasses. She left the office and returned to the lab, pushing through another door into a room with walls lined with cages. Some contained brown, bored looking hamsters and others bleached white, dead critters.

Val started to open up all of the cage doors, reaching in and taking out the survivors, bundling them all into the empty peanut butter tub still inside of the cardboard box. The very least she intended on doing was releasing the poor, tortured creatures that evening. Anyway it's not really theft if there's no victim is it? In this case, they were reducing the number of victims, lowering the number of lives lost, of humans and rodents by hopefully taking down the entire corrupt project.

Tabitha had followed her through, taking photos of the animals and their cages with the I-pad, photo after photo of the lab and its equipment. She'd already taken photos of the documents and newspapers lying on the desk in the office and the main lab. A secure chemical cupboard was situated in the end wall of the rodent lab. Val opened it with Jon's lanyard card. Val stood back, rubbing the outside of her thigh to ease the residual pain she had from her fall whilst Tabitha took centre stage, crouching down and rummaging through the assorted chemicals like a zealous collector at a car boot sale.

Inside, amongst various alkalis, acids and other flammable substances, Tabitha found a large jar labelled HVN-1 .She'd picked out the words dissociative and dopamine excitor on the side and on opening the screw top lid, revealed a lilac-grey powder within. She realised she'd found the research drug. It matched the description she'd heard and seen on the news. There were several more, smaller tubs of it in the cupboard too.

Tabitha paused in her search and turned the I-Pad around to face her. She browsed through the settings options to turn the annoying 'click click' sound off and then continued in the magnificent documentation of their heinous discoveries.

'What are we going to do? What are we going to do now, Val?'

Val placed the box of nervous rodents down on the work surface, they were beginning to scratch and squeak with distress, but Val ignored it, looking wistfully at the floor in her own little world. She took a long sad sigh and then looked directly at Tabitha.

'We try it. That's what we do. Before we ruin this young lad's life, we try it. Try and learn why he sold the stuff. If it's that amazing, I need to know.'

'What?'

Up until now, Tabitha had thought Val's plan was pretty crazy, she'd tagged along as she was a woman of her word and strangely felt some pang of loyalty to the lady she'd known for just over a fortnight but she was sure she'd be going to prison for what they were doing now. Even though what they'd unearthed, what they'd discovered in the labs was atrocious and surely illegal and the scientists here were clearly working against the codes of ethics, Tabitha felt like they'd bitten off more than they could chew figuratively and literally. She spat out the dry husks of protein powder that were still circulating her mouth, sucking up any last drops of water like she'd been chewing on a silicon sachet and stared directly at Val in total disbelief.

It was no use lying. As thoughtful and intelligent as Val was, she couldn't waffle her way out of this. She'd seen what the drug could do. She'd seen what it did to their eyes with her own eyes. Her cancer was rapidly infiltrating every nook and cranny of her body and Val was aware that she didn't have much time left on this blue and green marble to rectify all that needed rectification. Bleach. HVN. Drop out. She wanted to experience it for herself.

'I need to see my son. Tabitha, before I die. I need to see him. I need to make things good.'

'But, he's dead... Stephen is dead Val. I don't understand. You've dragged me into this... Into this place... And now YOU want to get high?'

'Oh dear girl, no, no... If I wanted to get high, I've got a cupboard full of pharmaceuticals at home, I'm practically rattling with pills dear. No dear girl, I want to make my peace with Stephen. If this drug is as good as they say, if I think about him hard enough, if I picture his beautiful red curls and freckles. I can be with him, I don't know. Apologise, make my peace. It makes no sense I know, I don't know where he is now, if there's an afterlife or if he's just pushing up daisies, worm food. I at least need to try. Do you understand? Can you try to understand?'

Tabitha was crying too now. The women both stood still, facing each other in the middle of an otherwise empty underground network of laboratories/ It was quiet enough to hear a pin drop, quiet enough almost to hear their tears hitting the floor. Tabitha drew two neatly folded travel tissues from her pouch and handed one to Val, then she wheeled through the black executive roller chair from the adjacent office and guided Val into it like a transit reversing down a narrow back street. She pulled out a lab stool and perched alongside her friend.

'I can't let you do this, Val. We need to collect evidence then leave. What happens if an alarm goes off or a guard comes?'

'Damn it woman. It only lasts a few minutes. This is why I wanted to come alone. If it wasn't for my stupid leg you wouldn't be here with me now.' Val sulked, although secretly she was glad to have Tabitha with her. She was going to take the Bleach, Tabitha would have to fight her to the floor to stop her. She knew Tabitha wouldn't do this, and although she resented her trying to stop the flow, she was glad to have support in case it was the last thing she did indeed do if it affected her like it did her son.

Val started to cry again, years of emotion were flowing through and out of her now like an opened reservoir. She slowly lifted her glasses off in between sobs and coughs, folded them up and tucked them into her biker jacket breast pocket. The white tissue Tabitha had given her was now saturated with fresh, red blood and lay crumpled in a ball in her lap. Tabitha passed her the rest of the packet and rubbed her back until the crying and coughing fit passed.

'See love, I don't have much time left. I need to do this.'

Her eyes were red and slightly glazed with tiredness tipping over into old age, Tabitha put her hand on the old lady's thigh and spoke. 'I'm with you Val. I'm with you. Let's do this together. I'll help you find Steve.'

Val drew out a black and white portrait photo of her son and passed it to Tabitha. Tabitha looked at it and passed it back to Val safely. Now was not the time or place to share her own personal sad past, but Tabitha knew exactly what Val was feeling.

Tabitha got up from her stool and searched around the laboratory, opening cupboards and drawers to gather enough basic laboratory equipment for their very own experiment. She would help this dying friend achieve what she wished to achieve.

A place for everything and everything in its place. The order, the cleanliness the ability to control where everything was and what happened. Tabitha felt very much at home in the laboratory. Is this what she had been searching for? Looking for hopelessly whilst prodding around in other peoples' homes? This sterile, lifeless cell of a room, everything filed away alphabetically or by size or material?

She returned to Val and their make-shift trap-house with a silver spatula, plastic pipette, the lid of a mini Petri dish and some fresh water from the dispenser all balanced on a dissection tray. She took off her jumper and placed it over Val's knees to keep her warm for her trip. Tabitha took a miniscule heap of the powder and added several drops of water, stirring it with the end of the pipette then sucking up the solution ready to dispense it.

'One drop or two, Madam?' she asked, mimicking a waitress in an American diner, waving the pipette frivolously.

'I'll have whatever you're having,' Val replied. 'Actually, make it three. Living on the edge et cetera.'

'Let's start with one – just to be safe shall we?'

'Oh, poppycock dear,' Val swiped the pipette from Tabitha, sucked up several mils of the liquid and squirted it into the corner of her own eyes before plonking the plastic dispenser down on the tray with casual disregard and blinking rapidly to spread the drops over the surface of her eyes. Tabitha followed suite, taking a slightly lower dose than her fearless ally before sitting herself down gently in the corner of the laboratory on the cold floor so that she had nowhere to fall from. Moments passed, their stillness allowed the laboratory strip lights to turn off and the two women sat in near darkness. They were each totally unaware of their surroundings as their eyes rolled bleach-white and their limbs flailed around fitfully until they both flopped back and slid down in their seated areas, travelling to their respective nirvanas.

Tabitha was the first to come round, and after regaining her bearings she dusted herself off and slowly stood, stunned and silently hysterical. Her movement triggering the lights to switch back on. She drew close to Val's chair, crouching down by her knees, hugging herself tightly to them like a young child needing comfort, weeping more so now than before the Bleach. More tears fell in the few minutes that she waited for Val to rouse in than she'd shed in the past three or four years. Tabitha was inconsolable with both grief and joy. Grief that she'd buried. Grief that she'd been refused permission to acknowledge. Grief that could move worlds, but also unbridled joy.

She hadn't visited Stephen. She'd travelled down some rollercoaster that surpassed time and vision, her past and her future stretched out in all directions of which she was both joined to and separate from. She'd reached her baby girl. Her baby who would now be nearly eight years old. A baby whose birthday she still marked, alone, with tears and a candle each year that passed. A baby girl whom she'd loved and lost. Tabitha had birthed a stillborn daughter at thirty eight weeks. She could still smell the sweet scent that hung at the nape of her baby's neck, a smell only a mother can smell. Not biscuits this time but lavender. It permeated into her every pore. She could feel the same sun shining on her skin that shone through the hospital window nearly eight years ago. It had been a feeling of sheer joy and relief the moment the birth was over yet a feeling of pure agony when the baby did not make a sound and she realised she would not be taking her home with her that sunny day, or ever.

She'd somehow communicated with her daughter and now knew, after years of searching for something to fill the void that her death had left, a void partially patched up by the birth of Oscar several years later but still a huge hollow chunk taken from her, that her baby girl was safe and happy and that they would one day be together again. She left her with a wordless message to live her life to the full, to seek out only relationships that fill her with love and unity, friendships that give her beautiful butterflies. Butterflies that flap their wings in peace, scattering light and love and compassion. To embrace those loving butterflies, not the angry, hungry ones she'd been fostering to her detriment for so many years now. She must make connections with others still on the living plain, those that offer reciprocated kindness and companionship through this strange trip called Life. Life is after all just an adventure that we must all travel through before being reunited with the loved ones we have lost along the way. Do not do it alone and unhappy, Tabitha, and certainly do not do it with a partner who makes you feel worse than if you were indeed truly alone.

Val opened one eye, smiled a smile that stretched from wrinkly ear to wrinkly ear, her skin folded up around her cheeks like corrugated cardboard. She clutched Tabitha closely to her knees and closed her eyes again, trying to hold on to the amazing connection that she'd just experienced. Was it with her mind? Her body? Her senses? Every particle of her psyche? She had no idea, but she'd accomplished what she'd set out to do. She had seen Stephen. She had made her peace. He was safe and he was loved.

The ladies sat crying and smiling, wiping their own tears and wiping each others as they tried to explain in humble words what they'd each just experienced.

The ladies were still immersed in this dreamlike state of awareness and awakening until the box of rodents on the lab table started to edge forward and eventually tipped over. The scratching had been getting more frantic and the box had started to move towards the edge of the desk. Tabitha jumped up and caught it and tucked it under her arm.

'Val. Come one. Let's get out of here. Please. We've done everything we needed to do. Let's get out of her before we get caught.'

'Yes. Yes, love, yes dear. You're right. Have you got photos of the powder? And the paperwork from the office? And the lab photos?'

'Check,' Tabitha saluted.

'Good,' she dithered as Tabitha pulled her to upright position and passed her walking stick to her.

'Good. Well done dear.' The old lady looked like she had gained ten years that evening and now looked tired, pale and weak. Tabitha linked her arm through Val's and started to walk the lady back out of the double doors they had come through, box under the other arm.

'Wait a minute, dear just one more thing.'

Colour suddenly rushed to her skin and she pulled her arm away from Tabitha's support. She walked as fast as she could to the side of the lab, drew her stick into the air like a freshly withdrawn Excalibur and screamed at the top of her failing lungs. The sound that came out was rough and raspy, pained and deep. Waves of emotion came riding through Val's weakened body as she smashed shelf after shelf of glass lab-ware, she opened the waist-height cupboards along the back of the lab and pulled out everything she could muster the energy to pull, smashing and crashing it all came out and down, spraying glass and metal, powders, liquids and chemicals all over the once highly cleaned floor. Not a cupboard was left unturned. The damage she created must have run into tens of thousands of pounds. When she ran out of breath, the screaming stopped and so did the smashing. She leant over the bench, panting as her heart and lungs tried to catch up with the muscles she'd used in this mad outburst of rage. The place was destroyed. An alarm started within the lab, something had been opened that shouldn't have, or the noise had caused something to start ringing, whatever it was they needed to get out of there as fast as they could. Tabitha pulled Val over to the wheeled chair from the office, plonked her in it with the box of hamsters on her lap and pushed her along the corridor at maximum speed, backing out through the double doors as and when they came to any like a hospital porter guiding an emergency patient on a trolley bed. They came to the lift and Val got up and into it, leaving the chair behind on the underground level. Up they went, back along the same channel of hallways they'd followed Jon down earlier in the evening.

As they made it through the final doors, the women were breathless even though hobbling along only a little faster than a slow walk as they used Jon's ID card one more time. They both moved as fast as they could down the gritty path in the dark to finally reach Val's motorbike. Tabitha placed the cardboard box on the floor whilst helping Val find her keys and ascend her trusty metal stead. In their haste they forgot to pick up the box again before they set off. They could see a guard approaching them by foot, and another small white security van with a noiseless orange siren flashing was coming around from behind the building. There was no time to stop and retrieve the rodents now. Tabs kicked the box gently with her foot as she drove off, freeing the dozen or so hamsters which climbed over each other to sniff the fresh country air, a fluffy ball of stubby legs and tails. They had escaped the confines of the box for a (probably quite short) taste of freedom on the grassy plains of Wiltshire. Liberation even if just for a second is surely sweeter than a life incarcerated.

Val and Tabitha took off together into the darkness of the night, too scared to look back, too happy for words.

They easily outran the pokey security van, but the women weren't naive. They knew other forms of security would be on their trail. They probably had Val's number plate too. As they approached Bristol, coming off the M32, Val pulled over into a lay-by and drew up her motorbike visor so she could speak. Her words came out muffled so she pulled off her helmet and turned to look at Tabitha.

'You need to get off here, dear. They'll be following us. This is your chance to get away. Avoid both of us sailing up the creak without a paddle.'

'But I can't.'

'Stop, Tabitha. This was always part of the deal. I am not taking you down with me.'

'But there would have been cameras. They'll know what I look like. It's...'

'Tabitha. Dear, do you know how many other medium-build thirty something young women with brown hair and, no offence, rather dowdy taste in clothing there are on the planet? You have been, fortunately in this case, blessed with an extremely generic appearance. You'll sail free.'

'But...'

'And if we are caught, I will claim full responsibility. Have no fear. Also dear, never forget, we did the right thing. Everything comes out in the wash, dear. Everything comes out in the wash.'

'But...'

Val cut her off, raising the palm of her hand to Tabitha's face which was once again tearing up.

'Stop, love. It's over. I've got to go. I've got stuff to do.' Tabitha knew she was right and dismounted, placing the helmet in the box at the back of Val's bike.

'I can walk from here. I need the air, or maybe I'll hop on the number five.'

'Do yourself a favour, dear, stop at the pub on your way home, have a gin and tonic for me, or a glass of wine. Raise it in memory of the ones we've lost. Never be afraid to talk about your feelings. Chat to someone new. You have a lot to offer. You're a kind soul, but you're lonely. Lonely and unhappy. Trust me, I know, I've been there. There are good people in the world Tabitha. Good people like us.'

'I will. I could do with a stiff drink,' Tabitha tried to hold back more tears.

'Look after yourself and that little one of yours. He's so precious. Savour every second,' Val smiled with her heart.

Val passed Tabitha the I-pad 'You know what to do with this, dear. Put it all to right won't you? You will be okay. And so will I.'

'Yes of course. I'm sure Emma can help me send it all over anonymously to the police. I'll visit their house first thing. I'll take some real chocolate too.'

'What about you, are you okay?' Tabitha knew this would be the last time she would see her dear friend. She was probably already living on borrowed time and the events of the evening had taken their toll on them both.

'Yes dear.'

'What are you going to do now?'

Well dear, I've got a few plans. Stephen told me about a couple of people I need to see. To see to, actually. Well one chap in particular. A chap who fostered him when he was fifteen that didn't exactly look after him the way that he should've done. I need to go and pick up Ol' Betsy and put right one more wrong before I throw my towel in.'

'But ... but will you be okay?' Tabitha didn't want to know the answer to this, she knew what Val was going to do and she knew it would probably be the last thing she did.

'I've got Stephen to keep me company now, don't you worry.' She winked and with that final wink, Val unzipped her leather jacket to reveal three small tubs of HVN that she'd pinched from the laboratory whilst Tabitha had been taking photos. She zipped it back up safely before lurching her good leg once more over the bike and taking off back up the motorway.

Tabitha slept like a log that night, and for the first time in years, she woke without stomach ache. She was welcomed to the day with a beautiful smile and a gentle slap to the cheek from her gorgeous boy. Tabitha stared at his beautiful blue eyes. His older sister would've had the same ocean deep coloured peepers. She pulled him up onto the bed with her and told him all about his older sister, a story which she'd never dared share before as her husband had told her it was not something that she should talk about. She also told Oscar about what she'd done the night before. She told Oscar that they needed to go and visit the student house together today as they had some business to attend to in order to make sure that the nasty people couldn't carry on hurting others. She told Oscar that then she was going to bake a cake and take it over to Mrs. Burrows and ask her if she'd like to spend some time singing or feeding the ducks with them today. She was going to file for divorce. She was going to reach out to those in her community, her precious community that shared the pleasures and pains that is life, those who may as yet still be strangers but those who are not ashamed of their emotions, those that offer love and comfort in times of need, those that would appreciate love and support from herself and her son in their times of need. She was going to do the things that gave her butterflies. The good sort. The beautiful Red Admiral, Monarch and Tortoiseshell variety. She was going to nurture that feeling of love fluttering in the pit of her stomach and release her joy to the world. Head held up high, she was going to knock on the front door of her neighbours rather than sneaking in around the back searching for something in secret that wasn't there. She had found what she'd been looking for that evening in the lab. She'd found permission to grieve. She was no longer going to feel alone.

Standing up from the bed, she swept Oscar up in her arms. They had a busy day ahead of them. They needed to drop the tablet off at the student house along with some Cadbury's dairy milk and discuss what the next steps were going to be in righting the wrongs that'd occurred with minimal damage to all involved. Together with the evidence they'd collected they would anonymously help the police put a stop to the drug related deaths in order to try and make amends. They'd work it out. Working it all out with friends was so much better than lolloping through life alone. She kissed her son on the nose and nuzzled in close.

'So Oscar, what gives you butterflies?' she asked, grinning from ear to ear.

'Erm... buying caterpillars?' he replied.

'Yes, Oscar, I suppose it would. We shall put that on our list of things to do.'

THE END

IF YOU LIKED IT PLEASE LEAVE A REVIEW!

(Amazon.co.uk / Goodreads.com / Facebook.com)

About the author:

SJ Townend is a new author dependent on word of mouth and good reviews for publicity and feedback.

She is also a science teacher, the mother of two small children and lives in Bristol. She enjoys combining the everyday with the extreme, the regular with the unexpected.

Her current work in progress is entitled:

Twenty Seven & The Unkindness of Crows

which is a bitter-sweet, nostalgic romance spanning the nineties and noughties. It will be published later this year.

For further updates and information, please follow her at:

https://www.amazon.co.uk/-/e/B086H51N7C

Twitter handle: @SJTownend

https://www.facebook.com/SJTownend/

Printed in Great Britain
by Amazon